City of Women

DOUG VILLHARD

MABEL

MABEL PUBLISHING

Cover design by Danielle Villhard

City of Women is a work of fiction. The roles played by E.G. Lewis and his family in this narrative are fictional; however, the imagined characters in this novel do abide by many of the generally known facts of Lewis's real life. Specific incidents and dialogue, and all characters with the exception of some well-known historical public figures, are products of the author's imagination and are not to be construed as real, including the chronological order of events. Where real-life historical public figures appear, the situations, incidents, and dialogues concerning those persons are entirely fictional and are not intended to depict actual events or to change the entirely fictional nature of the work. In all other respects, any resemblance to actual persons, living or dead, events, or locales is entirely coincidental.

*This book is dedicated to my daughters,
Danielle and Dia, who are poised
amongst their generation of women
to change the world.*

Act I:
The Same New Ed

CHAPTER 1

◆ ◆ ◆

From the moment Ed spies the woman anxiously stepping off the train, he knows it's about to be a good day. California, in 1913, is the perfect time and place to start a brand new life, and Ed is just the man to make it happen for her.

A porter drops the woman's luggage at her feet and hops back on the train, leaving her alone on the wooden platform as the steam clears. Ed notices immediately she's younger and more attractive than the others who've made the journey. The way her slender hand brushes back her raven black hair revealing her striking violet eyes, certainly catches his attention. He guesses she's just a few years younger than him in her late-30s and, given the brand and style of her clothes and luggage, is considerably affluent. His clientele to date—and really his whole career—has been women older than him, so this will be a welcome challenge.

Given all the advertisements surrounding the big sales event today, the woman is clearly confused to find a deserted train station. But then she spots a familiar face as she notices Ed sitting at a table, his eyes now on his newspaper, unassuming, drinking a coffee.

For days on the train, she's been staring at a photo of him in the brochure. She's read Ed's columns in his women's magazines for years, but she's never seen him in person. He's definitely older than his promotional photo, but even in his 40s, he's aged well and could still pass for being in his 20s. She wasn't expecting to find herself starstruck as she approaches his table, gathering the courage to attract his attention.

"Eddie?" she asks, finally getting him to look up from his paper.

"Well, hello," he replies, startled, as he rises to shake her hand. "It's Ed, actually. New city. New name."

As she shakes his hand, she's a bit surprised by his height now that he's standing. Ed is handsome with an athletic build, but he's decidedly short—shorter even than most women. However, now that she's sizing him up, she finds herself thinking his height might actually be refreshing for a change. He's certainly far less threatening than the other men in her life.

"And you are?" Ed asks.

"Mrs. Hattie Plah…Greenfield," she corrects herself, visibly affected by the gaffe of flubbing her own last name. "Miss Hattie Greenfield."

"New name for you too?" he smiles, shaking her hand. "It's a fresh start here in Atascadero. Welcome. What can I do for you?"

"Well, I'm here for the big sales event," Hattie says, looking around, realizing they are still the only two on the train platform.

"Oh my," he replies, "that is next week. A week from today."

Hattie is immediately embarrassed, yet certain she has the right date as she starts fumbling through her handbag, looking for the confirmation letter she'd received from Ed's office.

"It's okay," Ed says. "Regardless of the mix-up, and I'm sure it's on our end, you're here now. You've come all this way. Don't worry. I'll just cancel all my morning appointments and give you a VIP tour of Atascadero myself. All is good. My pleasure."

Hattie is still rummaging through her papers as Ed grabs her luggage and walks her toward his brand-new convertible Cadillac with three rows of seats. Ed tosses her luggage in the very back and opens the front passenger door. Her mind is still occupied with whether she had the right date, but she finally relents and gets in the auto.

Some men drive fast. And some drive recklessly. Ed does both. It's all Hattie can do to keep her hat from blowing away, her hair intact, and not be thrown out of the auto herself as Ed floors the machine relentlessly across dirt and gravel paths over undeveloped land.

With the dust hitting her face, Hattie can't fully take in her surroundings to see everything Atascadero has to offer. She's simply holding on for dear life, especially now that Ed is headed straight up what feels like it might be a mountain cliff. Afraid of heights, she can barely will herself to peek out to the side.

Finally, the path crests at the top as Ed slams on the brakes, skidding to a halt and generating a billowing cloud of dust. When it clears, Hattie finally regains her bearings, and what materializes is the most amazing view, a majestic lookout over an ample valley below.

"Atascadero is 23,000 acres," Ed says, proudly motioning out over the horizon. "It extends from that range of mountains to those over there. It's twice the size of Manhattan. Entirely undeveloped. Isn't it a marvel?"

Hattie has to admit that it is, indeed. Everything is so green, rich, and abundant. If the overall view wasn't beautiful enough, she notices wildflowers of every color growing everywhere. Not to mention rippling creeks that appear to flow endlessly down from the mountain tops. It's everything and more than Hattie had ever hoped California might be.

"Atascadero means 'abundant water' in Spanish," he says. "As you know, water is everything in California. It's the scarcest of resources. All the other towns popping up out here and competing for your attention have to fight for water. Los Angeles, for example, is the worst. But not here. We have water to spare. And not just to drink and use for cooking but also for agriculture, which will be our main enterprise."

Ed motions to the middle of the valley, using his hands to paint a fuller vision.

"Picture this. In the middle out there is a rectangular mall, like in Washington, D.C.," he says. "An administration building to one side, concert hall and theater to the other, sunken gardens in between filled with statues, fountains, and natural green space. Surrounding the mall is commerce. Stores and businesses of all kinds. Followed by 10,000 home sites—once we get all the infrastructure built, that is. Infrastructure first. Homes second. Remember that."

Hattie nods, hanging on Ed's every word as he continues.

"And on the outer rim of the valley, to be planted immediately, are segregated orchards for pears, oranges, pecans, apricots, peaches, figs, grapes, you name it," Ed says. "In fact, Professor E.J. Wickson, who heads the agriculture and botany departments for the University of California, confirmed for me that we have the amplest valley in all of California, in which agriculture and I quote, 'will grow in an abundance this country has never seen.'"

Hattie loves everything he is saying, but she can't help but find herself distracted by the lone, majestic home she sees off in the distance.

"Who lives in that one big white house way over there?"

"The rancher," Ed says. "J.H. Henry. A loner. He'll be moving out soon. This was all his. But now it's ours."

Hattie takes a moment to imagine what it must be like for one man to own all of this and to live here alone in a two-story mansion with a wraparound porch.

"Back to the orchards," Ed says. "Many varieties are already growing in my lovely wife's demonstration garden, which I'll show you in a bit."

Hattie has nearly forgotten he's married, being so caught up in Ed's vision and even in Ed himself.

"But my favorite, and I ask you to picture this," he says, "sprinkled throughout the homesteads in organized beds are the most beautiful flowers you've ever seen, whose seeds our community will sell. Our seed catalogs will soon sweep the nation, and just by owning a homesite, you'll be a part owner of the Atascadero Seed Company."

The prospect of being an owner of anything is more than exciting. She knows little about agriculture, but it appears that anything could grow in this valley. It's the prettiest view she's ever seen and with a considerably more pleasant climate than the East Coast, where she's lived her whole life.

"As you know," Ed says, "Atascadero is located directly between Los Angeles and San Francisco. Right smack dab in the middle. In short order, we're going to be the third-largest city in California. You'll notice over there the new California Highway 101, which cuts through the heart of Atascadero for 10 miles. We're also on the main rail line. And just over that mountain to the northwest is where William Randolph Hearst is planning his castle."

"A castle?" Hattie says, straining as if she could barely see it.

"Yes, a castle. He showed me the plans. It rivals any in Europe."

Hattie can only imagine what those plans must be like, not to mention the fact that Ed knows Hearst.

"And just a few miles over that mountain range to the west is the Pacific Ocean," Ed says. "We're building a highway, as we speak, straight through the mountains that leads to the beach. How do you like that? And as a homesite owner, you'll have access to private bungalows on Atascadero Beach."

Hattie certainly likes the sound of that, too, along with Ed's vision for the entire city. Nearly everything he's saying is in his brochure and in the numerous articles he's written in his magazines, but seeing it in person is much grander than any description in print. It definitely holds the promise of a fresh start and an escape she so desperately needs.

"But the real beauty of this planned community," he says, "is that we're all going to own it together. Fifty percent of the agriculture profits will go back to land owners, nearly all of them widows like yourself."

"I'm not a widow," she corrects him. "I'm, well…it's just that…."

Ed can tell she doesn't want to say, so he helps her.

"Seeking a fresh start," he says. "We all are. You're most welcome here. And it will be a wonderful place to raise kids."

"My son is already in college."

"College? Impossible. What's your secret for looking so young?"

"I am young," she replies.

"Well, that'll do it," he says. "To be young, gorgeous, getting your newfound freedom and life back. You're living a dream. One for which Atascadero is envisioned. You're our ideal citizen."

That certainly sounds charming, she thinks, as does being called "gorgeous," but if he only knew half of what she's endured.

Ed can tell he's asked enough personal questions and gets back to business.

"Anyway, you'll profit off the orchards without lifting a finger," he says. "It's an annuity for life to pay you back for your land and home purchase. But Atascadero is not about money. We are mission-driven here. We're focused on building a community of like-minded people who, like yourself, I assume, are interested in the arts, nature, education, and generally making the world a better place while also taking the time to slow down a bit and escape the rat race of the East Coast. We're on a mission to build a better tomorrow for women and their families. Is all this resonating with you?"

"Oh, yes. It really is quite the vision," Hattie says.

"It's more than a 'vision,'" Ed corrects her. "It's a utopia."

Hattie barely has time to let the word "utopia" sink in as Ed drives her back down the mountain even faster, accelerating through the most dangerous curves. Eventually, Hattie just gives in to the experience, takes off her hat, and lets the wind do its worst to her hair. Once she learns to trust him, the ride is really quite exhilarating.

She's never met a man like Ed before. One with vision. One so daring. One so alive. And one who only appears to know one speed, which is fast. Beyond fast. He's so full of energy and passion. Though it wasn't her intention, she can't help but feel a growing affection not just for Atascadero and its vision but for its founder, as well.

Ed again skids the auto to a halt. This time on the top of a grassy knoll within the valley. Once Hattie collects herself and gets her hair back in place, she notices orange stakes have been hammered out in all directions marking the homesites.

"Right here are some of my favorite views," Ed says, motioning out to the valley from inside the convertible. "All of the 10,000 lots in Atascadero are superb, and each has been plotted with thoughtful care by the most credentialed civil engineers, but the ones on this hill have a particular vantage point that can't be denied. Anyone would agree, I'm sure, you as well, that these are the very best and the most choice lots."

Hattie certainly can see what he means. She notices, though, that these particular stakes aren't just numbered but have a person's name written on each one.

"Have these already been purchased?" Hattie asks.

"Reserved," Ed says. "These are folks who asked me to go ahead and pick out lots for them. They haven't seen them yet in person, but as the requests come in, I drive out and reserve them. For example, look at this prime one here I picked out for Mrs. Fahrmeier, a recent widow looking for a change of pace and a better climate for herself, her youngest kids, and her mother. Check out what will soon be her view. Amazing, isn't it?"

Hattie agrees it is. It's definitely the best of the bunch.

"Now let me drive you down the hill a bit," Ed says. "We have some great lots down there you may enjoy. Still many with a fine view."

"Hold just a moment," Hattie says. "So, Mrs. Fahrmeier hasn't seen this lot yet?"

"That's correct. Technically, I can't lock anything down officially until the big sales event next week. But Mrs. Fahrmeier is going to love it."

He shifts the auto into forward, but again Hattie stops him.

"How about you sell this lot to me instead?" she says. "We'll just shift Mrs. Fahrmeier and the others over by one. No one will be the wiser."

Ed puts on the parking brake and thinks about it for a moment.

"You know what Atascadero also means?" he asks.

"Besides 'water'?" she replies. "What else?"

"Integrity. This entire community is to be built on trust. We're not just selling land plots here. I'm going to live here myself. So are you. Our mission is to build a community here. Mrs. Fahrmeier isn't just a name. She's a neighbor who is going to help us shape Atascadero into the most beautiful city and community ever created in the history of the world. And the bedrock of it all, everything Atascadero stands for, must be built on integrity."

Ed lets that sink in as he looks out over the homesites again, visualizing the great city that is to be. He attempts to shift the auto back into gear when Hattie puts her hand over his and forcefully shifts it once again back into park.

"I'll pay double," she says, keeping her hand firmly on his.

He turns and looks straight into those lovely violet eyes of hers. It's the first time he's actually taken a moment to really admire her since she stepped off the train. Yes, even though windblown, she could never be anything but elegant to him. But more so, she's determined. And she's also the type of citizen Atascadero is going to need. Because along with integrity, Atascadero is going to need women who don't take no for an answer. Women who get stuff done. Women who appreciate the problem-solving nature of capitalism.

"Triple," Ed says, not taking his eyes off her. "Triple, and the best lot in the entire valley is both yours and our little secret."

A few hours later, Ed puts Hattie back on the train. Mrs. Fahrmeier's sign and all the other signs are now shifted over one lot to the right to make room for Miss Hattie Greenfield, Atascadero's newest resident.

Before Hattie fully boards the train, she turns back around, lifts Ed's hands in hers, and pulls herself close enough that he can smell the floral notes of jasmine and lavender from her designer perfume. She takes a chance and boldly plants a lingering kiss on his cheek.

"It's a beautiful thing you're building out here," she whispers in his ear. "I love your mission. For the first time in my life, I've seen a place I could actually call home. And a man I long to share it with."

With that, she boards the train to see to her affairs back east before moving. Ed returns to his table back on the train platform. Yes, he's expecting to finally make his fortune in Atascadero, but it has never been only about the money. Women like Hattie, so desperately in need of a fresh start, remind him he really is building something special out here.

As the steam clears and the train pulls away, another younger woman is now standing anxiously on the platform, luggage in tow, brochure in hand. She notices Ed, who is back to reading his newspaper, as she approaches him.

"Mr. E.G. Lewis?" she asks, finally getting him to look up from his paper.

"Well, hello," he replies, a bit startled, as he stands to shake her hand. "Call me Ed. And you are?"

"Mrs. Agnes Smi…," she starts to say before correcting herself. "Miss Agnes McClennan."

"Welcome," he smiles, shaking her hand. "And what can I do for you?"

"I'm here for the big sales event," Agnes says, looking around and realizing they are the only two on the train platform.

"My goodness," Ed replies, "that event is next week. A week from today."

She's embarrassed but certain she has the right date as she starts fumbling through her papers. Ed simply puts his hand on hers to calm her.

"Welcome to Atascadero."

CHAPTER 2

◆ ◆ ◆

Later that day, Ed's wife, Mabel, cleans up at a wash basin inside their residential tent. Her voluptuous curves further exaggerate the height and size differential between her and her husband. She's aged almost as well as him, but few are blessed with his seeming fountain of youth.

Through the thin tent walls, Mabel hears Ed's auto screaming toward her from a mile away, and she knows at any moment, he'll skid to a halt and throw dust all over the series of tents that serve as Atascadero's temporary headquarters.

She listens as Ed does just that. She can also hear him enter the tent next door to drop off today's sales contracts and talk with Mr. Kramer, whom Mabel believes to be a weasel in human form, but whom Ed trusts to handle all their business affairs.

The tent fabric is so thin that Mabel can hear everything they are discussing, which sounds like it was another great sales day. Like clockwork, she knows Ed's next routine will be to hang a chalkboard sign outside their tent before barging in, which he does right on cue.

"A good day?" she asks, but the answer is always the same.

"A good life," Ed corrects her, stripping off his dusty clothes and dunking his head into Mabel's wash basin, causing her to back away from what she knows comes next, which it does, as Ed shakes his hair back and forth like a dog, splashing water everywhere, including the sturdy oak plank floor that, in contrast to the canvas walls, makes the tent's interior feel more permanent raised just a few inches above the natural earth.

Now that he's refreshed, he focuses on her.

"A good life," he says, "and a good wife."

He immediately starts kissing her neck, ignoring the fact that she hasn't yet finished washing up and still has mud on her arms from gardening. Mabel just stands still, shaking her head and smiling as he starts to fumble with her buttons.

"Really, Eddie? Right here in this tent and at this hour?"

"I'm fired up," he replies, now kissing the top of her chest and struggling with the rows and rows of buttons on her dress. "You try flirting all day long and see where it gets you."

"Try gardening all day and see where it gets you," she answers, playfully pushing him away so she can return to the wash basin to finish up in peace.

But that doesn't dissuade Ed as he now gently approaches from behind, lifts her light brown hair to expose the back of her neck, and, standing up on his tiptoes—given her height advantage—attempts a few kisses.

"We're so close, my love," Ed says between pecks. "Presales are going great. We have appointments scheduled for weeks on end. Some of my old banker friends in St. Louis are lining up. Senator Platt is still dead, along with his spider web of conspiracies. Atascadero, our beautiful dream, our mission, is nearly a reality."

Mabel teases him by shoving her backside into him, catching Ed off balance and sending him tumbling backward and crashing onto their bed. Once he gets his bearings back, he finds himself even more aroused.

He tries to sit up, but she gently pushes him back down and motions for him to patiently stay on the bed as she finishes washing off her arms and, to his delight, finally starts to disrobe.

"Let me hear again how much you owe me, Eddie?" she says, unfastening button after button in what seems to Ed like an endless plot to torture him. "Remind me again."

"Now, dearest, you know that answer. It's been well publicized that your $500 loan to me allowed us to option all of Atascadero."

"And when do I get that back?" she asks, "Plus my interest?"

"As soon as we have 10% of the lots pre-sold to qualify for a loan from the bankers who are going to give us $1 million outright to buy the land from J.H. and another million to develop it," he replies as part of a daily charade Mabel likes to put him through.

She's nearly got her outer layer off now as Ed is realizing he's still wearing his suit. He sits up to unbutton his vest, but she knocks him back down again. She's now moved on to unfastening her next layer.

"And tell me again, why did we have to get such a big tract of land out in the middle of nowhere?" she asks. "Why not start small near an existing city? I still don't understand why you passed on the San Fernando Valley? We probably have enough presales already for an initial development outside of Los Angeles."

"Because, as you know, I'm thinking about the customer. She doesn't want a solution that is simply viable. And neither she— nor I—want to deal with the politics of an existing city. She demands something that amazes and delights her. That's our mission out here. That's why I always go big."

"Speaking of big," Mabel says, "tell me again, when will we move out of this little tent and into the big ranch house? Not that I really trust that handsome rancher to actually ever let go of his prized Atascadero."

Handsome, Ed thinks. Now she really is torturing him.

"We have a signed contract with J.H.," he says. "Right when we get the bank loan, I promise the first thing we'll do is pay the old coot his million and send him out to pasture. I don't think he can handle the distraction of you much longer. He's been out here with only cattle for too long."

"Well, a bunch more women are on the way," she says. "And how about the idiot man right next door, just one tent away, with only tiny layers of cloth separating us."

"Shh. Mr. Kramer hears everything."

"He's supposed to be next door accounting and lawyering and advertising and all the other stuff you graciously allow him to do for you," Mabel says, "but instead, he just lurks, procrastinates, and stares. Those beady little eyes of his always counting, calculating, and storing useless information in his computational brain."

She can tell by Ed's face he's imploring her to quiet down, but she's made her point while disrobing down to her last undergarment.

"You want me to be quieter?" she asks, raising her eyebrows at him.

"Please."

"But yet, at the same time, you come in here all 'fired up'?"

"Yes," he replies, "my life is a conundrum."

"Well then get me back my money, with interest, and get me a real house—and in my name. Until then, you'll just have to remain fired up."

With that, she turns to reach for a clean dress, leaving him lying there, unsatisfied, on the bed.

Ed admires her curves, but more so, Mabel as his partner. She's made her point, and he, too, is sick of the tents. And sick of the additional promises he continues to have to make as he desperately tries to sell homesites each day to achieve the mission. But real estate development takes time, especially when all the prospective buyers have to travel across the country by train just to visit.

He needs this to work. He has to achieve success. His whole career, he's been so close, but it has never quite panned out. He knows he has to make Atascadero presales materialize within six months, or his option on the land will run out. Yet even at that, he'll never stop trying. If he has to, he's certain he can get an extension out of J.H. He'll never stop. Just like he's not going to stop trying right here and right now to seduce his wife.

It's a process for Mabel to get dressed again with so many layers and so many buttons to fasten, but it's much simpler for Ed to slip out of his suit before she's made much progress, which he does without her seeing, as he tries a new approach.

"Here, let me help you with that," he says, coming up to her from behind, helping to hold out the dress for her so she can slip her arms in. She obliges.

"Let me tell you something about that big house," he says, guiding her into her dress. "It will be beautifully decorated. No expense spared. All his old furniture tossed out. The latest designer brands shipped in. We'll add indoor plumbing. Indoor bath. New paint. It already has that amazing wraparound porch. And we'll add what I'm certain will become your favorite feature of all…."

"And what is that?" Mabel asks, maybe letting herself enjoy the vision for a moment.

"We'll add really, really, thick walls. The thickest."

Now that makes Mabel laugh. She turns to face her husband, who she now realizes has both disrobed and is a bit thicker himself.

Mabel believes in him. And she believes in Atascadero. But it's the fantasy of getting back into a real home that gets her through the day after seven years of following him around the country, always searching for the perfect piece of land and fending off government conspiracies.

"I'm just exhausted, is all," she says. "You have to admit these past years have been a long haul."

"I know, my love, but I also feel in my heart of hearts that this time we're almost there," Ed says, smiling, pushing himself up against her. "Can't you feel it?"

She can, which makes her laugh again. It's inevitable, and they both know it, that she, and everyone else they'll ever encounter, will eventually succumb to her husband's relentless charms as she drops her charade and takes charge, tackling him onto the bed.

Outside the tent, Kramer is indeed lurking. He is about to knock when he notices the little chalkboard hanging at the door. After reading it, he gets the hint to walk away, but not before lingering, listening just a little longer.

On the chalkboard, Ed has written, "Deep In Prayer."

CHAPTER 3

◆ ◆ ◆

Ed continues to give two tours a day for the next few weeks. He's gotten so good at his pitch that his close rate is now nearly perfect.

Today, he is showing a middle-aged widow and her young children the same staked homesites he showed Hattie. He has a slightly different pitch when kids are involved, pointing out all the creeks in Atascadero that are ripe for finding ancient Indian arrowheads.

He starts to show the kids a few arrowheads he keeps in his pocket when GUNFIRE suddenly erupts, seemingly all around them.

The widow and her kids duck and take cover in the Cadillac, but Ed doesn't flinch. He knows exactly what's going on.

Just as Ed expects, from behind some wild oaks, just over the ridge, the dark silhouette of a horse appears, and on it rides none other than the handsome rancher, J.H. Henry. He's around sixty, with white hair, a handlebar mustache to match, and tan leathered skin from decades of the relentless California sun. Despite the year being 1913, J.H. dresses as an old-time 1880s cowboy, complete with a spectacular hat that Ed has always assumed J.H. took from a man he killed in a gunfight years ago.

J.H. limberly jumps down off the horse and kicks at the coyote he's just shot to make sure it's dead. He's pleased with himself as he looks up to see a startled widow and her children peeking from the Cadillac.

"Been tracking this monster for weeks," J.H. says. "You kids want to help me skin it? The fur would make a great shawl for your mother. A real souvenir, for sure."

The widow is appalled, but the kids are maybe considering the idea as Ed steps in.

"Mrs. Jenkins," Ed says to the widow, "let me talk to Mr. J.H. for a moment. Why don't you walk the kids down the hill a bit and pick out a homesite."

"We're never getting out of this car," she replies. "There may be more monsters."

"Always," J.H. drawls. "I've lived here 40 years. Always there's a somethin' just a lurkin' around."

Ed realizes Mrs. Jenkins will never leave the Cadillac, but he does, hopping out.

"You all stay right here," Ed says. "You'll be fine in the auto. This is the first coyote I've ever seen on the property, I promise. Now let me talk to Mr. J.H. just a moment."

Mrs. Jenkins, still petrified, takes the hands of her children to pray together as Ed takes J.H. off to the side.

"J.H., please," Ed says. "Come on, sir. This is uncalled for."

Now that they are standing next to each other, the two men couldn't be more different. J.H. is at least two heads taller and with strong, ox-like shoulders.

"Look, Ed," the rancher says. "I've been meaning to talk to you about our deal. This seems like good enough timing."

"Really, this seems like good timing?"

"Well, the thing is," J.H. says, now with his hunting knife out, kneeling over the coyote to cut off its hide. "I got me a better offer, I'm afraid."

J.H. slices into the coyote. Ed does his best to muster a tough response while trying not to gag at the sudden sight of fresh blood and guts.

"Sir, we have an ironclad tight and legal deal, as you well know," Ed says. "We have paid the $500 in earnest money and have six months to pay you the million as the contract says."

"Actually," J.H. says, putting his boot on the coyote, gaining just enough leverage to really rip at the hide, "it says three months with a three-month extension. And we're already one month in."

"An extension that 'cannot' be summarily withheld," Ed clarifies.

"I know I'm just one of them dinosaurs or relics or whatever it is that you and that tempting wife of yours like to call me in the assumed privacy of your thin tent. But I do know how to read. And how to write. And in the final contract revision, my legal team changed *'cannot'* to say *'can* be summarily withheld.' And you and that idiot Mr. Kramer missed the edit."

Ed can feel he's starting to lose color in his face. He has the signed agreement back in his office and can't wait to race back and check for himself, but assuming this is true, he's now got to think quickly and clearly, which is getting harder to do with the smell of the flayed coyote now reaching not only him but surely Mrs. Jenkins and her kids.

"What do you mean by a better offer?" Ed asks him.

"Somebody out there in Washington, D.C. must really have their undercarriage all tied up in a knot over you."

Now that is Ed's worst nightmare. Even more so than losing this deal. *But how could that be?* Platt has been dead for several years. Shortly after that, Congressman Ashbrook and his committee completed their hearings and disciplined the U.S. Postal Service, but all of that is long in the past. Ed is now all the way out in California. He's as far as he could possibly go without leaving the country. *Could the conspiracy really be back?*

"As you know," J.H. continues, "before you came along, I had a $500,000 offer from the U.S. Army to buy this land for use for military exercises. But they putzed around, and your $1 million offer was higher, so I took it. But now that they got wind that it's 'Mr. E.G. Lewis' that done made the offer, they've countered with $2 million."

Ed's head is spinning, and the smell of the carcass isn't helping. He has to step back and take a knee. He fears the coyote's dead face with its tongue hanging out must be what he now looks like, as well.

"How many of them homesites you sold so far?" J.H. asks, almost finished carving off the hide now, ignoring the flies amassing and swarming around the bloody carcass.

"About 100."

"Of the 1,000 you need for the banks?"

"That's right," Ed says. Tracking against the goal every single day, he knows exactly where he stands.

"Well, the good news for you," J.H. says, now standing and holding the bloody hide. "You're 10% toward your goal with just 60 days left."

Ed doesn't need to be told the bad news, but it is clear J.H. is going to anyway.

"But the bad news," the rancher says, "is you seem to be averaging only two of these little homesite tours a day. Putting you on track in 60 days to be where at this pace?"

But again, Ed knows J.H. already knows the answer.

"Putting you on track to fail," J.H. continues. "Big time fail."

"But what about the women?" Ed asks. "What about what we're building out here? What about what Atascadero is about to become? Our mission? To give folks a chance at a new life?"

"Noble," J.H. says. "Noble indeed. But so is helping our military. And I ain't that great with 'rithmetic, but I'm pretty sure the army's $2 million is double your $1 million. And the government actually has money. I looked into you. All you've ever amassed over your career is broken promises."

Ed's mind is really spinning now as J.H. takes a few steps toward Mrs. Jenkins.

"Ma'am," J.H. says, holding up the freshly cut coyote's hide, which is dripping with blood and swarming with flies, "You sure you don't fancy a shawl or the like?"

But it's obvious by her face she's sure she doesn't.

"Next time, then," he says to her. "You all enjoy the rest of your time in beautiful Atascadero. Pleasure to meet you."

It's also obvious by her face that she won't be staying much longer.

J.H. turns and walks back past Ed toward his horse.

"Well, shoot, Ed," J.H. says, mounting his horse, "you might not be averaging two a day after all. Apologies for the widow over there. I done messed up your sales streak."

With that, J.H. rides off back over the ridge, leaving Ed, not to mention Mrs. Jenkins, aghast.

CHAPTER 4

Later that day, back in the administrative tent, Kramer frantically searches the final version of the contract, running his finger across it word by word. Ed paces, planning for the worst, when Kramer finally finds the clause in question.

"Replacing the word *cannot* with *can*," Kramer says. "Unscrupulous. Surely, I cannot have been expected to detect a level of deportment of this magnitude."

"Use normal words. Speak like a normal person," Ed says. "So, do we really only have 60 days left?"

Kramer doesn't answer, still reading over the document, looking for other unexpected edits, but Ed can tell that the answer is yes. Sixty days is his new reality. Ed, lost in thought, is still pacing around a circular woven rug on the wooden floor of the tent as Mabel enters. Neither Kramer nor Ed takes the time to fill her in. They know they don't need to. She's clearly heard everything through the thin tent fabric.

"Deplorable," Kramer says, pouring over the rest of the agreement. "Wanton chicanery. Dare I say skullduggery."

Mabel rolls her eyes. She knows Kramer also pulls stunts like this all the time. Kramer had first advised them all the way back in Connecticut, well before St. Louis, when Ed was in business with what turned out to be a devious uncle. She had hoped all of that would stay in the past, never to return again, including Kramer.

Mabel knows that a creative mind like her husband's needs a business partner with knowledge of the law to handle the details— like Ed's brother, John, had so faithfully executed for them in St. Louis. But she also knows that in Ed's current financial and reputational state, finding another person of John's quality and integrity hasn't been easy.

The best thing to do at this particular moment, Mabel knows, is to give Ed space to use his superpowers. He needs time for that exceptional entrepreneurial mind of his to figure a way out of this.

She also knows Ed has been adamant about only giving individual tours and avoiding large sales events. But Mabel has never understood why they couldn't experiment with an event. She's advocated that women might be better salespeople than Ed, but he'll never see that. He thinks he has to flirt, but she's had a plan in her head for a while now of taking women who have already put down a deposit and turning them into ambassadors who want to help promote the mission. It worked before with Ed's magazine sales, but he is convinced it could never work with a purchase as large as real estate.

She's hoping he's at least considering her idea of holding a real event, which is why she's shocked at what next comes out of his mouth.

"I need to make a trip back to St. Louis," Ed says.

This causes a fascinating thing to happen. Mabel and Kramer, for the first time in their lives, are suddenly both in agreement with each other.

"You can't raise capital there," Kramer says.

"Dearest, no," Mabel says. "After what happened? All those people who lost their investment in the magazine and the bank? Not to mention their jobs. How could you even show your face?"

"Time heals," Ed says. "They know my heart. They know the government evil we were up against. And John is still there."

At the mere mention of John, Mabel longs for the time when he was their advisor. She knows he is still in St. Louis outsourcing the presses and paying off Ed's debts. She allows herself to fantasize for a moment how wonderful it would be if Ed could persuade John to move to California.

"I think in many circles back there," Ed says, "now that Ashbrook's commission found us not guilty and condemned the Postal Service, I'll garner sympathy as I've already done with a few St. Louis banks—and maybe even earn back the trust of some previous investors."

"Investors?" Mabel says. "Eddie, no. No! You swore we'd never work with investors again. 'Presales this time, my dear,' you said. 'We'll be beholden only to ourselves and our customers,' you said."

"And the banks," Kramer says.

"Of course," Mabel says. "I understand there is no way around banks when it comes to real estate. But, Eddie, you promised no investors."

"No 'equity' investors," Ed corrects her. "I said I won't give up equity, and we won't."

"I'm lost," Mabel says. "You just said you want to raise money from investors?"

Kramer quickly catches on.

"He must be postulating securing a convertible note," Kramer says, considering the ramifications of the idea now himself.

"Exactly," Ed confirms. "I'll ask investors to give us a form of a loan that is riskier than a bank would give us at this point. In turn, it will have a higher interest rate, but we can still pay it back without giving up equity."

"Then why is it called 'convertible'?" Mabel asks.

"Well," Ed says, "technically, if we don't pay it back, it converts to equity. But we're going to pay it back."

Mabel is not pleased with any part of this plan, but Kramer seems to be warming to the idea.

"And we'll finally execute a wider mailing and advertise sales events, for which I've been advocating?" Kramer says.

Mabel's blood is really boiling now. That has always been her idea and not Kramer's. Before she can remind the weasel Kramer of that, Ed puts his hand on her arm to calm her.

"Not like you're envisioning, Mr. Kramer," Ed replies. "And that was actually Mabel's idea."

Mabel appreciates her husband's recognition as Kramer continues to protest.

"There's no avenue to raise any amount, even in a convertible note, without more aggressive presales," Kramer says. "We now have a restricted time frame."

"I have a slightly different take on it," Ed says. "A bigger event."

Kramer isn't following, but Mabel thinks she might know what he's thinking based on a crazy idea Ed had brainstormed a while back.

"Oh, no, Eddie," Mabel says.

"Yep, a land rush," Ed says. "Just like what famously worked in Oklahoma twenty years ago."

"Oh, dear God," Kramer says, having now caught on.

"We'll call it the 'Atascadero Land Rush,'" Ed proclaims. "I'll go to St. Louis and raise the money—in a convertible note—to promote the biggest real estate event the world has ever seen."

"The second biggest," Mabel corrects. "Nothing will ever be bigger than the Oklahoma Land Rush. The last thing we need is to attract the attention of Postal Inspector Fulton and other postal inspectors with false advertising claims sent over the mails."

"I completely agree, dearest," Ed continues. "Let me try again."

Ed pauses for effect.

"Picture the biggest real estate event the world has ever seen—*in California.*"

CHAPTER 5

◆ ◆ ◆

Ed, standing with packed bags for St. Louis, waits with Mabel and Kramer for the train to arrive. There is just one issue. Given the duration of the cross-country train ride, he'll be gone for about two weeks, and in that time he has 28 sales appointments scheduled.

He's well aware that Kramer has a tendency to creep women out making Kramer, to say the least, a less-than-ideal candidate to give any form of a sales pitch, leaving the job to Mabel. Though Ed knows she doesn't enjoy it and her approach will be much different than his, Ed believes she certainly could be very good at it. But that also means neglecting hours in her demonstration garden, whose crop experiments and samples are essential to the agricultural part of his plan. Mabel would never trust Kramer to tend the garden, not to mention the additional problem of J.H., who will certainly come a calling on her with him gone. Ed doesn't envy Mabel having to juggle all this without him.

As Ed is considering these challenges, he's suddenly distracted by something he never would expect to see out here: a Cadillac convertible, identical to the one he drives, pulling up to the train station and parking right next to his vehicle.

Having just parked, smiling and waving, is a man about Ed's age. He is sitting next to a younger man about half his age. The older man compares his auto to Ed's for a moment before he exits and jogs up to the train station.

The last thing Ed, Mabel, or Kramer would ever expect in the middle of nowhere is for another identical auto to pull up, but it is the enthusiasm of the older man that is most unexpected. He's just so happy. Full of life. With his hand outstretched, ready for a shake, he can't get to Ed soon enough.

"I'll be," the older man says in a Southern gentleman's drawl. "Mr. E.G. Lewis, I am so delighted I caught you before you take off. I'm just tickled to meet ya."

Ed accepts his handshake, still dumbstruck. He also shakes the hand of the polite younger man. Now that the two men are standing closer together, Ed can tell they are basically spitting images of each other. He assumes they must be father and son. Both have red hair and freckles. Ed imagines their pale skin must be no match for the California sun.

The older man seems to expect to be recognized, but it is clear by Ed's, Mabel's, and Kramer's faces that they have no idea who he is.

"Come on," the older one says. "You know me. I'm Lawrence Mitchel, and this is Larry Mitchel. We're Mitchel and Son. And in case you were wondering, Larry here is the son."

Lawrence laughs at what Ed thinks might be the dumbest joke he's ever heard, while younger Larry just shakes his head in embarrassment.

"I'm sorry, but who are you?" Ed asks. "What are you doing out here?"

"Mitchel and Son," Lawrence says again, getting no response, but younger Larry is more astute.

"Pop, it's obvious J.H. never mentioned you to them," Larry says to his father.

"That can't be," Lawrence says. "J.H. told me what kind of auto to buy and everything to match. I'm the one that done inherited the Eaglet Ranch just to the south of Atascadero's border."

"Baron Von Schroder's ranch?" Kramer asks.

"It was," Lawrence says, "but with him being a German national and all and with the threat of war, the U.S. government took away his land ownership privileges, reverting the option back, per federal law, to the prior owner."

"You were the prior owner?" Kramer asks in disbelief.

"My pappy was back in the day before selling and raising me in South Carolina," Lawrence says. "I was just mindin' my little accounting business when…look at me now. The Eaglet has landed back in my lap."

Ed looks to the younger Larry as if to confirm this improbable story. Mabel and Kramer express similar doubts.

"Dad was an accountant one day and suddenly a rancher the next," Larry says, nodding his head in fascination. "I had to take a break from college to come and see it for myself. But the best part, thus far, is getting to meet you, Mr. E.G. Lewis, I'm a big fan of you and your mission."

The younger Larry is certainly growing on Ed. Considerably more than the father.

"I'm a big fan, too," Lawrence says. "It's just genius how you promote Atascadero. And I intend to do the same with my development next door in Eaglet."

Now Ed's, Mabel's, and Kramer's jaws all drop at the same time. Younger Larry is even more embarrassed. Lawrence picks up a bit on their collective reactions.

"Not the exact same development," Lawrence corrects himself. "I'd never do that. Nothing at your scale. I wouldn't even begin to know how to finance all the roads, buildings, infrastructure, and commerce you are planning. Or know how to go about promoting it."

"He'd have no idea," Larry adds.

"No idea," Lawrence agrees. "I'm just planning some modest homesites at far cheaper prices. Just selling a little bit at a time until I catch some wind. Nothing like the high-end development and clientele you attract. It's simpler folks for me."

"Far simpler," Larry says.

"Far simpler folks that could only dream themselves to one day afford to build here in Atascadero," Lawrence says. "I thought I'd just catch a few of 'em on the way out of town who turn you down on account of price. And show 'em the Eaglet is still close enough where they can take advantage of Atascadero's public parks, civic center, swimming pool, and all the other fancy stuff you're planning. I'm thinking of sayin', 'Buy cheaper in Eaglet. Visit next door Atascadero for the good stuff.'"

Ed, for maybe the first time in his life, is speechless. He's trying to make sense of what he just heard, starting with what appears to be the nicest but dumbest man, just standing there in front of him, smiling, not seeming to grasp that he is developing a parasite city right next door. To make matters worse, Lawrence apparently sees zero risk in revealing his entire strategy to him.

"And this must be the beautiful Mrs. Mabel Lewis," Lawrence says, shifting the conversation. "I'd love to see that famous demonstration garden of yours I've been reading about. How delightful."

"Me too," Larry says. "I'm studying agriculture at college. There's no evidence our land is fertile at all despite being nearly identical to yours. In fact, all our soil tests came back just terrible. Barren, even."

"Infertile as a castrated bull," Lawrence says, laughing profusely and alone again at his own joke. "Just my luck. But not as bad luck as the bull's."

Lawrence laughs and laughs. Kramer is about to lose his mind if he has to listen to this much longer, and Mabel doesn't hear a lot of castration jokes. Ed isn't really listening as he is thinking back to something Lawrence said at the very beginning.

"So J.H. told you what kind of auto to buy?" Ed asks.

"Yes," Lawrence says. "J.H. suggested not just the make of Cadillac to buy, but he also gave me my whole strategy. He said, 'Don't spend money on advertising, get the exact same auto as Ed's.' He even suggested I just hang out here at the train station and talk to folks coming and going to gauge whether maybe they've decided if they can't quite afford Atascadero. J.H. said, 'Win them over on price.' He suggested I say, 'Why leave when you can still be a neighbor?'"

Kramer can't help himself.

"Is that right?" Kramer asks. "A neighbor is how you regard yourself?"

"A neighbor indeed," Lawrence says. "After all, I even want to share your same mission of helping fine women make a new life for themselves out here. Helping them discover a fresh start. I like it so much I'm copying it."

Ed can tell Larry is clearly embarrassed for his dad. As the train is now approaching the station, Ed is completely dumbfounded and also doesn't have enough time for a proper response.

But Ed knows one thing is certain: there's no way he can leave Atascadero with this hillbilly parasite hanging around the platform. Ed needs time with Lawrence to politely reset the strategy J.H. has planted in his mind. Being gone for two weeks isn't going to work.

The train comes to a halt, and a woman, clearly having traveled all this way for a sales appointment to meet Ed, steps off the train with her kids and mother in tow. The plan had been for Mabel to show her around Atascadero, but before Mabel or Ed can greet her, Lawrence swoops in, makes her acquaintance, helps her with her bags, compliments her kids, flirts with her older mother, and generally makes them all feel the most welcomed, cherished, and charmed they have ever felt in their entire lives.

Larry, shaking his head, looks at Ed, Mabel, and Kramer as if to apologize for his father. They are all watching Lawrence with such awe it causes them not to notice that two twin college-aged girls, wearing identical floral dresses, have also stepped off the train. Larry, however, notices since he never expected to see girls his own age out here in the middle of nowhere, not to mention their striking beauty.

Ed eventually glances in the twins' direction, immediately recognizing their also identical smiles, but he thinks they can't possibly be who he thinks they are, given they are supposed to be in the middle of their college semester in Chicago.

Mabel is still looking for an opportunity to cut in on Lawrence to begin the tour when Ed forcefully grabs his wife's shoulders and turns her attention toward the college-aged twins.

The moment Mabel's eyes meet the twins' eyes, all her cares in the world cease to matter any longer. She entirely forgets about the tour and runs to greet her nieces, Marcella and Rose, disappearing into their warm embrace.

As the train takes off again, instead of boarding, Ed simply drops his bags. He has no choice but to stay and attempt to sort out the chaos that, for whatever reason, continues to plague him no matter what he does in life or in his career.

CHAPTER 6

◆ ◆ ◆

Ed is supposed to be spending the day on a train, relaxing and preparing for meetings in St. Louis. Instead, he's had to perform his normal routine of charming prospective buyers in the morning and the afternoon while in between observing Lawrence receiving a tour of Mabel's garden and noticing the younger Larry clearly enamored with the twins by the way he steals looks at them. Marcella appears to most appreciate Larry's presence, which for some reason invokes a paternal response from Ed of wanting to gag at the thought of them together.

Hours later, Ed gets his final tour of the day back on the train so he can rush home to see why Marcella and Rose have arrived. He screeches to a halt outside the tents. Before he can even exit the auto, Mabel is waiting for him. She motions to the twins to make themselves at home in their tent.

"I need your uncle to take me out on the property for a moment," Mabel calls back to the twins, hopping into the front seat with him. "We'll be right back."

Ed gets the hint and drives off, giving them some privacy. He comes to a halt up on the cliff with the majestic view of the valley below as Mabel bluntly gives the news to him.

"You missed their tuition payment," Mabel says. "The university says you haven't paid in over a year, and it's finally reached a point where they were asked to leave."

Ed anticipated this might be the case, but it is the disappointment on Mabel's face that most affects him.

"They are embarrassed," she says, "and they had no place to go."

"I never assumed it would get that far," Ed says. "I thought we'd at least get some type of warning letter."

"We did," she says. "Mr. Kramer admitted he never gave them to you. He said he didn't want to distract you from more 'principal matters'."

Ed is livid. In his heart of hearts, however, he knows he doesn't have the money to pay their tuition anyway.

"What about their mother?" Ed asks. "Can't she help? Where is Claire? She's been such a mystery all these years. Do the twins even still talk to her?"

"They write her on occasion. She's apparently living in a small apartment in Memphis. And I didn't know this until today, but she's recently married."

"Married?" Ed says, trying to refrain from asking a thousand questions or hinting at any jealousy.

"The twins haven't told Claire yet about the tuition issue, but they are going to have to at some point. They decided their best chance to finish college was to come out here and help us get Atascadero off the ground. They want to help. They feel they have no choice but to help."

Ed is trying his best to process all of this, but his mind keeps going back to one thing.

"Who did Claire marry?" he asks.

"What's it matter? A saloon manager or something. The twins haven't met him yet. He had been a lifelong bachelor and runs a small saloon in Memphis or something. That's all they said."

Ed can't see Claire marrying a saloon manager. He'd assumed with her unparalleled beauty—and intellect—that she'd attract the likes of a doctor, lawyer, or an industrialist. Even a monopolist. In Ed's mind, any prominent man would go out of his way to woo her. *How did she end up with a saloon manager?*

If she had just stayed with them, Ed thinks, he probably would have met his pre-sales goals long ago with access to her talents. Oh, how Ed misses his old team of Claire, John, and Mabel.

"We have to get the twins back to school," Mabel says. "There has to be some money somewhere. Some way."

Ed doesn't disagree, but he can't help thinking that the twins could be an opportunity for them at the same time. He and Mabel could use the help. If he doesn't get Atascadero going, he certainly won't be able to pay their tuition in the future. It takes him a moment, but he thinks it through and realizes the twins shouldn't be burdened with Atascadero. This is his dream, not the twins' responsibility.

"I'll take them back to Chicago on the train tomorrow," Ed says. "I'll raise the money we need along with their tuition in St. Louis. But, in the meantime, it sure is wonderful to see them, isn't it?"

"They are so beautiful," Mabel says. "And smart. Just like their mother, whom I miss dearly. I miss my sister."

As does Ed. He'd love to get this resolved before Claire finds out. He's seen firsthand that the wrath of Claire is not something to ever be trifled with.

◆

The next morning at the train station, Ed is set to head to St. Louis. Joining him are Mabel and the reluctant twins, who he'll first be taking back to school in Chicago.

Lawrence and Larry pull up to the station in the Cadillac and jog up to the platform.

"It was such a joy to meet you ladies," Lawrence says. "Wasn't it, Larry?"

"It very much was," Larry replies, especially to the delight of Marcella.

"Well, they are back to college now," Ed says.

But the twins are clearly not happy about it. They were enjoying the adventure of California and the break from studies.

If ever there was a nervous talker who can't handle any form of silence, it is Lawrence. Marcella and Larry continue to make eyes at one another while Lawrence jabbers away.

Ed hates leaving town like this, putting everything on Mabel's shoulders, which isn't fair to her. What he really needs to do is take Lawrence aside and set him straight, and he's ready to do so, but the train arrives.

As they are saying their goodbyes, Ed can tell Mabel is certainly sad to see them all go, but he knows she's also mentally gearing up to start giving sales tours as she'll be greeting her first prospective customer any moment now.

Indeed, as the train stops, a woman, this time with her husband and kids, steps off. Occasionally, the women arrive with their husbands, but not often. When they do it is always the same: he'll soon reveal himself to be the type of man who is basically subservient to his wife. Atascadero, like Ed's mailing list from his women's magazines, attracts only strong, independent women— still married or not.

But before Mabel can introduce herself to the family, something very unexpected happens. Exiting the train at that moment are a dozen other women along with their families. Ed's quick glance at their faces reveals that he recognizes them all. They are a sampling of the women Ed has given tours to over the last month who have put down deposits.

Most familiar to Ed is Hattie Greenfield, the younger and more attractive woman compared to the others who had toured just a few weeks ago. Dressed as elegant as ever she's arriving with far more suitcases, and what Ed assumes must be the college-aged son she had mentioned, who is helping to carry her luggage.

Hattie is the first of all the women to notice Ed and rushes right up to him, hitting him with a wave of her unforgettable perfume. She envelops him in a deep embrace and delivers an even more tender kiss on his cheek than when he last saw her.

"Surprise," Hattie says, smiling exuberantly, exposing her polished white teeth in perfect contrast to her vibrant black hair cascading down her shoulders.

The other women, having also exited the train, apparently all having met each other on the ride, offer him a "surprise" as well.

"Ed, we know you said 'infrastructure first, homes second'," Hattie says, "but when you realize where you want to spend the rest of your life, and you've bought into the mission, well, you want it to start right away. We all do. Turns out we all had the same idea just to take a chance and come out here early."

Ed is not sure what to say. He has no accommodations for them. They know the plan is to first build out the infrastructure before any homes go up, not to mention, Ed doesn't even technically own the land yet.

Real estate is supposed to be easy, Ed thinks. Far easier than the magazine business or establishing a national bank. It was all supposed to be so easy.

He's still just standing there. Mabel is equally dumbfounded. Even Lawrence is at a loss for words, which Ed never thought he'd see.

Ed has no idea what to do or say when suddenly something wonderful happens.

"Welcome to Atascadero," Marcella says to Hattie and the ladies.

"We're a community of women on a mission to pitch in and figure it out together," Rose adds. "We're so glad you came."

Mabel and Ed watch in awe as the twins take charge. Soon, Larry and even Hattie's son, Teddy, are right in there alongside the twins, working together as a foursome, collecting luggage and forming strategies to use the two autos to taxi the families back to the tent site and make plans to assemble more tents from the pile Ed had shipped out from the supply left over from the 1904 World's Fair.

Hattie, revealing herself to be a natural-born organizer, is right in there with the four college-aged kids, taking the lead and organizing them all as a team. Lawrence is, of course, now back to babbling away and is in on the action, as well.

Instinctively, Ed, again, sets his suitcase down to join in to help when Mabel instead picks his suitcase up, shoves it in his hand, and pushes him onto the train just as it is pulling away.

"We've got this," Mabel shouts over the roaring train engine.

Ed is forced to helplessly watch the surreal scene continue to unfold outside his train window as he steams away.

CHAPTER 7

◆ ◆ ◆

Ed will always love and admire St. Louis. There's both a peacefulness and a sense of purpose to a river town, which seems to flow right along with the water, generating endless opportunities.

"There are two kinds of investments," Ed says to the standing-room-only crowd at the St. Louis businessman's lunch. "The first is an investment opportunity where the growth has a steady history, yielding modest but certain returns."

"Which has never been your style, Eddie," an old friend of Ed's shouts out from the crowd to thunderous laughs, as nearly the whole room knows the famous E.G. Lewis or of him.

Ed forces a smile, waiting for the chuckles to die down when, in the back of the room, he finally spots what he's been waiting for: his brother, John, arriving late and, true to his personality, taking a seat quietly in the rear with what appears to be a younger colleague.

It wasn't long ago that Ed introduced John to this very room at the same table John sits at today. They were both here the day it was announced the 1904 World's Fair would be coming to St. Louis. What a memory that will always be for them.

"Women are the next market opportunity in the U.S.," Ed says, seizing back the attention of the male-only crowd. "They are the future. Say what you will about them, but women are half the population. More and more are entering the workforce. And attending university. And wives always seem to somehow outlive us husbands."

That statement causes laughs in agreement from the crowd.

"Out in California, state laws have already been passed allowing women the right to vote," Ed says, this time drawing some boos from the audience.

"You may jeer," Ed says, "but women are flocking there as a result."

"California can have them," Ed's old friend shouts again, to further laughs.

"Well, women are arriving daily in droves out there," Ed says. "Just like families used to arrive in St. Louis. Just like you all did back in the day, or your parents did. Since the dawn of time, people will seek out the newest opportunities. And investment will follow them."

Ed can tell he's starting to connect to the crowd. They have quieted and are more focused on him.

"More than half of those headed to California are women," he continues. "Atascadero is the only city out there advertising directly to them. Atascadero speaks to their hopes, dreams, wishes, and desires. We're forming a community that accepts women on day one. Not with a future promise of a national constitutional amendment of equal rights, but a future that is ready, waiting, and designed for them today. That's our mission."

Ed pauses one last time for dramatic effect.

"You have two choices. Fight it. Fight it tooth and nail and resist change to your last dying breath. That's a choice you can make. That's investment option one. Invest in the steady but boring past."

Ed stares down his previous hecklers for a moment.

"Or, there is a second investment option," he says, finishing up his speech. "You men can profit off the future."

In the back of the room, John knows if there is anything for which his brother Ed has a gift, it is winning over a room. In this room, however, the majority still hates everything Ed just said about women's rights, but John knows Ed knew that going in and that he never intended to change all their minds.

John knows all Ed needs to do today is to win over a minority, and it is obvious he's accomplished just that by the number of men clamoring to shake his brother's hand now that he's finished speaking. Gone are the days of Joseph Pulitzer and Adolphus Busch ruling this room; both died a few years prior. New men have taken their places, and many of them were not burned by Ed's prior schemes.

John waits patiently for over an hour as Ed exchanges business cards with about a quarter of the room and schedules follow-up meetings with each interested party. When Ed has finished exhausting all the leads, he finally makes his way over and gives John a bear hug.

"Oh, how I've missed you."

"You never cease to amaze," John says.

"Just living the dream, brother."

"You mean selling the dream."

"Is there a difference?" Ed asks, to which John can't help but smile.

It is great to see him, John thinks to himself as they sit down. John hands Ed a cold Budweiser and a bottle opener. Gone are the corks of old as Ed admires the new innovation of the tin cap he's just pried open. Also sitting with them is John's younger colleague, a man in his late twenties, who waits patiently to be introduced.

"This is an apprentice of mine at the publishing plant," John says. "Meet George, he's shadowing me these days."

Ed shakes George's hand. Ed can't help but notice George is about his own height for a change. Ed would normally exchange pleasantries with George, but it's time to tackle the real business at hand in St. Louis, and he doesn't have time for small talk.

"Come out to California with us," Ed says. "We need you, John. We're building something wonderful. Purpose-driven. You've done enough cleaning up of my mess here. Move Marguerite and the kids out. Time heals."

John just smiles and politely shakes his head.

"One tiny problem," he says. "My wife hates you."

"Marguerite hates me? Let me talk to her."

"Her father lost a bunch of money investing in the magazine, the bank, University City real estate, everything. Time hasn't healed your investors who went in big with all they had and lost it."

"I'm so sorry, but Atascadero is the one that will finally change all our fortunes. I can make it up to everyone."

"Don't sell to me. Don't pitch me. Not me of all people. Let's just be brothers for once in our lives."

Ed can sense the resoluteness and even pain in John's voice.

"Can we try just being two brothers having a beer together who don't want or need anything from the other," John says. "Just brothers."

"Just brothers it is," Ed says, clicking beers with John. "I like that. Just brothers."

They both enjoy their Budweiser in silence. But only briefly. It's not long before Ed can't help himself and blurts out, "Mabel isn't going to take this well."

"How is our sweet Mabel?"

"Expecting me to bring you home. I made her a promise I wouldn't take no for an answer. I swore I'd bring my brother home."

"Maybe you will," John says. "But not me. Our youngest brother might just be stupid enough to join you."

"Where is he? Still in Connecticut? Working in construction, right?"

"He's trying to break into sales."

Ed hasn't seen him since a generous family at church took him in after their parents died.

"Sales, you say?" Ed says. "Fascinating. I haven't seen him since I went off to college."

"I was off to college. You were off getting married and selling fake gold watches."

Ed can't deny that may indeed technically be more accurate.

"Where did you last see him?" Ed asks.

"In my office."

"In St. Louis? He visited?".

"He lives here now. He's been working on the printing press floor for me for over a year."

Ed can't believe it.

"Where is he now?" Ed asks. "I'd never recognize him. He was just a toddler when we left. I have to see him while I'm in town. Why didn't you bring him?"

"I did."

With that, Ed takes a quick look over at George, still sitting there, waiting patiently for the revelation to kick in. Ed takes an even better look at him. George is hands down the most handsome Lewis, with golden flowing hair and the most magnetic smile, not to mention that despite wearing a suit and tie, he is showing evidence beneath of a strapping laborer's physique given his years of working construction.

"Well, hello," George says. "Big brother, I've been waiting patiently my whole life to someday reunite with the famous Mr. E.G. Lewis."

CHAPTER 8

These days, even a moment of anonymity has become increasingly rare and precious for Ed, especially on a crowded cross-country train ride filled with enthusiastic women and their families—with more joining at each stop—all headed to Atascadero.

Ed has positioned himself in the back of the train, facing backward, hat tilted down to block his face, looking out the window at the landscapes racing by. He holds tightly to his briefcase filled with a treasure trove of newly signed convertible notes fresh from his fundraising success in St. Louis.

Ed barely has time to reflect when a very excited George plops down in front of him, a notepad filled with fresh and frantic scribbles in his hand.

"It was just as you said," George says. "I barely had to ask a single question, and the women on this train all just spilled their guts to me. They are so excited and eager about the prospect of a new life that, I guess, they'll talk to just about anyone."

Ed knew that would be true, but he suspects they especially like talking with George. Even Ed is enamored with his brother's handsomeness. George naturally possesses assets that Ed can't teach, but there's still much he can.

George wants to show Ed what he's written down in his notebook, but Ed motions for him to pause just a moment.

"Before we get into all that," Ed says, "tell me, why do you want to go into sales?"

George attempts to form his thoughts. No one has ever asked him why he wanted to get into sales before. He just assumed everyone knew that answer.

"To make money," George says.

"Wrong answer. Though I answered that question the exact same way when I was first getting started. But selling is not about making money."

"What is it then?" George asks.

"Lesson number one: It's not *selling* that leads to riches. It's *solving*. Solving problems for customers is the key. Have you ever heard the old adage, the customer is always right?"

"Yes," George says.

"Well, I don't subscribe to that. And I don't want you to either if you want to work for me. You need to recognize instead that the customer is always selfish. Incredibly selfish."

George ponders that concept as Ed continues.

"It wasn't easy for them to make, save, or even inherit a single dollar," he says. "Once they have that dollar in their hand, they learn at a young age they will not just give it away to anyone who asks for it. They don't just run around throwing away their money. No, there has to be something in it for them to part with it. You have to provide real value to them. You have to solve a pain point big enough to get them to spend it."

George likes the term "pain point." Ed can tell George may be starting to catch on as he continues.

"As a salesperson, you have to solve a big enough problem that the customer is willing to part with their hard-earned dollar. They couldn't care less about our city and what we're building— unless it selfishly aligns with their needs."

George is paying close attention now, and that's a good sign, Ed knows. He lets the concept sink in a bit more before continuing.

"Now, what did you learn in talking with them?" Ed asks.

"Where to start," George says, flipping through his notes. "Everything. Escaping their pasts. Details of wills. Kids' education. Fashion. Anticipation of a new climate. Being able to vote. How much or little they have in savings. Anxieties of meeting new people. Hoping the real thing matches up to the brochure. Hoping Atascadero really is all about the mission of women. They spilled everything."

"That is what they said," Ed says. "But look closer. What are their problems?"

George isn't sure how to answer that. He starts repeating what the women said until Ed cuts him off again.

"George, you're not ready for sales just yet. I'm sorry."

"I don't understand."

"Keep thinking about it. Find the true meaning behind what they are saying. Catalog their real problems. Or, rather, think of it as if you are rank ordering their pain points."

"Rank ordering their pain points," George repeats, writing that down, thinking for a moment, and flipping through his notes when a thought comes to him. "Like, maybe, income."

"Yes, income, that's it," Ed says excitedly. "Yes, go on."

"Well, they all have some savings, or they couldn't make the trip. But it didn't necessarily come from money they earned themselves. So, they are worried about running out and how to make more."

"Yes, exactly," Ed says. "Now, as salesmen, what can we do given we now know this about them?"

George doesn't even have to think about that; he knows the answer.

"Make it a big part of our pitch?" he says. "That land ownership comes with 'a guaranteed income for life'. Just exactly how you already pitch it."

"George, my boy, you might just be a natural."

George is pleased with himself. He knows if he's going to rise above his history of manual labor, he's going to have to learn everything he can from his older brother Ed.

Rank ordering customers' pain points now consumes George, not just for the rest of the train ride but for the rest of his career. As he begins to rank them, he smiles, realizing that the top pain points are already the main part of Ed's standard pitch.

So that's how Ed does it, George thinks to himself. That's why his pitches always hit home with customers. They are simply designed to address their largest needs.

CHAPTER 9

◆ ◆ ◆

As the train arrives in Atascadero, Ed notices it's an entirely different scene than when he left. Two banners now hang proudly at the station. One reads, "Tour Atascadero," and the other reads, "Welcome Home." Women wearing ambassador ribbons pinned to their dresses wait for the train doors to open.

Droves of women and their families exit the train and self-select toward the correct banner with the help of the ambassadors. At the center of it all, directing traffic, is Hattie, holding a clipboard, welcoming families, checking them in, and overseeing the entire operation.

For the ones who have come for a tour, Ed notices there is now a fleet of Cadillacs lined up, allowing for multiple tours at once, with women, children, grandmothers, and, on occasion, husbands filling all three seats of the convertibles. Ed assumes Kramer must have wired some of the newly raised money to the dealership in Los Angeles.

Ed sees Lawrence is still hanging around, meddling. However, when Lawrence reaches the point of talking too much, it appears Hattie has a system where she gently puts her hand on his shoulder, signaling him to focus back on the assigned task of handing out a freshly picked wildflower to each woman upon arrival. Nice touch, Ed thinks. He's already very impressed with the leadership Hattie is showing.

When Hattie finally spots Ed, her face is immediately flushed with emotion.

"Ladies, ladies," Hattie says, quieting down everyone on the platform. "Ladies, look who's returned. Our fearless founder, Mr. E.G. Lewis."

Everyone is shocked to realize Ed must have been on the train with them the entire time. Cheers ring out as he's greeted with hug after hug. All the women are admirers of his magazines, columns, women's suffrage editorials, and Atascadero sales collateral— always adorned with his favorite headshot, which they've been staring at the entire journey.

George can now see why Ed kept to himself on the train. In Atascadero, George realizes Ed will never have a moment to himself, ever. He'll always be in the limelight. As impressed as George is with his brother, he's even more impressed with Hattie. Not just her leadership, radiance, and confidence, but also her attractiveness. George was expecting an army of middle-aged widows out here, which it mostly is, but never in his wildest dreams did he ever expect to encounter someone like Hattie at the helm.

Eventually, Hattie briefly makes eye contact with George and politely nods, but George can tell it is Ed who really has her affection. She seems entirely smitten, staring at his older brother longingly. This is just another reason, George thinks, that he can't wait to learn everything he can from his brother. *Everything.*

Once the crowd is accounted for, processed, and paired with ambassadors, Ed introduces George to Hattie and she ushers them into a new convertible Cadillac. This time she's doing the driving, taxiing them around the property. Ed can barely get a word in as Hattie updates him on all the successes since he's been gone the past two weeks. But it is the changes to the camp itself that Ed finds most impressive.

56

There are now the makings of an entire tent city. Tents are perfectly arranged in straight rows. Electricity is strung to each one. Water and sewer lines have been dug. Ed estimates the tent city is probably only one-tenth the size of the one he had erected at the World's Fair, but it is well on its way to eventually matching it.

The wooden floors of the tents provide a perfect platform to hold the weight of elaborate furniture residents have shipped out. Rather than storing their belongs, they are settling into their tents as if they are decorating and furnishing a finished home.

What also surprises him is the way Marcella, Rose, Larry, and Teddy all work together as a team, along with a few other teens and several husbands. Hattie explains how those four have taken the lead in constructing the tents and infrastructure. Atascadero, as of yet not having any skilled laborers, has become reliant on its own volunteer community.

George, given his construction background, can't help but notice that the way the electricity has been run, not to mention the sewers and even the way the workers are holding hammers, isn't quite up to professional standards.

To make himself most immediately useful, George hops out of the auto and introduces himself to Marcella, Rose, Larry, and Teddy. Then George removes his suit coat and tie, strips down to just a sleeveless undershirt, and pitches right in to help and politely teach a few things to the volunteers.

Ed is pleased to see that George is a go-getter and is literally willing to roll up his sleeves. Ed also can't help but notice his brother's bronzed and toned physique from years on construction sites. George's muscles are also catching the attention of every single woman in the camp. His brother possesses so many assets Ed can't teach him.

"What do you think?" Hattie asks Ed, finally having him alone to herself.

"He's a god," Ed says.

It takes Hattie a moment to realize Ed is talking about George.

"No, silly, Atascadero. How'd we do in your absence?"

"How'd you do? Please. You all are amazing. Amazing! It's a thing of beauty. All of it. And especially you."

Ed meant her performance, but she takes it to mean more than that as her face goes flush again.

"Now, where's my dearest?" Ed says, looking around. It takes Hattie another moment to realize he's talking about his wife.

"Tending the garden, I'm certain. She's been there the whole time, having delegated everything to me."

Ed starts to walk in the direction of the garden when suddenly he thinks of something and returns back to Hattie.

"Hattie, I'm curious, have you ever had a real job in your life?"

She's embarrassed to answer but shakes her head no. Ed suspected that to be the case.

"You do now," he says. "Atascadero needs a Claire. I need a Claire."

"A what?"

"Sorry, a right-hand man, I mean," Ed corrects himself, "a right-hand woman. Someone who believes first and foremost in our mission. Someone who has my back at all times. Someone folks go to before me to get answers. Basically, my chief of staff. How'd you like that job?"

Hattie thinks for a moment.

"I thought maybe I'd already earned that job," she says.

"Indeed you have," Ed says, liking her even more. He reaches to shake her hand, which she gladly accepts before pulling him into an extended hug and stealing yet another kiss on his cheek.

Hattie releases Ed and watches him walk toward the garden. It is her first real job. It's also the first time in her life she's ever really felt valued. She also can't deny feeling a spark of something toward Ed, the kind she hasn't really ever felt in her life.

As Ed makes his way to the garden, he spies Mabel in the distance talking to a couple whose backs are to him. He'd hoped to sneak up on her, but it's impossible, given the direction Mabel is facing.

Ed can't wait to tell her how proud he is of her and how right she was regarding how sales should be organized. Her ambassador strategy, along with the money he raised in St. Louis for the Land Rush, should do the trick in the weeks they have left. And he wants to tell her all about George. And that John asked about her. And that he needs an update on Lawrence and is curious about how much damage that bottom feeder is causing. And ask if the rancher J.H. has kept to himself.

Most importantly, however, he wants to tell his wife he's missed her. He's not going to be the same man he used to be, previously distracted by work. The trip reminded him that she is his family and the most important thing in the world to him. There will be no other distractions this time or ever again. She's his wife. She's his life.

Mabel is intently listening to the couple, especially the woman whose back is to Ed. Neither Mabel nor the woman has yet to acknowledge him, but the man does, immediately stretching out his hand, which Ed accepts.

"I'm Alphonse," he says. "It's amazing what you are building out here."

"Thank you," Ed replies. "All the credit goes to my wife."

Mabel, still in an animated conversation with the woman, has an intense look on her face. Ed inches closer, attempting to cut in and interrupt. Eventually, the woman can feel Ed's presence and turns toward him. Ed immediately recognizes her face.

He wasn't sure if he'd ever see her again. Despite being several years older now, she looks as perfect and as radiant as ever and not a gray hair in those gorgeous blonde locks of hers.

Ed barely makes eye contact with Claire—Mabel's sister and the mother of the twins—when Claire hauls off and punches Ed square in the face, dropping him to the ground like a sad sack of potatoes.

CHAPTER 10

◆ ◆ ◆

A few minutes later, having retreated to Ed and Mabel's tent, Mabel applies a cold rag to Ed's face while Alphonse attempts to apply another to Claire's bruised fist, but Claire pushes him away.

"Get the twins," she says to Alphonse. "We're taking them back to college. Far away from here."

Outside the tent, Marcella and Rose are beside themselves. The last thing they want to do is leave. Larry and Teddy attempt to comfort them. Claire hasn't caught on yet that the tent doesn't really provide any privacy and that basically all of Atascadero can hear them. But even if she knew, she wouldn't care.

Claire continues to go on and on about how all she's ever wanted is for her girls to have the opportunities she never had. She points her finger right at Ed.

"How dare you not pay their tuition and put them to work out there," she says. "When will you ever change?"

Ed takes this tongue-lashing straight on, nodding as if he's intently listening, when he's actually taking a moment to size up this Alphonse fellow who has somehow tamed the heart of the legendary Claire.

Alphonse is tall and thin with a tight mustache and perfectly coiffed hair. He's actually more of a dandy than Ed would have expected for Claire. Ed always assumed she'd find someone more like George, or even him. More rugged, handsome, built.

Alphonse doesn't seem her type, but he appears to have one thing going for him: he knows to keep quiet when Claire gets angry, especially when it has to do with her girls.

Ed certainly knows to keep quiet in this situation, as well. He's never going to win a battle with Claire. Instead, he looks to Mabel for help. The only person on earth who can stand up to Claire is sweet Mabel. Claire is still fit to be tied, going on and on, as Ed practically begs Mabel with his eyes to help him out. Finally, she obliges.

"What did it feel like?" Mabel asks Claire, startling her a bit. Claire is not used to being interrupted.

"What did what feel like?" Claire asks.

"Punching Eddie in the face."

"Glorious. It felt glorious."

Mabel dares a little smirk. So does Ed. And even Alphonse. It takes a long while, but eventually, Claire lets her guard down.

"I've missed you," Claire says to Mabel, opening her arms. The two sisters embrace, something Claire realizes they should have done when she first arrived.

After a while, when Claire has calmed down a bit, Mabel talks directly to her sister, ignoring their husbands.

"Look, the twins are yours, not mine," Mabel says. "I could never love them more than their mother, but you know how much I do love them."

Claire starts to tear up. She knows Mabel wanted to have kids more than Claire ever did. Too often life just isn't fair that way.

"I know," Claire says. "I know you love them."

"The very next morning after they arrived, we had them packed up to return to college."

"I didn't know that," Claire says, confused. "I assumed Eddie just put them right to work."

"I'm not saying that wasn't his first instinct, but he didn't. He came to the conclusion, just the same as me, that they should go back to school. He was all set to take them to Chicago himself."

Ed nods, not that Claire cares or is even looking at him.

"Well, why didn't he?" Claire asks.

"I'll admit, it was actually my fault," Mabel says. "I realized I couldn't do it alone."

This is not at all how Claire had envisioned it in her head upon receiving the letter from the twins that they had left school. She was certain the blame was Ed's alone.

"The twins have missed too much of their spring semester at this point," Mabel says. "We'll get them back there in the fall. Eddie has the money now. I'll make sure Kramer sets it aside."

Claire could never trust Ed, but she has no reason to ever doubt Mabel. Ever. Ed can tell Claire might be appearing to reach a point of acceptance, but she still appears unsure of something.

"The twins are not the only issue," Claire says.

"What else?" Mabel asks. "What else is wrong?"

"Alphonse and I are going to have to stay here too for a while."

"Great, but why?"

"Alphonse lost his job when he decided to travel out here with me."

Alphonse, not seeming to be upset or embarrassed by the revelation, nods it is true.

"I'm so sorry," Mabel says. "I had no idea."

"It's okay," Alphonse says. "I was planning to find something in Chicago when we took the girls back."

"We'd love for you both to stay here," Mabel says. "There's plenty of work for both of you. Eddie always says if he'd had Claire out here from the start, he would've had skyscrapers built by now."

"I say that all the time," Ed says, ecstatic about his sudden fortune to have Claire back again.

"Well, my days of making all your crazy ideas work are behind me," Claire says. "I think I'll just help Mabel out in the garden. Besides, it appears that Hattie woman has my old job covered."

She'll never be you, Ed thinks to himself.

"If I'm being honest," Claire says, "We have to stay. I just can't bear to leave the twins again."

Claire looks at Alphonse, not for approval but to make sure he understands.

"Where they go, I go from here on out," Claire says.

It appears obvious by Alphonse's face that he must comply, which he does.

The sisters again embrace. Ed shakes hands with Alphonse. Alphonse hugs Mabel. The twins, having heard the entire conversation outside, now rush into the tent to get in on the hugs.

Ed wonders for a moment whether Claire might like a reconciliatory hug from him, but quickly realizes she definitely does not. Regardless, for the first time in a long time, Ed's family—his team—is back in action again.

CHAPTER 11

Much further up the mountain, J.H. sits on horseback overlooking the valley. He's spent years of his life out here avoiding women. Only a month ago the only visible man-made structure he could see from this vantage point was his mansion. But now the burgeoning tent city full of women is all that occupies the horizon.

If Ed had been here the last few weeks, J.H. would have stopped all this, but women have always proved to be too much for him. Especially swarms of women. Cattle can be controlled and prodded. Even ranch hands. But not women, in his experience. Certainly not for long.

There's something about that Mabel he just can't quite put his finger on. There are dozens of women now in the camp, but none compare to Mabel. Not even close. How Ed was lucky enough to land her he'll never understand.

But J.H. suspects everything Ed attempts is doomed to fail. He knows men like Ed. Ed is a house of cards, and J.H. always has the ace up his sleeve. In fact, that is exactly how Atascadero came into his possession all those years ago in a famous card game with Patrick Washington Murphy, who had been sent by his father Bernard to run to run the rancho after Bernard himself had won it in a card game from Pedro Estrada who was given Atascadero as part of the 1860 Mexican Land Grant. Both Patrick and Pedro were handed Atascadero making it easier for them to wager it.

J.H. knows that no matter the risk, sometimes you're dealt the cards. Sometimes you're not. But the worst would be sitting on Ed's side of the table, thinking he has it won. J.H. can still see young Patrick's face after he laid down his cards and reached for the pot, assuming he had won, without first waiting to see what J.H. had in his hand.

Along with J.H.'s cherished memory of a devastated Patrick's face, not to mention the disappointment of the father, Bernard, and Pedro's face before that, he'll soon be adding Ed's and all these women's faces to his collection. He'll soon cherish those memories just as much as the ones of the past but, if he's being honest with himself, the look on Mabel's face might be a little harder for him to witness.

Regardless, Ed has already played his hand, and J.H. is still holding his tight to his vest. In the end, J.H. knows he always wins. Always. It's just a question of if he can win over Mabel, too.

CHAPTER 12

◆ ◆ ◆

The next morning, Ed's new management team joins him in the administration tent. In attendance are Mabel, Claire, and Hattie along with George, Alphonse, and Kramer. They gather around the board where Kramer is refreshing the number of tours scheduled and lots sold.

"When I left for St. Louis, we were at 100 sold of the 1,000 we needed for the bank loan," Ed says, watching Kramer do the math, always in his head without a need ever to write it down.

It's still surreal for Ed to see what Atascadero has quickly become since he left for St. Louis just two weeks ago. He is amazed by all the tents going up, women giving tours, families moving in, communal dinners, a city starting to form, and, most of all, now having his family and team reunited.

Ed used to start his day with a coffee and a newspaper at the train station. Now, instead of giving tours, he's a stop on the tour. This morning, he has already shaken hands, given hugs, and even helped Hattie close a deal. He also loves seeing the college-aged kids—Marcella, Rose, Teddy, and even Larry—organizing the food lines. Having all the organizational tasks expertly under control creates time for Ed to get back to his war room with his executive team to plot out his strategy.

Ed watches Kramer change 100 lots sold to 300. Not bad. Better than Ed had anticipated. Kramer sets down the chalk, walks across the floor to the side of the tent, and goes back to his routine of opening and sorting through the mail. Now that Ed sees new totals, he's ready to form a plan.

"Okay, 300 of 1,000 with 30 days left," Ed says. "We appear on pace to get to maybe 500 sold before the land rush. So, we need the land rush to bring in another 500. Or the final half."

They all pause a moment and take in the numbers. Ed tries to read their faces, but it is Claire he's most interested in as he passes out drafts of promotional mailers for the land rush event.

"This is the new mailer Mr. Kramer and I came up with," Ed says. "We now have the funding to send it out of St. Louis to our list of several hundred thousand former magazine subscribers. I want to know what you think. Especially you, Claire, since this is the first time you are getting a real peek behind the curtain. Thoughts? Also, Alphonse? George? Anyone?"

Alphonse, looking over the mailer, just nods and cedes to Claire. Ed likes that Alphonse is continuing to show signs of being content to stand on the sidelines, where Ed prefers him to be as well. George, Mabel, and Hattie are still reading and processing the mailer.

All eyes are back on Claire now as she reads over the mailer and thinks this through. Hattie and George have heard so much about Claire that they are fascinated to get a peek into her famous mind. As such, they wouldn't dare offer a thought ahead of her even if they had one.

"It will come down to two things," Claire finally says. "The first is your relationship with your bankers. When was the last time you spoke to them? Any wiggle room on the 1,000 presales?"

Now that Ed thinks about it, it has been quite some time since he's spoken to them. He didn't get to see them while he was in St. Louis because his main contacts were out of town on business.

He's not sure the last time Kramer has corresponded with them either.

"And the other thing is the U.S. Postal Service," Claire says, holding up the mailer. "You are promising everything under the sun here. You even literally have a California sun shining down on the claim—'with every lot purchase comes agriculture income for life'."

Ed was wondering if anyone in the room would pick up on that. Despite saying it as part of his sales pitch for quite some time, this is the first he's ever considered putting it in writing.

"The last time I saw you was seven years ago, Eddie," Claire says. "What were your two biggest challenges then?"

"Banks and the U.S. Postal Service," he says sheepishly.

The room lets out an audible sigh. Mabel, too. When Claire puts it that simply and that directly, which is her gift, it's easy to see that all the effort they've put in over the last seven years in many ways has done nothing but get them right back to where they started.

"Mr. Kramer," Claire says, "as a lawyer, or whatever it is you are purporting to be these days, do you have concerns about Eddie's language in the mailer?"

"Not if we succeed in our endeavor," Kramer says. "But if we do not, the mailer could be used by the prosecution to impeach our credibility or to demonstrate that we have a consciousness of guilt."

Everyone starts to look uncomfortable now, avoiding eye contact with Ed while beginning to realize the serious consequences as Kramer continues.

"However, the mailer is of secondary importance," Kramer says. "Edward, during your sojourn to St. Louis, you articulated the bankers were temporarily indisposed due to professional commitments elsewhere."

"I said they were out of town. Use plain speak." Ed implores. "Where were they?"

"Visiting D.C.," Ed says, not realizing the ramifications of that until now. At the time, he just thought of them as being out of town. But saying D.C. out loud just now sends goosebumps up his spine, triggering warnings of conspiracy.

"I propose that we transfer our banking business to a Los Angeles-based financial institution," Kramer says. "The requirement for a locus geographically discontiguous from the District of Columbia has become evident. Might I suggest one of Hearst's banks in Los Angeles?"

Ed needs a moment to think. The last time he spoke to Hearst about this, the proposed terms with Los Angeles banks were nowhere as good as the St. Louis ones, but he might not have a choice at this point.

Before Ed can continue the meeting, a flustered woman barges into the tent with an apologetic ambassador hot on her heels.

"Ed, sorry to interrupt, meet Mrs. Maryanne Raymer," the ambassador says to Ed. "All the way from Lincoln, Nebraska, here with her children."

"My pleasure," Ed says, crossing the room and reaching his hand out to Mrs. Raymer, who doesn't take it.

Mrs. Raymer is a stout, broad-shouldered woman with a set jaw. She's all business, forgoing any first-meeting pleasantries. She stares Ed down with her furrowed brow.

"I expected more out here. I'm not impressed."

Ed glances over at the ambassador, who mouths the words, "I'm sorry." But Ed isn't flustered in the least. He takes a breath and musters up his famous charm.

"Nice to meet you, Mrs. Maryanne Raymer. When I was growing up in Connecticut, there was a girl in my school that I had the biggest crush on. Her name was also Maryanne. I love that name. Mabel and I had always hoped to have a little girl and name her Maryanne."

Ed glances over to Mabel, who doesn't immediately affirm Ed's statement, but eventually nods a bit as if to say, "Sure, I'll go along with it." Mrs. Raymer ignores all this anyway, taking the conversation back to business.

"Your brochure talks about roads and orchards and homes and municipal buildings and water and infrastructure," Mrs. Raymer says. "Not tents. Not a tent city. There's no mention of tents anywhere."

Ed ignores that complaint and continues on with his story.

"But instead of calling that girl back in grade school Maryanne like everyone else, I always called her Mare for short," Ed says. "Do folks ever call you Mare?"

"Folks call me Mrs. Raymer," she says. "Or the widow Raymer. Besides, when I think of 'mare' I think of an old horse."

The team does their best to hide their smiles, especially since Mrs. Raymer does look like an old horse, come to think of it.

"No, I called her Mare because she was like the 'mayor' of the schoolyard. Mare was the smartest of all of us. Kept us all in line. A natural leader. Before we dared do anything or played anything, we looked to Mare for approval. She ran the place. She was also the prettiest girl in the entire school. I hadn't thought of Mare in all these years until I just laid eyes on you."

Most in the room can't help but roll their eyes, but the flattery does seem to catch Mrs. Raymer off guard just a bit.

"Well, that's, um, fine, but the brochure isn't…." she says.

"You know what Atascadero needs?" Ed interrupts. "It needs a mayor. Someone to help keep us on track. Hold us accountable to our mission. Organize the other ladies and help shape our community. Could you see yourself being our mayor, Mare?"

"Well, I mean, I hadn't considered…."

"A city like Atascadero isn't a brochure," Ed says. "It's a place to start over. It's even a chance for a new name."

Mrs. Raymer wants to get back to her complaint, but the vision of a new name, a new city, and a fresh start may be winning her over a bit.

"Mare, the whole rest of the country is complaint-ridden. It's still so new that we're constantly innovating all the time, trying to get it right. And most complaints fall on deaf ears. Especially those, let's face it, issued by women to men. But out here is a chance for women—for you, Mare—to finally be heard."

Mrs. Raymer starts to say something, but Ed stops her.

"And a chance to listen," he says. "I'm listening to you, and what I'm hearing is a need to create a culture in Atascadero of folks who feel they can finally speak up. I love that about you. What do you say? How about you make Atascadero your home and, in turn, you help us make it better? What do you say, Mare?"

"Mare," she says, for the first time, trying the name on for size. "But the brochure…."

"Improving the brochure will be your first course of action when you get out here and get your family moved in. Now let my brother George and Hattie here walk you outside and show you what home lots we have left. How do you like your morning sun?"

"My morning sun?" Mare says.

"Do you like it to hit your front porch or back porch?" Ed asks. "George and Hattie will show you all the options, and I'll join up with you in just a moment."

George and Hattie stand and walk Mare out of the tent. Once they are well on their way, Ed is back to where he left off, focusing on Claire.

"Here's what we do," he says. "First, we send the mailer because we need the biggest response possible by the deadline. If we don't get that, we're in bigger trouble. Second, Mr. Kramer and I will head immediately to Los Angeles to line up another bank."

Ed looks out to gauge the room's reaction but notices everyone is smiling and laughing.

"What?" he says to them.

"Mare?" Mabel says, to which everyone laughs. Especially Alphonse. Even Kramer.

"Have you all forgotten our purpose?" Ed says. "We're mission-driven out here. I love Mare. I hope we attract hundreds more Mares. California was built on missions."

Claire has heard enough.

"As I said, I think this time around I'll be smart like my sister Mabel," she says, "I'll help in the garden. I'll let Hattie, George, and the others make your crazy ideas happen."

"Come on," Ed says. "It's not that bad. We've been in worse situations. I need you in the thick of it. Why the garden?"

"So, we at least have food to eat," Claire says.

CHAPTER 13

It takes Ed and Kramer a few different stops in Los Angeles to figure out Hearst is indeed in town. Eventually, one of Hearst's traveling secretaries gives Ed an address where they might find him before the day runs out.

On the drive there, Ed takes Kramer out to look at the new Los Angeles Aqueduct that has just been completed. Ed has read that the water delivered via the aqueduct, considered to be the greatest engineering feat of all time, second only to the nearly completed Panama Canal, is the missing key necessary for Los Angeles's continued explosive growth.

The population in Los Angeles isn't even in the top fifteen cities in America, but Ed suspects it is about to grow even faster now that they have water. Luckily, he has water covered from the start in Atascadero.

The aqueduct is indeed impressive, Ed thinks, but he is also amazed at how all the Los Angeles roads are laid out in a perfect grid as he drives north of town to meet with Hearst. On the East Coast, the roads are all paved on old horse and buggy paths that go in all directions. West Coast cities like Los Angeles certainly have an advantage in that they are all planned out thoughtfully from the start.

Ed parks the auto in front of what appears to be a new development that is going to be a high-end subdivision. A motion picture is being filmed on the property, making it hard to find a place to park given thousands of people are there to watch the filming. Like the rest of the crowd, Ed and Kramer pay 25 cents each to get closer to the action of an actual movie being made.

Neither Ed nor Kramer has really seen anything like it before. A fake railroad track has been laid along with the shell of a locomotive that is actually made of wood and propelled by an auto that is hidden inside. There are horses, wagons, and hundreds of extras dressed like last-century settlers. It takes Ed a moment to notice the irony in that the film is recreating the Oklahoma Land Rush.

It takes Ed and Kramer a while longer to spot the camera, director, and the VIP chair area. Ed is looking for Hearst when Hearst instead finds Ed.

"Eddie," Hearst says, his large hand outstretched. "Welcome back to Los Angeles. My girl called ahead and said you were in town."

Ed is excited to see him. Hearst and Ed are about the same age, but Hearst towers over him. Hearst may be one of the tallest people Ed has ever met, and Hearst could say the opposite about Ed.

After some small talk and meeting Kramer, Hearst invites them to duck under a rope line and sit in the VIP area behind the director. Without warning, the director yells "Action!" and chaos erupts before them as the onlookers cheer. There's no need for the crowd to be quiet as there is no sound associated with motion cameras. There is only the picture itself and the sound of the organist playing along with it in movie houses.

Horses, wagons, and extras in costume recreate the Oklahoma Land Rush. Ed is fixated on what must be the lead character in the center of the action, one of the most beautiful teenage girls he's ever seen. Her blond hair, and the way it is lit to draw all eyes on her, is a striking contrast to the other actors around her.

As the director yells "Cut!" Hearst is the first to clap and holler in her direction, to which she smiles back at him and waves.

"She's going to be a huge star," Hearst says. "Marion Davies. Remember that name. And that face."

Ed has certainly noticed her beauty, as well, but to him, she's just a kid. But Ed can tell Hearst's attraction to her is different.

As the director sets up for the next shot, Ed wastes no time pitching Hearst.

"I'm all set up in Atascadero," he says. "Land is optioned. The presales are amazing. We've got our own 'land rush' sales event planned in less than a month. Banks are lined up. We're going to give Los Angeles and even San Francisco a run for their money before long."

"Wonderful," Hearst says, not really paying full attention, his eyes still on the young starlet.

"Maybe you'd like to send some reporters up to cover the story," Ed says. "I'll give you an exclusive."

"I only deal with exclusives," Hearst says.

"You got it," Ed says, "but the real reason we're here is that I have something confidential to tell you."

The word "confidential" does get Hearst's attention as he turns to look at Ed.

"I want to renege on my St. Louis banks and instead work with Los Angeles banks," Ed says. "I feel local California banks would be better."

"Local is always better," Hearst says. "I bet further from D.C. is also better."

"What have you heard?"

"Whispers. Just whispers like whether you really still have banking deals or not in St. Louis."

Ed tries to keep a poker face.

"Well," he says, "all the more reason to keep it local."

"As a matter of fact," Hearst says, "I'm an investor in the Los Angeles bank that is backing this very subdivision development we're filming at."

"Is that right? You don't say."

"I thought filming the opening day of the most expensive film ever made here might draw some attention to the new neighborhood," Hearst says. "I'm building a new estate here myself to show others the full possibilities. I even have my army of reporters and photographers here covering it."

Despite all the commotion of the scene around him, Ed had already noticed that. When walking in, he also noticed the coordination of the entire event with billboards for the new subdivision in plain sight for all in the audience watching the scene.

But Ed knows that a movie, or even a new subdivision, or even a new bank wouldn't get Hearst out here. Hearst's involvement has everything to do instead with that young starlet. And he suspects that the army of photographers and reporters is really here to cover her, ensuring instant fame.

"My bank executives are over there," Hearst says. "I can wave them over in a heartbeat, but they are going to want two things. Given the position you are in, I'd suggest you give both to them."

"What are they?" Ed asks.

"That they be granted an exclusivity period in Atascadero. Who doesn't like to be the only newspaper or bank in town?"

"Who doesn't? And the other?"

"More presales," Hearst says. "St. Louis may have required only ten percent, but we'll be requiring double that. Twenty."

Ed doesn't say yes or no, because he knows it doesn't matter. Hearst holds all the cards and has him over a barrel. Ed has no choice but to nod as Hearst motions the bankers over to meet Ed and Kramer. As they make their way over, Hearst has one more thing to say to Ed.

"And none of your 'mission talk' and 'building a better place for women' and all that hoo-ha," Hearst says. "These guys want to make money."

Ed's instinct is to protest and stand up for what he most believes in, but in the end he acquiesces. While pitching the bankers—and to distract himself from the fact that he's selling out—he glances around a bit more at the surreal scene around them, taking in the sprawling movie set and land development. It also helps to distract him from having to listen to the terrible business deal he's being forced to take.

Ed eventually notices Hearst is back to eyeballing the starlet, who is now talking with the director. Ed thinks about the pressure the director must be under organizing such a large film set and hopes the director is smart enough to keep all the billboards out of the frame.

Advertisements for Hearst's neighborhood are nearly everywhere, facing the crowd and the main road in nearly all directions, all reading the same: "Between the City and Sea—Welcome to Los Angeles' Newest Development—Beverly Hills."

CHAPTER 14

At first, George was disappointed he wasn't invited to go with Ed to Los Angeles. He had hoped to shadow Ed in all his endeavors, especially when there might be a chance to meet with important people. But the next best thing is getting to spend time alone with Hattie.

Each morning, George reports to her in the administration tent to see what he can do to help. His favorite tasks are giving tours or filling in for Ed as the closer, but lately, it's the current residents that Hattie needs the most help with as she flips through a stack of work orders.

"How about you knock these out today?" Hattie says, reading through them. "Loose dresser knob, a gash in tent fabric, a splinter in flooring—probably just needs some sanding down—and…."

Hattie pauses a moment reading the next one, which causes her to smile.

"And Agnes needs your help. It just says, 'Need George again. Squeaky bed springs.'"

At first, like a dummy, George would jump at the opportunity to grab his toolbox and get out into the community to help. But he's quickly caught on that what's actually happening is the women are manufacturing complaints just to get him alone in their tents with them. Nothing out of sorts ever actually happens on these service-order visits. Still, he's starting to realize that after simply receiving a visit from George, the women then brag about it, building up a bit of a cachet for themselves.

"How about *your* bed springs?" George asks.

"What about them?"

"Well, you've always got me out there helping everybody else. Anything in your tent that needs attention?"

Hattie gives him a stern but playful look as she hands him the stack of work orders.

"My tent is not the priority at the moment," she says.

Hattie takes a brief moment to enjoy that handsome grin of his. He's certainly been more forward the more time they spend together.

"I'm just saying," George says. "I got all the tools here and everything."

Before she can come up with a clever response, Claire's husband Alphonse, of all people, enters the tent. He's mostly kept to himself since he's been here, so his presence is a surprise to both Hattie and George.

"Hope I'm not interrupting," Alphonse says.

"You are," George says.

Alphonse is immediately taken aback as Hattie quickly reassures him.

"Ignore him," she says. "What can I do for you?"

"I had an idea I wanted to run by you, Hattie. I can't help but notice the camp is getting a bit, well, restless. Have you noticed that?"

"Indeed," she says. "Why do you think I send George out into their tents every day?"

George looks at her as if to say, "Very funny," as an idea comes to him.

"Alphonse," George says, "how about you open a saloon or something?"

"A saloon?" Alphonse says.

"Like you worked at back in Memphis."

"What? A saloon? No, it wasn't a saloon. I worked at a theater."

"A theater?" Hattie says. "Interesting."

George and Hattie glance at each other. Apparently, they had been given some misinformation. Alphonse shakes it off.

"With your permission," Alphonse says, "I was thinking we might put on a stage play. I'll direct it, of course. Something with lots of female parts. And requiring scenery and costuming. What do you think? Something to both distract and bring the community together."

"I think that sounds wonderful," Hattie says.

"Anything that might cut down on work orders sounds great to me," George says.

"Great," Alphonse says. "I'll make it happen."

As Alphonse turns to leave, he gets one more thought he can't help but share.

"George, any interest in playing the male lead?"

"Is it a Lothario?" Hattie says.

This causes Alphonse to nearly fall over in laughter as he shares a moment with Hattie. George has no idea what a Lothario is.

"I'm sorry," George says. "Theater is not for me."

"A shame," Alphonse says. "So much of acting is simply looking the part."

"Now Ed would make a great lead," Hattie says. "That's a real draw for sure."

"Indeed," Alphonse says. "We'll have to work him into it somehow."

"If my brother plays a part," George says, "then so will I."

Alphonse gives them both a smile and a nod as he heads out of the tent, leaving George and Hattie alone.

"So, Ed would make a better lead than me?" George says. "You'd take my brother over me?"

Hattie is not sure how to answer that other than by being honest.

"Well," she says, "I would."

She gathers up her clipboard and heads to the train station to start her day. George, watching longingly until Hattie disappears from view, flips reluctantly through the stack of work orders, wondering if the day will ever come when he'll be given a request to service her.

CHAPTER 15

Returning from Los Angeles a few days later, Ed expects that the tent city will be a few rows larger, which it is, but there is something else he hadn't expected to see.

Apparently, George, the twins, Larry, Teddy, and some other men in the camp have constructed a large wooden stage at the base of the mountains on a strategic spot where the natural acoustics in all directions are superb. An audience can sit anywhere on the surrounding hillsides and hear even a whisper coming from the stage.

Ed enjoys sitting there watching early rehearsals of Atascadero's first stage performance. He especially enjoys observing Alphonse, who is amazing in the way he expertly coordinates a cast of nearly a hundred, with everyone seemingly wanting to get in on the action.

From what Ed can tell, the storyline has something to do with the women of King Arthur's court and their husbands, the knights, who are away on a mission. There are also a few scenes of Lancelot and Guinevere, who, to Ed's delight, are to be played by George and Hattie in the final production. Hattie is often too busy for the rehearsals, and Ed chuckles at the sight of the other women fighting for a chance to get to stand in for Hattie and play a love scene with George.

Ed himself is expected to play King Arthur in the final scene, but Lawrence has been gracious enough to stand in for him throughout all the rehearsals. Ed watches Lawrence off to the side practicing Ed's single line over and over while wielding a big wooden sword that George must have constructed. By all accounts, Lawrence is absolutely terrible even as a stand-in, but it keeps him busy.

On the hillside, enjoying the rehearsal, Ed flips through a stack of mail and paperwork. The early response to the mailer has been strong. However, there are dozens of notes from folks saying they can't make the Land Rush event but are asking if, instead, it would be alright if they wired money.

Ed knows there is a telephone line that goes to J.H.'s home, but no telegram lines. He expects the banks in Los Angeles to have telegram lines, which gives him the idea to make an important tweak to the next mailer. As he scans the mail, he is reminded that all the best ideas in his entire career have come from listening closely to customers, just like when he came up with the idea for a postal bank years ago based on the feedback from readers.

As he's reminiscing, Mabel and Claire sit down next to him, still dirty from gardening.

"As you can imagine, Eddie," Mabel says, "Claire has already rearranged my entire garden to maximize light, water, harvest order, and even color."

Ed just smiles as Claire doesn't show any real reaction. Ed knows that optimization is just who she is.

"Look at those four," Claire says, motioning to the stage. "I don't like how close they are getting one bit."

The college kids have agreed to a dance number in the production that Alphonse has choreographed. Ed notices Marcella and Larry are natural dancers. Rose and Teddy, not so much. But they stumble along the best they can, and all four of them always have big smiles on their faces whether they get it right or wrong.

"Remember John's wedding?" Mabel says to Claire and Ed. "You two drew quite the crowd that night on the dance floor."

"Don't you dare mention that to Alphonse," Claire says. "The last thing I need is more pressure from him to get me to join the production."

"I wish you would," Mabel says. "Everyone adores Alphonse. I have a feeling there will be many more of these shows."

Again watching Alphonse, Ed notices how he masterfully coordinates the cast. Ed trusts Alphonse will use the magic of theater to transform what appears to be madness and chaos into an organized, entertaining show by the end.

Ed hopes that same magic pours over into his own entrepreneurial pursuits in Atascadero itself. He certainly needs to find some magic. And soon. He hasn't gotten up the nerve yet to tell Mabel and Claire about the new bank terms requiring them to double their pre-sales goals with just a few weeks left.

Ed is lost in that thought when suddenly, ARTILLERY BLASTS ring out in the hills behind the stage, and given the especially excellent acoustics, the explosions feel as though they are happening right next to them.

The entire theater production is in pandemonium now, with women running in all directions, many of them tripping and falling. Ordnance and shells continue to hit the hills at a volume that shows no sign of stopping. Children are covering their ears. A lovely evening has turned into pure panic and mayhem.

Ed tries to imagine the source of the cannon fire, but the answer suddenly unfolds as swarms of uniformed U.S. Army soldiers charge down the hill, waving guns affixed with bayonets, wearing gas masks, and screaming war cries at the top of their lungs.

CHAPTER 16

◆ ◆ ◆

Lieutenant Malone, a young army officer, hat in hand, is beside himself, standing with Ed, Mabel, Claire, Kramer, and Alphonse.

"I'm going to be court-martialed for this," Lt. Malone bemoans.

The war games scene has turned into one of considerable reconciliation. Army medics are apologetically tending to the wounds of some women and children who have scraped their hands and knees as a result of having fallen down, not to mention several women who have outright fainted and are being slowly brought back up to a sitting position.

"How could you not have seen us?" Alphonse asks, unable to get his mind around what happened.

"Well, this stage wasn't here just a few days ago," Lt. Malone says, "but I should have checked again. We were assured this ridge was a safe place to practice our maneuvers."

"By whom?" Kramer says.

But Ed already knows that answer.

"By the landowner," Lt. Malone says. "J.H. Henry."

Mabel and Claire shoot a look of daggers at Ed.

Lt. Malone appears as if he may actually start to cry. The threat of him doing so actually overcomes Alphonse, who puts his hand on Lt. Malone's shoulder to comfort him.

"If I'm not the worst soldier in the army, then I don't know who is," Lt. Malone says, touching and appreciating Alphonse's hand. "My father insisted I join. If we are ever to go to war, I'm going to get everyone killed."

Lt. Malone's eyes are watering now as Alphonse continues to comfort him.

Ed takes in the scene around him. All the young soldiers are exhibiting the same genuine remorse as Lt. Malone despite enduring the wrath of some very upset women. The threat of war is momentarily less daunting than the fury of enraged mothers yelling in the young soldiers' faces and showing them the wounds of their children.

As Ed takes in the aftermath of this madness, an opportunity occurs to him.

CHAPTER 17

◆ ◆ ◆

A few evenings later, J.H. sits high on the ridge, watching his beautiful valley, now overrun by strangers, being abused as backdrop for an elaborate play production complete with period costumes, a replica of King Arthur's castle, and voices ringing out from the amphitheater, polluting his land.

Given the amateur nature of the production, Alphonse has to shout out a line here and there when someone stumbles, but it appears to all to be in good fun, especially now that the women in the play have an added reason to perform.

Out in the audience, laughing along with the jokes and clapping loudly after each dance number—all to J.H.'s further disgust—is the entire regiment of soldiers led enthusiastically by Lt. Malone. The audience of young men has put a real kick in the step of the entire camp the last few days, quite the opposite of J.H.'s intended plan.

J.H. is starting to realize that Ed, just like a cockroach, is proving to be a bit harder to kill than he thought, but the game isn't over yet. As J.H. ponders his next move, a voice surprises him.

"Enjoying the show?" Mabel asks, having somehow successfully snuck up on him and on his own property.

Without invitation, Mabel sidles up next to him. At first, she doesn't say anything, watching the show herself, especially since the dance scene with Marcella and Larry, accompanied by Rose and Teddy, is now unfolding.

Mabel has watched them practice it a hundred times, so she's not surprised to see them nail the actual performance. Finally seeing some younger women on stage makes it the favorite number thus far of the young soldiers, as well.

"I have a theory about you," she says to J.H. "I'm thinking 40 years ago, some young woman did a number on you. And you've been out here hiding from the world ever since."

J.H. holds his cards very close to his vest, but Mabel can tell she might not be far off in her assumption. She can also tell there is no way he's going to reveal anything to her.

"You know what our camp is full of?" she asks.

"Squatters and degenerates?"

That makes Mabel laugh. She even elbows his arm a bit.

"You have a quick wit," she says. "I like that. Not what I expected. Handsome and also funny."

He knows she's trying to butter him up, but standing this close to her, smelling her perfume, that touch to his arm, well, he has to admit, it may be working. She did after all call him handsome.

"You'll never find a more eligible group of women," Mabel says. "Most of them have had someone do a number on them, too. I've had more than one of them say to me, 'Who is the handsome rancher who's always keeping to himself?'."

"This is Ed's big plan? Send you up here to flatter me? Charm the old coot?"

"No. He'd be jealous if he knew I was up here," she says. "He knows I admire you. He's backstage, getting ready for his big scene. He's none the wiser."

"Is that right?"

"That's right. But I just can't get my head around you."

"How so?"

"We're about to give you a check for a million dollars. Making you the most eligible bachelor one could ever imagine."

"The army is going to make me twice as rich. And allow me to stay and keep living here."

"Oh," she says. "Apologies. I get it now. You prefer bayonets to bonnets."

A wry smile forms on his face.

"Now you're being clever. I very much prefer bonnets."

"Start showing it," she says. "Lean into life a bit. Let me take you down there and introduce you to a few of the gals. That would be a real reason to stay on here. It would give you a new mission."

"I'm just fine up here."

"If you change your mind," she says, "you know where to find us."

"Not for much longer. I bet Ed didn't tell you the full truth about Los Angeles. I know about the new banks. I know about having to double the presales. I know everything and even a bit more. One thing you'll soon learn is that I always, always have the ace up my sleeve. Always."

"All I can say," she says, "is that it must be awfully lonesome. Plotting schemes. Destroying dreams. I guess I'll leave you to your evil doings, then. But you know what's more fun? Maybe try being the hero for a change."

As Mabel walks away, great applause rings out as the college kids finish their dance number. J.H. can't help but steal a look or two at Mabel leaving. He is feeling something he hasn't felt in 40 years. The very thing he's worked hard to avoid ever since.

On stage, Hattie, dressed as Guinevere, and George, dressed as Lancelot, come out for the final scene.

Many emotions are now drifting through J.H.'s brain, including something he thinks about every day, which is his own Guinevere running off with a Lancelot all those years ago.

Leaving him stuck out here all these years, like Arthur, to rule over a lost Camelot.

Ed, dressed as King Arthur, wooden sword in hand, waits off stage for his cue as George and Hattie are having their big scene where Lancelot professes his love, encouraging her to run off with him. Hattie, in character, unsure, relents as George, in character, emits even greater efforts of persuasion.

Ed notices Lawrence in the front row, nervously watching the scene, mouthing all the words of both characters in anticipation of Ed's big line. Ed had thought about just giving Lawrence the part, but it was obvious from Alphonse and the rest of the cast that the poor guy just wasn't going to cut it. Even Lawrence had seemed relieved when Ed took over in the last rehearsal. After a couple more lines, Ed's big moment on stage is approaching.

As Hattie and George's scene crescendos with George embracing her, their big kiss imminent, suddenly, a very large and intoxicated man steps onto the stage. The soldiers in the audience assume this is part of the show, but the cast knows otherwise. Alphonse starts to run on stage, but Teddy beats him to it.

"Dad," Teddy says. "Dad, no!"

But the man, Ted Sr., is drunk and enraged. Teddy has seen this look on his father too many times before in his life to count. It's exactly what he and his mother have worked so hard to escape.

As Teddy attempts to slow his father, Ted instead locks his eyes on his wife, Hattie, with George still performing their scene. George's back is to Ted, but he can tell something is wrong by Hattie's face, which suddenly shifts to one of pure terror.

Teddy attempts to stop his father, but he's no match for the larger Ted, who grabs his son and tosses him into the scenery, sending painted castle walls down on top of him. Rose rushes on stage to help uncover Teddy from the rubble.

All of this distracts George enough that he's not ready for Ted's clenched fist, now sailing through the air, sucker-punching George across his jaw, dropping him immediately to the stage floor.

No one is left now between Ted and Hattie. Ted grabs her by the arms, shaking her and taking full advantage of his superior strength. His grip against her struggle causes her dress to rip, but she's unphased. Alphonse attempts to break them up, but an enraged Ted sends Alphonse also flying into what was left of the remaining backdrop.

Hattie continues to put up enough of a fight that Ted reaches back his hand to slap her across the face. The audience has finally caught on now that this isn't scripted. Lt. Malone, Larry, and even Claire are rushing to the stage, but they are too far away to reach Ted and Hattie.

Just as Ted is about to strike her, he suddenly writhes in pain from a fierce and sudden strike across his back. He instinctively turns to see that Ed has hit him as hard as he could with the wooden sword.

As Ted turns toward him, Ed witnesses the most intense rage he's ever seen in his life. Ted seems to recognize him as he loosens his grip on Hattie. Ted's savagery is now directed squarely at Ed. Given Ed's much smaller height and frame, he's no match for Ted, except that Ed has already reloaded his swing and, this time, directs the wooden sword toward Ted's temple, where he delivers a powerful blow.

The sound of the sword shattering against Ted's cheekbone is one Ed will never forget, as the crash knocks Ted immediately to his knees. But even this isn't enough to subdue the monstrous foe.

Ted, now on his knees, is nearly eye level with Ed. Ted's fist cocks to deliver a blow, but Ed again is the quicker one and smashes what is left of the broken sword directly against Ted's face.

Before Lt. Malone, Larry, or Claire can scramble up to the stage, Ed delivers several more blows until Ted, in a bloody mess, finally falls unconscious to the stage floor. Ed, caught up in the adrenaline, is about to strike Ted again when Lt. Malone puts Ed in a bear hug to prevent him from doing so.

Hattie is beside herself as Army medics now hop on stage to attend to George, Teddy, Alphonse, and even Ted. Hattie doesn't realize her dress is ripped open. Claire approaches her, grabbing up what's left of her dress to cover her.

As Hattie turns her attention to her son Teddy, she sees George and Alphonse still on the ground. Teddy is being helped to his feet by Rose. Hattie is about to head over to see what she can do to help but finds herself instead pausing just a moment to look over at Ed, shining in King Arthur's armor, triumphant. Her hero.

CHAPTER 18

◆ ◆ ◆

The following morning, Ed watches as a battered and bruised Ted Sr. slowly starts to regain consciousness.

Ed imagines Ted must be feeling a wicked combination of being both hung over and having received multiple blows to the head. As Ted groggily attempts to place his hand on his face, Ed enjoys watching Ted eventually figure out he's handcuffed to the wall. It takes Ted a bit longer to realize he is chained to a storage car in the back of a train. Then a bit longer to realize Ed is there too, just out of reach.

"I have some good news and some other good news," Ed says. "Which do you want first?"

Ted is still trying to focus and apparently isn't yet ready or able to answer. Ed continues, "Let's start with the good news for you. Waiting around for the county judge and sheriff, we decided, was going to take too long."

Ted has finally found the focus to join the conversation.

"My lawyers will make this go away," Ted says.

"Maybe," Ed says. "My understanding is you have quite the wealth and privilege on your side. Rather than fight all that, we've decided to instead ship you off. The cuffs will come off when you're fully back on the East Coast. In the next train car are some soldiers who have orders to see to that in a few days when you get there."

Ted gives his chains a pull, realizing he is indeed stuck and about to travel.

"That's the good news for you," Ed says. "The good news for Hattie and Teddy is that that was the last time they'll ever see you. Because if you step foot in this county ever again, you'll be immediately arrested, as they are filing later today both a restraining order and an arrest warrant. Not to mention my brother George, the one you sucker punched, is hell-bent on simply shooting you on sight if he ever lays eyes on you."

Ed can see the rage beginning to form again in this very dangerous man.

"Before you say or do anything more that you'll regret," Ed says, "you've got a couple of days now ahead of you to think it over on the train ride. More good news for you."

Ed stands to leave, but he can tell Ted is going to certainly insist on having the last word. Ed braces for it as he begins to step out of the car.

"I'm done with that bitch," Ted says to him. "Over time, my boy will come around. But you're the one I have my sights set on now."

Ed had told himself he was just going to walk out no matter what Ted said, but now that he's attacked him personally, he's finding it a bit harder.

"Sights set on me?" Ed asks, turning back around.

"Sights set on Atascadero," Ted says. "I am going to ruin not just you but also this entire place. Your whole stupid-ass mission. You have no idea what I'm capable of."

Truth be told, the focus on Atascadero does rattle Ed, but he doesn't see any point in engaging further as he finishes stepping through the door and closes it behind a now-shouting Ted.

"It's all about to come tumbling down," Ted warns. "Your banks in St. Louis and Los Angeles. All of it. Even Hearst."

In the next train car, Ed slumps against the door. He can hear Ted going on and on, saying phrases like "The Postal Service," "military contracts," and "fraud orders." All Ed's worst nightmares are reverberating from the beast of a man who Ed fears might somehow free himself and bust through the door at any moment.

Eventually, Ed regains his composure and steps outside onto the platform as the train steams away. He feels like he can still hear Ted yelling, but that has to be in his head, given the noise and distance of the train. It's not until the steam has fully cleared and the train is safely on the horizon that Ed allows himself a sigh of relief. He barely gets a moment before noticing something unusual on the side of the train station.

He spies against the wall what appears to be Alphonse and Lt. Malone privately talking to each other, except it is noticeably odd how close they are standing to one another. Their body language is confusing. The back of Lt. Malone's hand is softly caressing Alphonse's cheek where bruises have appeared from last night's events. The two of them are passionately close to one another. To Ed, this definitely does not appear to be a normal interaction between two men.

Ed doesn't want to witness any more of this, or to speculate, or for them to notice him, so he proceeds to a safe vantage point across the train platform. In his haste, Ed nearly runs right into a uniformed man on the platform.

Ed has seen this uniform before. So perfectly pressed. Not a single wrinkle. Perfectly polished shoes. All buttons majestically shining, somehow even glimmering in the California sun. New to the uniform, Ed notices, is a large badge on the chest that reflects so much light it causes Ed's eyes to squint. A holstered gun on the man's hip is another new addition.

Ed's eyes follow the stripes up the sides of his pants. Despite the heat, white gloves cover the man's hands. Ed's eyes continue up a pressed seam on the sleeve all the way up to the man's face, and, sure enough, Ed's nightmare is confirmed.

"It's always the same with you," Postal Inspector Robert Fulton says. "New town. New name. Same old Eddie."

CHAPTER 19

◆ ◆ ◆

In the administration tent, Fulton examines mailers and other documents that Ed and Kramer have laid out before him on the desk. Fulton is about to express his serious reservations regarding the mailers when the tent flaps are violently opened behind him. He tenses the moment he hears her voice.

"Ed and Mr. Kramer," Claire says, "Out! Get out!"

Kramer immediately books it out of the tent. Ed starts to waver, but the daggers in Claire's eyes quickly send him out right behind Kramer, leaving Fulton alone in the tent with Claire. Fulton's back is still to her, as he lacks the courage to turn and face her.

"You've got some nerve coming all the way out here," Claire says.

Fulton takes a deep breath. At least once a day, he recalls being curled up in a ball during the raid on the Woman's Magazine Building in St. Louis, which ended with Claire pointing her finger at him and calling him every terrible name imaginable.

But at the same time, he's missed her. *Oh, how he's missed her*. In advance of his arrival to Atascadero, he had confirmed she was now residing in Memphis. He'd done all he could to avoid this situation, but yet, somehow, here she is.

If there were any other exit out of the tent than past her, he would take it. He's seriously considering what would happen if he were to throw himself against the side of the tent. *Could he get out? Would the tent fall on itself? Could he escape in the melee?*

His mind is spinning in all directions, exploring all possibilities. Some people's first reaction is to fight. His, though, has always been first to scheme and then to flee.

"You've got some nerve," she says, "but, I must admit, I'm glad to see you."

Fulton wonders if he heard her correctly. *I'm glad to see you.* Could that be his new daily memory of her? Could he instead replace the shame he's felt every day for years with *I'm glad to see you.*

"You're glad to see me?" he says.

"I'm glad to see you."

It takes more courage than he's ever mustered in his life to slowly turn and face her.

"Believe it or not," she says, "I didn't hate our time together in St. Louis."

"Didn't hate," Fulton mouths those words to himself, logging every word she says in his brain to replay later, over and over, for the rest of his life.

"But why are you here?" she asks. "What is it this time?"

Fulton is now regaining his composure. If Claire wants to get right into it and discuss postal business, that is fine by him. Just like the old days. Just like the best days of his career—and his life.

"Your brother-in-law, Eddie," he says, holding up one of the mailers and reading, "'Income for life.'"

"It's bold," she says, "but not preposterous. I'm helping him. Planting the orchards is our first priority."

"He hasn't even planted them yet? New orchards take seven years to first harvest."

Fulton gets out his notepad and immediately starts to scribble down a few notes with a look of pure disgust on his face. Claire tries a different tack.

"What's with your gun?" she says. "And your badge? Are you some kind of sheriff now, out here in the west?"

"Postal Inspectors are now federal law enforcement officers," Fulton says, without looking up and still scribbling in his book. "Per the order of Congress, I am authorized to carry a firearm, make arrests, execute federal search warrants, and serve subpoenas. There are roughly 200 federal laws I'm sworn to enforce to preserve the safety, security, and integrity of the U.S. Postal Service from criminal misuse."

"So, are you authorized to shoot me?"

"If I am met with a provocation of harm—" Fulton starts to say before Claire interrupts him.

"I'm kidding," she says. "I'm joking. Please don't shoot me or anyone here."

"If provoked, I am obligated to protect myself…."

"It's not necessary out here," she says. "Why don't you focus on Los Angeles or San Francisco? I read all the time in the newspapers about illegal lotteries that Chinamen keep setting up, each time claiming to be 'just off the boat' and 'unaware of U.S. laws'."

"That is extremely frequent. Illegal lotteries are the number one postal offense out here. But the mere mention of a new scheme being orchestrated by Mr. E.G. Lewis also draws attention, as you might imagine."

Claire can imagine.

"Need I remind you," he says, "at one point, one-sixth of all U.S. mail had something to do with Eddie? And the censure of the Postal Service from the Ashbrook Committee caused many policies and rules to change. The Postal Service has improved, but here I find Eddie hasn't."

"The government took him to court fourteen times, and they lost every case."

"We did," Fulton says. "But maybe we need one more."

"Did you bring one of your famous fraud orders with you?"

"I can't issue those any longer. My powers are considerably tempered now. First, I must make my case to the U.S. Attorney's Office, and then they decide if or when to prosecute. But that's not why I'm here."

"Then why are you here?"

"I came here to persuade him to stop," he says. "Just stop. Stop. Stop. Stop. I don't trust him. I'll never trust him. But out of respect for you, I'm here to beg him to stop. Just stop. Don't make me make a case against him."

"He won't stop," Claire says. "He can't. He's in too deep. He's on a mission."

Fulton lets out an audible sigh, instinctively resting his hand on his gun.

"But now I'm wrapped up in this too," she says. "As are my girls. How about I run anything else we plan to mail by you first, just like in the old days."

There's another phrase for Fulton to memorize. "The old days," he mouths out loud, storing that in the depths of his mind forever.

"We have one more mailer we have to get out," Claire says. "Just one more encouraging folks to wire if they can't attend the Land Rush event. How about you roll up your sleeves and help me word it just right? What do you say?"

"I could never roll up my sleeves," Fulton says, shuddering even to think of the wrinkles that would cause.

But without actually rolling his sleeves, he does take her up on it, and they banter ideas around for the rest of the day. What turns out to be one of the longest and most exhausting afternoons of Claire's life is, yet again, one of the best and most rewarding afternoons of Fulton's.

Just like the old days.

CHAPTER 20

Ed holds a loaded pistol in his hand for the first time in his life. All the planning and preparation over the last two months comes down to him successfully pulling the trigger.

Over three dozen Cadillac convertibles are lined up on the starting line, each with three seats full of smiling patrons ready to race all over Atascadero to select a homesite. Many of the autos are Ed's, but others have been brought in on loan from Los Angeles and San Francisco. Also lined up are hundreds of people on foot and even a few on horseback.

In the VIP area sit the Los Angeles bankers, construction company executives, politicians, and newspapermen from across the entire state of California just in time for J.H.'s 90-day deadline.

Ed and Kramer have been tallying up presales multiple times a day over the last week. Judging by the final attendance, all they've been able to say to the bankers is that it's going to be close. If the deal were 10% down, they'd be fine, but 20% down is a taller order.

But the real truth, Ed knows, is that the Land Rush event is really just for show. It will be the wires he is expecting at the bank's headquarters in Los Angeles that will make or break them. In fact, Kramer is stationed on site today in Los Angeles to oversee it, leaving Ed to his ceremonial duties as the Grand Marshal of today's Land Rush event.

Before Ed pulls the trigger to start the race, he takes a moment to enjoy the smiles and anticipation of all in attendance, especially his team. He nods and makes eye contact with George, the twins, Teddy, Larry, and Alphonse, who have each been so instrumental in advancing Atascadero to where it is today.

He even takes the time to nod at Lawrence, who legitimately seems to be the happiest person of all in attendance, with a genuine appreciation for Ed and the event. From what Ed can tell, Lawrence has been able to attract only a few dozen interested buyers to his cheaper Eaglet housing development next door, not that Ed couldn't use every one of them today.

Ed had hoped to formally acknowledge J.H. in front of the crowd, but J.H. remains holed up in his house. Ed had hoped to do the same with Postal Inspector Fulton, who is onsite but hiding somewhere in the back to avoid being photographed or labeled a willing participant in the day's activities.

But it is the trio of Claire, Hattie, and Mabel who monopolize his attention. Ed takes a moment to blow a kiss in their collective direction, leaving each of the three most prominent women in his life to interpret the gesture in her own way.

It's finally time to pull the trigger, but instead, Ed surprises the crowd by lowering the pistol to make a final proclamation.

"On a day like today," Ed says, "and at an event this momentous, I feel a pistol start just doesn't do it justice."

A murmur begins to roll through the crowd, wondering what Ed has in store when he motions to Lt. Malone, who is high up on a ridge, next to a legion of soldiers standing at attention.

A subordinate hands the new technology of a radio receiver to Lt. Malone, who says a few words into it as he looks up over the ridge into the sky. The crowd follows his eyes to witness something all in attendance have only ever seen before in newspapers. They let out a gasp as a military biplane suddenly flies in low and circles the crowd. There are only a handful in the entire U.S. fleet, but one is here today.

Everyone marvels at the flying machine and its propeller soaring over them. Once the shock subsides, a cheer rings out through the entire valley, especially as the pilot waves to the crowd on each pass.

After he's flown over them a few times, the pilot reaches a safe point far out in the distance and pulls out a contraption that was apparently stored near his feet. He holds it out over the side of the plane, lets it drop, and flies away.

Moments later, the contraption hits the side of the hill, and the biggest bomb the crowd will ever witness in their lives explodes, sending fire and smoke high into the air. After a moment, the crowd cheers again, despite the pungent, bleach-like chlorine smell that now wafts across the valley.

Lt. Malone and his men cheer as well. Ed can't help but notice Alphonse appears especially proud of Lt. Malone for pulling off this military display. Before Ed has much time to dwell on their relationship, all the attention comes back to him, which reminds him the bomb was supposed to trigger the land rush event, but the crowd is still too in awe to realize it.

Ed, still holding the pistol, fumbles to aim it high in the air before finally pulling the trigger. Never having fired a gun before, he is caught off guard by the recoil, but the shot and sound are successful enough. Ed clears the smoke away with a wave of his hand, relieved to see the autos, horses, and even those on foot are finally off to the races.

CHAPTER 21

◆ ◆ ◆

Later that evening, J.H. is still holed up in his front parlor, where he's been all day. His only solace is knowing this is the last day he'll have to deal with all this nonsense, as he's certain there's no way Ed's land rush event was big enough to secure all the necessary presales.

He knows a particular moment is, however, inevitable as he hears a knock on his front door and recognizes Ed's voice.

"J.H.," Ed says. "I need to talk."

J.H. lets him sweat it out for a few moments, but Ed begins knocking insistently until such a point as J.H. finally has to relent and open his front door.

He is, of course, expecting Ed. But he is not expecting to see that hundreds of women, children, and even husbands from the camp have surrounded the entirety of his home. J.H. can't help but notice all of their eyes are on him as Ed, holding a tally sheet in his hand, leans in a little closer to whisper so only J.H. can hear.

"The bankers just behind me have a check made out for a million dollars with your name on it," Ed says. "A million dollars. You're about to be one of the richest men not just in California but in the world."

J.H. looks over, and the bankers are indeed there and holding a check. J.H. looks back at Ed.

"There's no way you have the presales," J.H. says. "Your little event today was all for show. I know for a fact you are short."

Ed leans in even closer.

"We are a little short out here today," he says. "I just need to borrow your telephone for a moment to confirm the wires in Los Angeles have us covered, and the million is yours."

As J.H. looks at Ed's face, it is reminiscent of young Patrick Washington Murphy's face when he too thought he'd played the winning hand.

"I refuse," J.H. says. "This is private property, and I refuse the use of my private telephone. And you don't have time to drive to a neighboring town at this hour. You've lost."

J.H. steps back a little to take in Ed's face at the news. Watching all the color disappear from Patrick had been the highlight of his life until now. *How often in life does one get to win twice at the same game over the same plot of land?* J.H. is still waiting to enjoy Ed's full reaction, but surprisingly, Ed remains stoic.

J.H. can't understand why Ed doesn't at least protest regarding the use of the telephone. He takes a moment to scan the crowd when he suddenly comes to the realization they are all staring at him. But their faces are different from how he first read them. They do appear disappointed. Not at the situation but at him. At him personally. Their piercing looks are suddenly beginning to eat at him.

He just wants to shut his door, but the magnitude of the crowd is proving to be too much for him. He might have found the courage to close it, but his eyes unexpectedly connect with Mabel's out in the crowd. Her look of disappointment is somehow greater than all the rest combined. Again, he wants to shut the door, but he can't for some reason. He's frozen, staring at her.

Without protest, Ed walks past him into the house, picks up the telephone receiver, and asks to be connected long distance to Los Angeles and then to the bank. Once he's connected, he asks for Kramer. While Ed is doing that, J.H. remains locked in a trance with Mabel. What causes him finally to break out of it are the voices of a few women in the camp who suddenly start singing a familiar hymn they all know. J.H. certainly knows the tune, remembering it well from attending church in his youth. The women sing:

> *Onward, Christian soldiers, marching as to war*
> *With the cross of Jesus, going on before.*
> *At the sign of triumph, Satan's host dost flee;*
> *On, then, Christian Soldiers, on to Victory!*

Soon the entire crowd joins in, and their voices carry over the entire valley and echo throughout the house, making it hard for Ed to hear on the telephone or for J.H. to hear what Ed is saying.

> *Hell's foundations quiver, at the shout of praise;*
> *Brothers, lift your voices, loud your anthems raise!*
> *Onward, Christian soldiers, marching as to war.*

J.H. is having trouble controlling his emotions now as the voices continue. His eyes again find Mabel's. He's locked back in on her, not realizing Ed has finished his telephone conversation, stepped outside, and whispered a few words to the bankers.

As the song ends, Ed again joins J.H. on the porch, where only the two of them can hear each other.

"We don't want to take Atascadero from you," Ed says. "With your blessing, we want to build a great city here. With a mission like the world has never seen before. And one in which rancher J.H. Henry will always be known as the man who generously made it happen."

J.H. suddenly remembers what Mabel said to him. "Rather than be the villain, Here's a chance to be the hero."

Ed can tell emotion is starting to overcome J.H. as he turns to the crowd.

"Mr. J.H. Henry," Ed says, but now loud enough for all to hear him, "may the good people of Atascadero have your blessing to build the most beautiful city in the world on your magnificent plot of land?"

J.H. looks out over the crowd again. Everyone appears to be waiting with bated breath for his answer. Mabel especially is waiting. This is decidedly not how J.H. saw today playing out. He expected another memory like that of young Patrick. Instead, well, this memory may be shaping up to be significantly and surprisingly even better.

"Yes," J.H. says. "You have my blessing."

Cheers erupt from the crowd. The bankers hand Ed two checks. Ed turns one made out for $1 million over to J.H. It's the largest check J.H. or any in the crowd have or will ever see in their lives.

Spontaneously, nearly one by one, all the women in the camp now approach J.H. for a handshake or a hug or to simply view the check. At first, the human contact appears more than J.H. may be able to handle, but eventually, he gives into it, accepting embrace after embrace. It's also not lost on any of them, including J.H., that he is now suddenly the most eligible bachelor any of them will ever meet.

In the melee of celebration, George fights his way through the crowd to make his way to Hattie. When she sees him, she immediately throws her arms up and grants him the warmest of embraces. George spins her around just in the same way they'd rehearsed their big moment on stage that was never to be, thanks to Ted Sr. Slowly, he brings the spin to a stop. At first, her instinct is to break away and celebrate with other people, but she can tell by the way he is holding her that he is not finished just yet.

Hattie looks up at George, and it is clear that he has something to say to her. He's about to say it when the overly emotional twins nearly tackle them. The twins immediately hug Hattie, followed by Larry and Teddy, who do the same to George. Even Lawrence piles on them. Whatever George was going to say to Hattie will have to wait as the crowd swallows them.

Ed receives just as many hugs himself, if not more, until, finally, he gets a moment alone with Mabel. He shows her the other check from the bankers. It also has $1 million written on it with a memo that reads, "Atascadero infrastructure."

"In addition, they've set up a bank account in your name only," Ed says. "In it, you'll find your $500 loan to me, paid back, plus interest. This house here is to be titled in your name only, too."

Mabel seems happy, but she isn't as excited as Ed expected her to be.

"Unless that is," Ed says, "you've come to prefer the tent?"

Mabel shakes her head at that thought and laughs as they share the moment together. She knows the bank account and home are only in her name just in case something goes wrong with his business, but that's not what's on her mind.

"Even with the wires, there's no way you reached the 20 percent mark, correct?" she says.

"Correct."

"Meaning," she says, "that the convertible notes just converted, didn't they? That was your last-minute negotiation with the bank, wasn't it? You threw in the investor's loan to seal the deal?"

Ed doesn't answer. Instead, he pulls Mabel closer to him to enjoy the scene. He just wants to look out at the crowd and enjoy with his wife a moment of pride for what they've accomplished thus far, the mission they've always believed in, and the community they are about to build.

But, yes, it is not lost on him that he also now has many, many new investors he'll have to deal with on top of everything else. Not to mention Postal Inspector Fulton is probably out there in the crowd somewhere and will never, ever let up. And Ted Sr. and mysterious foes in D.C. And who knows what else. But those are worries for another day.

Ed barely has a chance to let it all sink in when he notices Claire making a beeline for him through the crowd with Alphonse hot on her heels.

Claire leaps up on the porch, fist clenched, and would have struck Ed in the face again if Alphonse hadn't caught up to her in time and gotten between them. Even Mabel has to step in to keep her from striking.

Ed can't imagine what this can possibly be about. He now has all the money they need to send the twins back to college. He's come through on everything he promised. But Claire is so mad she can't even seem to form words as she's still trying to hit him.

"What is it?" Ed says. "What did I do now?"

Claire doesn't answer except to point out into the crowd where Ed sees a bunch of women gathered in a circle. In the middle of the circle, Ed sees Marcella and Rose. With, of course, Larry next to Marcella and Teddy next to Rose. Except, Ed now realizes that the twins are each showing something off to all the women around them. Hattie and Lawrence are there, as well, and both also seem especially overjoyed. George, too.

At first, Ed doesn't understand what is upsetting Claire, but then it dawns on him as he looks a little closer. He sees the twins are each sporting brand new engagement rings.

Act II:
The Promise of Promise

CHAPTER 22

◆ ◆ ◆

Oscar Willet will never forget his first day in law school when his professor gave a lecture on the twenty different types of law Oscar and his classmates might one day practice.

When the professor got to bankruptcy law, he asked the auditorium full of wannabe trial lawyers, "Now, can I skip over bankruptcy? Or do we have any vultures in this classroom?" Before the professor could move on, Oscar confidently raised his hand.

"Ah, there is always one out there. You have to squint to see them circling amid the clouds," the professor said. "But there is always one. And apparently, a real live one at that."

All eyes turned toward Oscar to reveal a peculiar-looking young man with skinny arms and legs, a large nose, a pudge of a belly, poor posture, and early signs of hair loss, which has begun to reveal his naturally wrinkly and pale scalp and neck.

"So, what is it about bankruptcy that interests you?" the professor asked. "Dead clients are more interesting to you than live ones?"

The auditorium of law students chuckled.

"I don't want dead clients at all. I prefer they still be alive," Oscar said.

"You'd rather feast on them while they are still alive?" the professor asked, eliciting groans and laughs from the audience.

"The client might be broke, but they aren't dead. Their assets, their business, their land, their contracts, and their autos, for example, might still have value. Besides, real vultures play an important role in nature. They consume meat before it decays, and, in turn, they prevent harmful pathogens and toxins from releasing into the environment. I'll be doing the same—extracting what value is left before it evaporates."

"So, feeding on carcasses does give you pleasure?"

More chuckles rang out from the crowd.

"Helping my clients gives me pleasure. Earning sizable commissions by selling off the assets also gives me pleasure. Stumbling upon the right dead elephant at the right time can set someone like me up for life. In turn, I'd be extracting what value might be left for the shareholders, creditors, and employees, and maybe even helping the founder of the business get a little something in return, that is, if he doesn't wait too long to engage my services."

The professor is actually quite impressed with Oscar's knowledge of the subject, and Oscar's classmates are paying more attention, as well.

"Ladies and gentlemen," the professor says, "as evidenced today, a lucrative option in which to practice law can indeed be feasting on misfortune. Well done, Mr. Willet. I'll enjoy watching your career…from a safe distance, that is."

Oscar couldn't care less about the professor's choice of words or his classmates' laughter. He is resolute in his choice of bankruptcy law. Shortly after law school, he discovered a territory of the country that is ripe for dead elephants—California. He quickly realized no other state in the union attracts more entrepreneurs and risk-takers. Along with risk comes the potential for colossal failure.

What Oscar has also learned during his career is that what's even more important than one's territory is timing. Left to their own devices, failed business owners will always wait too long, trying desperately to stay alive, their assets quickly becoming tarnished in the process. Oscar has pioneered an approach that is unique to the industry in that he circles until just the right moment when the company is indeed almost dead, but its owner hasn't entirely accepted that fate just yet.

Dividing up the assets, selling them off, and earning a commission for doing so isn't the hard part. The hard part is timing it just right when the owner is willing to turn it over to Oscar while the assets still have plenty of value, but before the courts get involved in a lengthy and public process.

All these years later, he's still longing to stumble upon the really big elephant he fantasized about back on the first day of law school, one that could set him up for life. Thus, he can hardly contain himself when one day he receives a package in the mail from an anonymous sender.

In it, he finds a stack of advertisements, sales collateral, and newspaper articles about a new city development in California in the middle of nowhere between San Francisco and Los Angeles that has just received an exorbitant amount of bank and investor financing. Each month, more and more clippings arrive anonymously, which Oscar savors as he adds them to the file.

He patiently keeps tabs on Atascadero over the next four years, watching all that bank and investor money being spent while more and more assets get created. Hundreds of miles of roads are built. Hundreds of acres of agriculture are planted. Water and sewer lines are laid. Lakes are dug, and parks are cleared. Sculpture gardens are commissioned. A highway is even built through the mountains connecting Atascadero to the beaches of the Pacific Ocean, where The Cloisters Hotel & Resort is nearing completion, along with a golf course.

Oscar watches in amazement as the largest outlay of cash is put into Atascadero's city center with plans for three of the largest buildings ever constructed in California. The first is a massive printery with the largest rotogravure press west of the Mississippi, which will allow for magazines and newspapers to print full-page photos en masse for the first time. The second is an administrative building four stories tall with not one but two rotunda ceilings. Finally, the third is a large community center complete with a massive public swimming pool. If those buildings weren't enough, next up are plans for a performance theater in Atascadero to rival any in New York City or those being planned in Los Angeles.

In total, Oscar reads there are now nearly 800 construction workers in Atascadero feverishly creating new assets daily, utilizing a mix of workhorses, oxen, and modern construction machines. The temporary tent city for future residents has grown to over 1,000 dwellings. Despite all this development, not a single family home has been built, and this is what is most fascinating to Oscar. The city's founder is famous for insisting on "infrastructure first," which somehow all the residents have bought into.

Oscar envisions the founder to be some kind of cult leader whose followers seem to forget they are going on years now of living in tents. Instead, they appear mesmerized by the mission of building a utopia that always remains just around the corner, out of reach.

This entire scenario is almost too good to be true from Oscar's perspective because he knows business accounting financials are a simple formula of revenue minus expense equals profit. The expense is infrastructure—roads, city centers, buildings, sewers, water lines, and electricity. The revenue comes from the value of the 10,000 home sites, which are still sitting idle. It's not that the profit is missing. It's that it is yet to be extracted.

Like clockwork, every month, copies of anonymously mailed clippings and sales mailers continue to arrive which Oscar adds to his file. Utilizing his unique approach, he has been patiently circling and waiting for just the right time to pay Atascadero a visit.

Circling is an art. Timing is everything. Sometimes, it has nothing to do with the stage of the company or enterprise or the development itself but instead that of the larger economy. When the economy is at a weaker point, Oscar's choice of law really picks up. The deeper America gets now into 1917, so does the threat of a worldwide conflict in Europe.

Oscar has never seen better timing than at this point in his career. He's never seen an elephant bigger than Atascadero. Nor has he ever seen a pied piper and dreamer of the magnitude of E.G. Lewis.

CHAPTER 23

◆ ◆ ◆

Four years after acquiring the Atascadero property from J.H., Ed, Alphonse, Lt. Malone, and Kramer are spread out evenly, each holding a stake in an open field on the undeveloped end of the city mall directly across from the newly constructed Administration Building. Ed stands on one corner of an imaginary rectangle and begins to position the other men.

Before he builds something, he likes first to see how it looks laid out. On Ed's command, they each drive their stakes into the ground and step back to admire their work.

"Alphonse, what do you think?" Ed says. "You happy with the size of the stage and the seating?"

"If you build this," he says, putting both hands to his mouth, barely controlling his excitement, "it will be the biggest theater in which I've ever set foot. There's nothing like it in the U.S. outside of New York City."

Not that anyone is paying attention to Kramer, but he nods in agreement.

Lt. Malone can hardly believe the audacity of it all. Alphonse has explained to him over the past three years they've known each other that Ed views the Atascadero landscape differently than everyone else. Anyone looking out at the city would be drawn to the construction of the four-story Administration Building. Or the

Community Center. Or the 1,000 tents all aligned in perfect rows. Or the water plant. Or the roads. Or the massive printery building where the presses have already been installed.

Alphonse has taught Lt. Malone to watch Ed's eyes because if he looks closely, he'll see that Ed is always thinking about what is yet to come versus what is already built.

Lt. Malone knows that dreamers dream, but Ed is always dreaming. Always. Ed has turned J.H.'s old parlor into what the community calls the Headquarters House, even though Ed calls it Mabel's house. Out the windows of Ed's office is the best view of the valley. Lt. Malone envisions Ed looking out with no limits to his imagination. Even when Ed's wildest dreams are already being realized and built around him, he appears never to take the time to admire his work. He's always onto the next thing.

Lt. Malone would love to be lost in the future, but his own future is precarious, given what appears to be a looming world war. He tries to avoid those thoughts at all costs, hoping instead to finish his obligations to his father and the military before war breaks out. His only escape each day after drilling his troops is to assist Alphonse with theater productions.

"Alphonse, what is going to be the first production on the new stage?" Lt. Malone asks, arranging himself so he is now standing at center stage and looking out to the future audience. "Something classical? Maybe Shakespeare?"

Before Alphonse can respond, Lt. Malone transforms his mannerisms and voice into that of Juliet.

"'O Romeo, Romeo, wherefore art thou Romeo?'" Lt. Malone says to Alphonse, causing the others to laugh.

Alphonse launches into character himself.

"'A rose by any other name would smell as sweet,'" Alphonse says, longingly back at him.

Alphonse and Lt. Malone take each other's hands, spin around, and the two of them probably would have continued on with the entire scene if Kramer, to everyone's surprise, didn't launch himself into the action as well.

"'A horse, a horse, my kingdom for a horse!'" Kramer says dramatically to the invisible audience, imagining all the lights and attention on him for a change, until, that is, collective laughter shames him back to reality.

"Now that would be funny," Lt. Malone says.

"The most titanic villain in all of Shakespeare," Alphonse agrees.

"Indeed. Can you ever imagine Richard III performed live on stage in Atascadero?" Lt. Malone asks.

The two of them laugh and laugh at Kramer's expense when Ed eventually comes to his aid.

"Don't listen to them, Mr. Kramer. Never underestimate a good villain," Ed says. "They get all the best lines."

"Especially when they have just murdered their own young nephews to shore up their case for the throne," Lt. Malone says.

"'True hope is swift and flies with swallow's wings,'" Ed says. "'Kings it makes gods and meaner creatures kings.'"

"My goodness," Alphonse says. "We have our lead."

"Yes," Lt. Malone adds, "you just need to add a hunch to your back and drag your leg a little."

Ed does just that, transforming before their eyes from hero to villain as he launches into a Richard III hunchback pose, limping around and cracking them all up. All but Kramer. At first, they assume Kramer is just being a bad sport until they realize he's now looking at something behind them. Alphonse and Lt. Malone soon stop smiling as well.

Ed eventually turns his head around to see the source of the sudden embarrassment. Mabel, Claire, Hattie, and even Mare have walked up on them with serious looks on their faces.

"Not fans of the villain?" Ed says, trying to lighten the mood.

Mare pushes a copy of a newspaper into Ed's face. Ed grabs it and tries to focus on what this is all about, thinking in short order Mare really has established herself as the mayor around town. Kramer steps over to look more closely at the headline as well.

"The U.S. has declared war on Germany," Mare says. "It's official."

As Ed and Kramer quickly read the article, it is Lt. Malone who is suddenly the most visibly affected by the news. His face turns ashen white. He appears to lose his footing as Alphonse instinctively grabs his arm for support.

"The contractors have already stopped work this morning," Hattie says. "The younger workers are headed by train back to their hometowns."

"Why would they do that?" Alphonse says.

"To enlist, of course," Kramer says, still reading. "Anticipating a draft, they are eager to volunteer their services and preempt their conscription."

"They want to what?" Alphonse says, still propping up Lt. Malone.

"Eddie, we need you to talk Larry and Teddy out of it as well," Mabel says.

Finally, Ed is starting to realize what is going on.

"It's bad enough those two married my daughters," Claire adds. "But now they want to run off like every idiot young boy and get themselves killed."

Claire doesn't realize how her harsh tone especially affects Hattie, given the prospect of her only son Teddy going off to war.

Her comment also causes Lt. Malone to stumble, needing even more support from Alphonse now.

"Ed, you need to quit all this theater and infrastructure nonsense," Mare says. "Get our boys focused. Start building homes with what you have left of the workers. Have you ever been over to Lawrence's Eaglet development next door? You know Larry and Marcella live there now, right? Have you ever visited? I don't think you have. Larry and Lawrence are building real homes. They are up to 50 now. People here are about to defect. They want homes. I want a home. We want the homes you promised us."

"Everyone just calm down a moment," Ed says. "Just give me a chance to think for a second. I can fix this."

"Your brother George and Lawrence are trying to talk the boys out of enlisting right now," Mabel says. "They are down at the printery. You need to go help them."

Ed hears her, but he's still in the middle of processing everything, including wondering if the stakes in the ground are in the optimal location. He's considering maybe shifting them over just a little more to make sure the stairs leading into the theater match up perfectly with the stairs leading to the Administration Building when Mabel takes him by the hand and squeezes it hard.

"Dearest," she says, "focus on real priorities. Go talk those boys out of going off to war."

CHAPTER 24

♦ ♦ ♦

Ed steps into the printery and is excited to see that George has the new rotogravure presses running for the first time. Ed pulls a fresh copy of the new *California Illustrated Review* magazine off the line to admire it.

He loves what George has done with the inaugural issue. It is not only chock-full of photos, which can only be accomplished using this new printing technology, but also the content of the magazine isn't just promoting the allure of moving to California, but specifically Atascadero. There's even a prominent column written by none other than E.G. Lewis.

Ed strolls through the printery, flipping through the magazine while envisioning content for future issues, when he gets close enough to hear George and Lawrence in a serious conversation with Larry and Teddy.

"Let Lt. Malone and the professional soldiers handle this," George says to them. "It's not your fight."

"You want Atascadero to be labeled yellow?" Teddy says.

"That's what they are doing," Larry says. "Printing in newspapers which towns are volunteering and which aren't."

Lawrence is absolutely beside himself. He has no idea what to say when he notices Ed walking up to them.

"Thank goodness," Lawrence says to Ed. "Help us here. Stop this madness."

"It is madness," Ed says. "They print that stuff and label towns just to sell newspapers. It's only propaganda. Newspaper publishers love war. Nothing sells copies like war coverage. That's all it is."

George and Lawrence nod along with Ed, but the boys aren't buying it.

"I know you guys would fight if you were our age," Teddy says. "I know you would."

"We're going to do our part here," Ed says. "I've already been planning to apply for a government cannery contract. We're going to send dehydrated fruits and vegetables to the front lines. I can get a carve-out for you two and the other boys in town to help with the production lines. You'll be labeled essential workers. I got it all covered."

"I didn't know that," Lawrence says enthusiastically. "I love it. Perfect, Ed, just perfect. I knew you'd know what to do. Just perfect."

"And I haven't mentioned this to Eddie yet," George says, "but I'm thinking of going to New York City and striking a deal with the National Press Association to publish photos from the war in the magazine. We'll probably change the name to a wartime *Illustrated Review* but still talk about the virtues of Atascadero. You boys can help me with that. We're going to do our part here."

"Very clever," Ed says, liking the sound of that.

George, Lawrence, and Ed all seem pretty proud of themselves and their arguments.

"You expect us to can food and print war photographs?" Teddy says. "While everyone else our age is fighting tyranny, and we're here doing that?"

"We need you here," Ed says. "Teddy, your mom needs you. Larry, your dad needs you."

"I really do, son," Lawrence says. "The little success we've had selling a few homes is because of you. I barely know what I'm doing."

George puts his hands on the boys' shoulders.

"We need your help starting these businesses," George says. "The cannery and the printery are going to create a lot of jobs for the women here in Atascadero. We need you. They need you."

But Ed can tell they are still not fully getting through to the boys. It is obvious to him now that he's going to have to reluctantly step in and play his trump card.

"If you won't stay for any of us," Ed says, "then stay for the twins—your wives. They need you."

Lawrence especially likes that tactic, wishing he would have thought of it himself. George likes it too. It's perfect. They nod along with Ed, looking the boys in the eyes to gauge their reactions. Surely that has to win them over. It has to.

"Our wives want us to fight," Teddy says.

Ed's, Lawrence's, and George's jaws drop.

"They'd fight themselves if it were allowed," Larry says.

"We have their full support," both Teddy and Larry say together in unison, nodding to confirm.

Lawrence is absolutely beside himself now. He clearly is not going to be able to keep himself together. He absolutely can't believe it.

George, however, can't help but think for a moment how brave the twins are. He's loved this foursome since the day he met them when they were leading the efforts to assemble the tent city. Of course, George now realizes they are going to want to pitch in and fight. Of course they are now that he thinks about it. Those four have been doing that for the last three years. It's just what they are wired to do.

Larry and Teddy are emotional now. They didn't want to bring their wives into it either, but it is the truth. Larry is struggling with his dad's reaction, but he remains as absolute as ever on his decision.

What timing, Ed thinks to himself. Just as he is finishing up the infrastructure and he is right on schedule to build homes, a war breaks out, and everyone loses their minds.

He's often debated with himself what part of a business is most important: the mission, the idea itself, the market, the competitive landscape, or the capabilities of the team who is tasked to execute it. Mission, idea, market, competition, or team?

It is becoming apparent to Ed that the answer may be something else entirely. Maybe, in the end, it all really comes down to one thing.

Maybe it's all about timing.

CHAPTER 25

◆ ◆ ◆

The next morning Hattie is getting ready to start her day, but she's been crying all night at the thought of Teddy heading off to war.

There is a knock on the outside of her tent. She does her best to dry her eyes and make herself presentable as she opens her tent flap, assuming it is one of her ambassadors hitting her up with a question, when instead, she's surprised to see George standing with his packed bags.

"May I come in a moment?" he asks.

Hattie holds the door flap open for him as he enters.

"How long will you be gone?" she says, making small talk and trying to answer the question herself by judging the thickness of his suitcase.

"It all depends on something I have to talk to you about," he says anxiously.

"And what is that?"

"Look, I'm just going to come out and say it. You and me. Are we something, or are we not something?"

Hattie's not sure how to answer.

"When I come back from New York, I think it is time we marry," he says. "All of Atascadero is rooting for us. Marry me. Just quit messing around and marry me already."

Hattie is, of course, caught off guard, but she also knows a conversation like this was inevitable. Here she is in the presence of a wonderful and adorable man who absolutely loves her and has an amazing future ahead of him. But she also knows her answer.

"I can't," she says.

George's face reddens in anger.

"You'd rather hold out hope for a relationship that is impossible," he says. "IMPOSSIBLE. Even today, you'd take him over me?"

She doesn't have a response for him.

"I'm headed to the train right now. I'm going to be standing at the platform waiting *not* for the train but for *you* to come to your senses. But if you don't come see me in time, I'm getting on that train, and I'm moving on. Do you understand me? The moment I sit down, I'm moving on."

Hattie nods that she does understand as George storms out with his suitcase and heads to the train station.

She needs to collect herself. If Teddy's decision to enlist wasn't enough, now she's got this to deal with. She gets herself together and steps out of the tent, only to find a gaggle of her immediate tent neighbors waiting for her. It's obvious they have overheard the conversation. Among them is Mare.

"If you don't head to that station right now, then you are the dumbest person I've ever met," Mare says, sharing the sentiment of all the other women in the circle, who are nodding along.

CHAPTER 26

◆ ◆ ◆

Ed usually paces during meetings, but today he's exhausted, sitting behind his desk while Kramer forces him to look at sales figures.

"New tours have come to an abrupt halt," Kramer shows him. "Scheduled tours are being withdrawn. Amidst the ongoing war, an increasing number of existing homesite buyers are seeking the return of their deposits, preferring to delay their purchase plans until the world conflict is resolved. A paradigm shift is afoot. Demand for Atascadero has evaporated."

Ed, of course, knew this was coming, but he never imagined it would happen this quickly. It's one thing for sales to dry up. It's another to have a retention issue with current customers. Together they are a perfect storm.

Out the window, he watches George, far in the distance, waiting anxiously for the train. It's been a pleasure to watch his younger brother mature into an amazing salesman over the last few years. Ed could never have imagined not going along on this trip himself just a few years ago. But now, he'd never dream of cramping George's style. Ed has complete confidence in him.

As Ed is thinking about how to respond to Kramer and how to stop the defection of customers, Hattie barges into his office.

"Mr. Kramer, out," she says. "Now."

Kramer starts to protest, but he can tell by Hattie's face she is resolute, and he quickly leaves. She makes sure the door is fully shut before turning her attention to Ed, who is now up on his feet again.

"Hattie, I know," Ed says. "I know we need to talk Teddy and Larry out of enlisting. The twins, too. We have to try. It's all that has been on my mind."

"It's not that," Hattie says. "Well, it is that. Yes. We have to try. We have to. But it's not that. It's….it's something else."

"What is it then?" Ed asks.

"I need to tell you something."

"What is it?"

"Something about my past and why I came here."

"I already know."

"You already know?"

"We all witnessed it at the play when Ted Sr. showed up."

"Yes, that. But something else."

"Come here," he says to her. "Come over to me. You look upset."

She complies, and Ed surprises her with a hug. He's never done that before. It's a serious hug, one that seems not just to last forever but one that, after a few moments, takes away all her worries. She nearly disappears into his embrace. When Ed does finally let go of her, he also surprises her with a beautiful kiss planted squarely on her cheek, just like she did to him the first day they met.

"Pasts are pasts in Atascadero," Ed says. "Let's focus on our future together. Yours and mine."

Hattie certainly likes the sound of that. She works to regain her composure as Ed looks around the office and picks up his briefcase.

"Now I need to take the auto out for a bit. I have an idea to really max out the printery. When I get back, can you have lunch with me? Maybe up on the outlook? I have a few ideas to run by you. I want you to be the first to hear them. I'd absolutely love your feedback. What do you say?"

He pauses before heading out the door and turns back, waiting for her answer on lunch while giving her that grin he's made famous from his brochure photo. That photo, and his matching look right now, will always take her breath away.

"I'm your girl," she says.

"You bet you are," he says, heading out the door. "The best."

Out the window, Hattie watches Ed hop into the auto and zoom away. Behind her, out on the horizon, Hattie doesn't even notice that George has now boarded and his train is steaming away in the other direction.

She puts her hand to her cheek where Ed kissed her. She can still hear him saying, "The best."

CHAPTER 27

The drive up to the mountain where Hearst is building his castle is a tricky one. Almost any storm knocks down loose limbs, littering the road and making the drive even tougher. But when Ed finally gets to the top he can see why the outlook has been named La Cuesta Encantada—Spanish for "The Enchanted Hill." The castle site is just 40 miles northwest of Atascadero, and the view, encapsulating mountains, forests, and the ocean, is simply spectacular in all directions

Ed waits patiently as Hearst finishes up a conversation with a woman Ed recognizes. Ed's women's magazines have run many stories on the famous architect Julia Morgan throughout the years. She was the first woman to be licensed in California and the first to embrace a new technology of using reinforced concrete that allows her buildings to be the only ones in San Francisco to survive serious earthquakes.

Ed would love to reacquaint with Julia, but instead, he gets to meet someone even more famous, a bona fide movie star, as none other than Marion Davies taps him on the shoulder.

The last time he saw Marion in person, she was a teenager in the land rush movie set in Beverly Hills. She has matured, having starred in many films since then.

"I know who you are," Marion says to Ed.

"You know who I am?" Ed says.

"My mother subscribed to all your magazines when I was growing up. She used to read your column to me."

Ed gets a better look at her now. Four years later she is no longer a teenager, nor does she exhibit any form of innocence. Marion, like most movie stars, has a different look than a model, more glamour than beauty. Movie stars look more like everyday people than fashion models, but they have a little something extra. Mostly it is the familiarity of people knowing their face. But there's also a glow. A radiance. Or maybe the better word, which nearly takes Ed's breath away, is fame. Ed often forgets that he shares the gift (or curse) of fame on occasion himself.

Ed has a million questions for Marion about her mother and his magazines, but Hearst interrupts them.

"Marion, dearest, come tell Julia your thoughts on the veranda design you were sharing with me the other day."

"Yes, more windows and more sun," Marion says. "'If you got it, flaunt it,' Mother always says."

But before she walks over to them, she whispers something back to Ed.

"I also learned to flaunt it from your magazines. All the others are always talking about keeping one's husband happy. Mother and I read your magazines to learn what to do if you really want to get ahead in this world. We've made it our mission to look out for ourselves."

With that and a wink, she walks off to express her veranda ideas to Julia as Hearst gives Ed a strong handshake.

"What do you think?" Hearst says, gesturing to the view.

"Spectacular," Ed says, actually referencing Marion even though Hearst assumes he is talking about the castle plans. "One in a million."

"Thank you," Hearst says. "Lasting memories are going to be made here for sure."

"Indeed," Ed says. "Millicent and your five boys are going to love it up here."

At the mention of Hearst's wife and family, Ed can tell Hearst had almost forgotten about them. Clearly, he was dreaming up other kinds of memories for the estate.

"Anyway, thanks for meeting with me," Ed says.

"Sorry I've been so busy," Hearst says. "It's a brilliant time for newspapers. As you know, nothing sells more copies than a war."

"War has a slightly different effect on real estate sales."

"Indeed it does. And you owe my bank a small fortune, don't you?"

"I do. I do indeed."

"Well, banks have two major goals. One, get our money back. Two, earn a profit on the interest."

"I'm aware."

"So, should we start the default proceedings to at least get our money back?"

"Not at all. That's not why I'm here at all. I've asked around, and it appears you are running all your printing presses at full capacity. Just so you know, I have some extra capacity at my press. What would you think about me printing some weekend copies for your papers in San Francisco and Los Angeles? And maybe even your special editions? I have the capacity you need."

"That does sound better than a loan default," Hearst says.

"I'm here first to help you, not just me," Ed says.

"How generous of you then. We do need capacity. We'll try you out. And maybe that will prolong that little noble mission of yours and the harem you're forming out there in Atascadero."

"Well, that's not how I'd describe it…."

"But I'm going to have one requirement, which I don't want you to be surprised about when my team sends over the contract."

Ed knew something like this was going to happen with Hearst. It always does.

"Of course. And what is that?"

"My competitors are also maxed out, and new printing press manufacturing, as you know, is halted during the war. If I work with you, then I need you to only work with me."

The problem with giving a customer exclusivity, Ed knows, is that, in the end, you don't actually have a company if you do. Instead, you just have a contract. If that contract goes away, then you don't have a company at all. Granting exclusivity is never a good decision. But, without hesitation, even knowing it is a terrible decision, Ed has little choice but to agree, given he can't go to one of Hearst's competitors anyway since Hearst would surely call his loan in retaliation.

It's also not lost on Ed that Hearst would force exclusivity on his business partners, but Hearst would certainly never allow himself to be held to exclusivity in his own marriage.

CHAPTER 28

◆ ◆ ◆

Alphonse and Kramer are in the office of a construction materials warehouse in downtown Atascadero, messing around with a movie projector. Alphonse has never operated one before. For the life of him, he can't figure out how to load the film.

"Let me run back to the office," Kramer says. "I think we may have left the directions there."

Alphonse doesn't acknowledge Kramer leaving as he continues to mess with the projector. The entire world seems to be changing overnight, and Alphonse would like to keep up with it in some fashion. He's starting to think that maybe towns in America are not going to want to keep putting on local stage productions. Maybe showing movies is the future. But if he's going to be part of the future, it starts with him figuring out how to run this stupid projector.

"Flip it over," Lt. Malone says to him, startling Alphonse, who didn't hear him enter the warehouse.

"You nearly gave me a heart attack," Alphonse says.

"You have it backward," Lt. Malone says, taking the film out of his hands.

Lt. Malone flips it around, loads it into the holder, pulls out some film, and threads it through the projector. He flips the power switch, and the magic of film plays out before their eyes as Charlie Chaplin materializes on the wall.

"I've had to show many war maneuver training films to my troops," Lt. Malone says.

Before long, they are both engrossed in the film. The only sound in the room now is that of the projector running, giving life to Chaplin's Little Tramp character, who appears silently on the wall in a film titled *The Adventurer*.

Lt. Malone takes a seat next to Alphonse, watching as Chaplin, playing an escaped convict, eludes police officer after police officer during a man-hunt with shots being fired at him from all directions.

In no time at all, Alphonse finds himself laughing out loud, watching Chaplin's slapstick of finding creative ways to keep escaping. At one point, he even feigns his own death before rolling down a hill to safety.

"When you get back from the war," Alphonse says. "We're going to have turned this warehouse into a first-class movie theater. How'd you like to help us run it? Claire, I know, will want to collect the money and optimize the whole thing. I'm thinking I'll play the organ music myself. And you'll greet people on the way in and play the host. What do you say?"

It's at this point Alphonse realizes that Lt. Malone isn't listening. Lt. Malone isn't even really watching the film. Instead, he appears to be lost in his nightmares. With all the shooting in the film and the risk of death, Alphonse is catching on that maybe this isn't appropriate content for what Lt. Malone may be dealing with.

"I read in the paper that you and your troops are shipping off in a few days," Alphonse says.

Lt. Malone nods.

"Mare and I have been talking about it, and she's thinking of hurrying and cleaning this place up to host a proper dance and send off for you and your troops. What do you say?"

Lt. Malone doesn't react.

"I told her that there needs to be a ton of planning to pull off an event like that. I spoke to Claire as well," Alphonse says. "I'm thinking maybe the two of us—you and I—should go camping this weekend. You get a few days off, right?"

The prospect of some time away for just the two of them does seem to get Lt. Malone's attention.

"Just to get away from the world a bit and to plan out the party is what I told Claire. What do you say?" Alphonse says. "Maybe I can help you take your mind off a few things."

Lt. Malone nods. But what he really wants to do is to slip back into his pity party and disappear into his misfortunes about having to be one of the first units to have to report to the war.

If Teddy and Larry really do enlist, he thinks, they'll at least have basic training to delay their going overseas. He knows that professional soldiers like him and his troops won't just be going over immediately, but they'll be sent right to the front lines since, in theory, they actually know what they are doing.

At this point, Kramer comes back into the warehouse with the projector instructions, but Lt. Malone and Alphonse don't notice him as they are back to watching the movie. Alphonse can't help but laugh a little at Chaplin's antics. Kramer also is caught up in the film, feeling it is certain that the Tramp will eventually get caught by the police officers. Surely he can't escape forever, Kramer thinks.

Kramer is about to say something to Alphonse and Lt. Malone to announce his presence when he notices Alphonse has put his arm around Lt. Malone, who has begun to sob. Kramer watches as Alphonse wipes away a few of Lt. Malone's tears as the two continue to embrace as the film comes to its climax.

At the very end of the film, the Tramp, along with his girlfriend, Edna, are cornered by the main police officer, this time with absolutely no way to escape. With quick thinking, the Tramp introduces the police officer to Edna. As any gentleman would do, the police officer takes off his hat to make her acquaintance, giving the Tramp just enough time to slip off into the night.

Which is what Kramer does as well.

CHAPTER 29

◆ ◆ ◆

That evening, after visiting Hearst's castle site, Ed slips into bed next to Mabel, but he never really falls asleep. His brain is always whirling. If Ed actually sleeps three to four hours a night, Mabel would be surprised.

In fact, he keeps a notebook on his bedstand along with a candle, which he often lights in the middle of the night so he can jot down an idea before it is lost. It's the same idea notebook he used to read to her from when they were first married back in their apartment in Nashville. It must have hundreds of ideas in it by now.

It dawns on Mabel that this is one of the rare evenings in the last four years that she and Ed have had the Headquarters House to themselves. Shortly after they moved in, Hattie reported jealousy from other couples in the tent city, wishing they also had some privacy. So now, on a rotation managed by Hattie, couples are granted time alone in the Headquarters House or at The Cloisters Hotel at the beach. Mabel has always felt Hattie goes out of her way to ensure someone is always signed up and that she and Ed are never alone. Surprisingly, no one is signed up for this evening.

Ed appears not to realize it is just them in the house, as he's just staring at the ceiling. While Mabel would very much enjoy reminding Ed they have the house to themselves, there are a few things on her mind that just won't go away.

"Eddie," she says to him, getting his attention. "Help me understand something."

"Anything, my dearest. What is it?"

"Why did Hattie come running into your office this morning? What was that all about?"

"Something about her past. I don't know. Later we had lunch together. She seemed back to herself as the day went on."

"That's all you are going to say about it?"

"Look, if I know anything about Atascadero, and the thousand women that live here, then I know that eventually everyone will know everyone's business. And somehow, I have a feeling you already know all the details, maybe more than me."

He is, of course, right. Mare tells her many things.

"She clearly has feelings for you," Mabel says. "Watch yourself."

"Nonsense. When you work closely with someone," he says, "feelings sometimes can get confusing. But *feeling things* and *acting on things* are different. I'm older now. I'm wiser now. I'm more in love with you than ever before. I don't want to punish someone for maybe having misplaced feelings. Especially someone I care deeply about."

"Just a warning."

"I'm the one that has a real concern, I fear," he says. "Why does J.H. keep coming back to town every few months? Why isn't retirement enough for that millionaire? My understanding is he's got himself a mansion in San Diego now. Instead of staying down there, he also bought one of our best lots, which he camps on way too often to make any real sense if you ask me."

"A 64-year-old man is your concern?"

"Adonis knows no age."

That makes her smile. Mabel is human. Of course, the thought of handsome J.H.'s size twelve boots under her bed has crossed her mind. She could make that or any reality happen for herself if she wanted to. But it is Ed, her little dreamer, who is her reality.

"There's nothing wrong with reading the menu every so often," Mabel says.

"But ordering off of it is different?" he asks.

"I think you know the answer to that."

Ed smiles as he gets closer to her.

"I'll give you a menu then," he says. "One with lots of options."

"Is that so?"

Launching into his best French maître d' accent, he says, "My, my, mademoiselle. What be your pleasure? Anything at all. I'll whip it right up."

"Let's see…."

"Anything at all, mademoiselle."

"OK, then, I'll take a peaceful and good night's rest, please."

Ed can't entirely hide his disappointment, but then realizes Mabel is kidding.

"I would like to sample the menu, but I have one more thing on my mind first."

"Anything at all, mademoiselle. I am here to serve."

"Cute. But this is a serious question. How are we doing financially? How much money is left? I just don't see how Atascadero is going to work. What are we doing about all the deposits we are returning? Would we be better off trying to find a buyer? Maybe consider a development closer to a bigger city like Los Angeles or something? Chalk it all up to the timing of the war and move on while we can. Regroup after the war ends?"

Ed doesn't even know where to start. Here he thought this evening was going in a much different direction. Nothing kills the mood more than financial discussions between spouses in bed, especially when one of them has the audacity to suggest they throw in the towel on their entire dream and the dreams of all the women they are helping. *Does she even care about the mission?*

Timing is everything, and her timing is terrible. His mind races through a hundred different responses, but all of them, he knows, will lead to the same eventual outcome. He decides to go with the inevitable as he simply gets out of bed, walks out of the room, and slams the door behind him.

CHAPTER 30

◆ ◆ ◆

A few days later, after getting back from camping, Alphonse throws an elaborate send-off for Lt. Malone and his troops to the frontlines of the war in Europe.

All the actors who typically perform in Alphonse's plays have a part. Sonnets are performed. Poems composed just for this event are read. Atascadero veterans who fought in the Civil War—on both sides—and the Spanish-American War are honored for their service. Each of those veterans has some words of wisdom for the younger soldiers, mostly tips about how to stay warm and not freeze to death.

Ed is invited to say a few words about support for the war itself and the need to stand up against tyranny. He had prepared a basic outline of what he intended to say, but standing up there and seeing the faces of the young men who were about to risk their lives causes him to pause and go off script.

"I'm far from someone who should be addressing you young men," Ed said. "My generation was fortunate enough to miss the Civil War and now to miss what is shaping up to be a Great War in Europe. I was too young for one and now too old for this current conflict. But I do know a little about standing up to tyranny."

Ed reminisces to himself about the time he stood up to Senator Platt in D.C. and the conspiracy against him. He also thinks of all the fights he's had in his life, but he always had his brother John and even Claire and Mabel there to defend him.

"And there is nothing easy about a fight," he continues. "Nothing. It's not romantic. It's not even heroic. It's just that as long as there are humans, there will be conflict. And as long as there is an America, there will be a sense of duty to aspire to making not just America better but making the entire world a better place. When evil surfaces, America must always rally against it."

Ed lets this sink in as he decides how he wants to close out his talk. He decides to make eye contact with Teddy and Larry and speak to them directly.

"But when I find myself in the middle of a conflict," Ed says, "which seems to happen more often than I like—"

"Way more often," Claire blurts out to thunderous laughs from the crowd, to which Ed can't help but accept and smile.

"As I said, more often than I would like," Ed continues. "But in those conflicts, I look for every way out of it before I'd ever consider throwing a punch. I'd attempt every possible avenue to talk my way out of it. Or to build an alliance to help me. There are many tactics one can do without actually resorting to violence."

"But you would throw a punch, wouldn't you?" Teddy asks Ed in front of the entire community.

"Push comes to shove," Larry adds, "what would you do if this time were yours?"

Ed isn't prepared to be put on the spot. Now his eyes drift to the twins, then Claire, then Mabel, and finally Hattie, who has so much to lose, depending on what he might say. Not to mention all the other wives and mothers in the room.

"In every situation, I'm the smallest man in the room," Ed says. "The last thing I ever want to do is fight. How could I ever stand a chance? I'd avoid fighting at all costs."

If he had stopped there, he would have forever had the support of the women in the room and the women in his life who don't want to see their men go off to war.

"But every time in my life that a fight has been unavoidable and the world is looking at me to help those who can't help themselves," Ed says. "Well, you're damn right I'd throw a punch. Every time I will fight."

With that, all the soldiers and young men in the audience erupt into cheers. Some of the women join in. This is Alphonse's cue to strike up the band and shift the evening over to what everyone was longing for, which is the biggest dance and celebration in Atascadero's young history.

Ed can tell he is now persona non grata with many of the women closest to him. He imagines them thinking, who is he to say such things when these are not his sons or husbands or his life at risk? He knows it is easy for him to say, given he'll never actually be called to battle himself. But who is he to tell a bunch of young men not to defend their country and the American way of life?

As Ed continues to ponder the effects of his words and actions, he notices someone he wasn't expecting entering the dance hall. Ed's eyes light up upon seeing that his brother George is apparently back unannounced from New York. Ed rushes over and gives him a big bear hug.

"Please tell me you have some good news for me ," Ed says. "We need some."

"I do," George says. "My time in New York has been very successful. I've lined up content, photos, advertisers, and even distribution. We are all set to give the new wartime *Illustrated Review* a go."

"That's my boy," Ed says. "The apprentice becomes the master. Love it. Well done."

By now, Mabel, the twins, Teddy, and Larry have all spied George and are hugging and welcoming him home. Even Lawrence gets in on it. Ed looks around for Hattie when George suddenly announces something.

"But the most successful part about the trip to New York is someone I met that I'd like to introduce to you all," George says, motioning to a woman who's been standing off to the side. "Lucile, honey, come over here and meet everyone."

They all turn to see a striking, light-haired, and tall French beauty walk over to them. George immediately takes her hand, kisses it, and introduces her to the family.

"Meet Lucile," George says, "my wife."

"Your what?" they all say nearly at the same time.

"I met her in the magazine circles in New York about fifteen minutes after I arrived there. My first meeting was at a photo shoot. She was modeling dresses. We hit it off instantly. She was looking to get out of New York. I was looking for, well, I guess I was looking for her. And here we are."

Everyone's jaws are basically on the floor. They don't know whether to look at George or Lucile. They all can't help but look around the room to try to find Hattie as well. But Mabel is the first to extend her arms and welcome Lucile into the family, followed by the twins, Claire, and the rest. Ed takes his turn and tries to make small talk and crack some jokes with Lucile, even attempting his French maître d' accent. Lucile smiles, but she doesn't seem to understand anything Ed is saying.

"Wait, everyone," George says, "I forgot to mention Lucile is still learning English. She's catching on quickly, but we have to slow things down just a bit. Especially you, brother. And no accents. Never do accents."

Now that they all realize Lucile doesn't speak English, they go back to her one by one, simply restating their first names.

Ed just smiles to himself. Of course George would marry a French model who doesn't speak English whom he just met on a business trip. Of course he would.

"Law-RENCE," Lawrence says over and over to Lucile. "I'll quiz you every day until we get it. Repeat after me. Law-RENCE."

Lucile can't quite get it right, so Lawrence continues saying his name over and over.

Well, she has that to look forward to, Ed thinks to himself when he suddenly notices a generous hand outstretched to Lucile.

"Welcome, I'm Hattie."

Now that is a name Lucile seems to have been anticipating as she takes not only Hattie's hand but pulls her in for a deep embrace.

"Quelle beauté," Lucile says. "Je dois vous remercier d'avoir envoyé George dans mes bras."

Hattie graciously smiles, having no idea what Lucile is saying as Lucile goes on and on in French. Finally, Hattie is able to extend a hand to George.

"I couldn't be happier for you," Hattie says to him.

Before George can reply, the twins lead them all to the dance floor to celebrate. Ed notices the whole room is in awe of George and Lucile, who are the most attractive couple they may ever see together in their lives, that is, besides when George and Hattie were paired together in the Camelot play.

Ed notices George and Lucile can barely communicate with each other, but they sure move well together. Love certainly is a universal language. Ed also admires Teddy dancing with Rose and Larry with Marcella. Lt. Malone sits next to Alphonse at the piano where they play together and lead the band. With the war looming, Ed can only assume nights like tonight will be few and far between.

Ed is deciding if he should force Mabel to dance or if he'd be better off asking Claire or Hattie. But before he can decide, none other than Lawrence approaches Hattie with his hand outstretched.

"I'd like to say I can cut a rug, but it's more often I cut up the rug," Lawrence says, laughing hysterically at his own dumb joke, to which Hattie feigns a smile. "But if you'll do me the honor, maybe we can give it a shot together? What do we have to lose?"

Ed assumes dancing with Lawrence is the last thing Hattie wants to do, but Ed is also realizing that Lawrence may soon literally be the only eligible man left in town—Kramer always excluded. Hattie, ever so kind, agrees to dance with Lawrence as they join the others. Lawrence, despite being far from debonair, does get the job done.

Ed makes eye contact with Claire, who shoots him daggers as if to say, "Don't you dare." Instead, he holds his hand out as a peace offering to Mabel, who is notoriously not a dancer. But on this rare occasion, Mabel takes his hand, recognizing a night like this may not come around again anytime soon.

CHAPTER 31

The war, which Claire despises more than anything in the world, has now pressed her into service, as well.

It's been a few months since Lt. Malone and his troops shipped off for Europe. Shortly after, her sons-in-law Teddy and Larry left for basic training. She begrudgingly spends her days now going back and forth between the cannery and the printing press, optimizing each for Ed despite having vowed never to help him again.

She steps out of the printing press into the bright California sun to head back over to the cannery, a trek she's made several times today already, when she nearly runs straight into Postal Inspector Fulton.

"You have to make time for me," he says, holding some papers. "I have a million questions for you based on your memo here."

"Keep up, and you can ask them," Claire says, not slowing down while continuing past him.

Fulton has to run to keep up with her.

"It took Eddie years in St. Louis to reach a million subscribers," he says. "Somehow, he's going to get there in months, according to your memo, with the way the wartime *Illustrated Review* is selling out at newsstands."

Fulton will never understand this new magazine that George designed. There are scarcely any words. Only photos. *What does this say about America that people would rather look at photos than read? Surely that can't be a trend that will continue*, Fulton thinks to himself.

"The magazine's growth is not my problem," she says. "My job is to get the finished product out on the loading dock by deadline. Your job at The Postal Service is to transport it."

"What more would you have me do? The Postal Service has already run three spur tracks in the past month, and we entirely re-routed our trains. Do you realize Atascadero is now the third busiest post office in California? I need to understand better your growth projections in this memo. I'm looking at your math here. Your figures can't be right. Not to mention the sheer weight of the canned products, assuming they are true and the math is right."

"My math is right. It's always right. Pay more attention to the diagram. I don't know why I do your job for you, but you're welcome."

"What is the diagram? I didn't understand. Is it some kind of stacking guide or something?"

"It's a way to get thirty percent more canned food and printed papers per standard Postal Service shipping palette. The previous guidelines cooked up by your hotshots in D.C. for how to stack them are wrong. I redesigned it."

Fulton stops and looks at the diagram again. Indeed, that is what she did. *How did he miss it?* He's been wrestling with this issue for months. She simply put a few scribbles down on a piece of paper that he is certain will not only solve his biggest challenge but also become the new best practice nationally across the entire U.S. Postal Service once he shares it with his superiors. He'd give anything just to be able to climb inside Claire's mind, even just for a minute.

When he looks back up, she is gone from his sight. He assumes she has already entered the cannery. He has to run to catch up and find her amongst the hundreds of people who now work on the assembly line. After a few moments, he spots her across the busy floor and sprints until he catches up with her.

"And the change of address forms in Atascadero," Fulton continues. "They are getting out of hand. Every morning you must wake up to realize more and more people are defecting from the tent city. From looking over the address forms, they are either moving away or building homes in next door Eaglet."

"Tell me about it," she says, making little tweaks to each assembly station as she walks by, slightly moving a packing box higher, lower, left, or right.

Fulton notices that the women at the stations don't even seem to realize or care about the tweaks Claire makes, but each tiny change immediately speeds them up by a matter of minutes, which he knows all adds up.

To Fulton, it seems that the female workers appear to just socialize with each other all day. If he were in charge, he'd make them all quit talking and work faster. He's mentioned that to Claire before, and she agrees, except she said something about how, with all their loved ones away at war, socializing at work is a form of therapy that she could never stop, even if it were to lead to more efficiency.

"I'm aware of the change of address forms," Claire says. "All day long, I have to optimize the production line to reduce jobs because we can't count on the same number of workers as the day before."

"How is Eddie even solvent?" Fulton finally has the nerve to ask.

That gets Claire to finally stop and look at him for a moment as he continues talking.

"I did some math on the train on the back of your memo. I've factored in a lack of new real estate sales along with a defection of customers," Fulton says. "I see no way the cannery or the press can make up for that. He's not going to make it. Look at my calculations. See what you think."

Claire is about to answer when out of the corner of her eye, she notices something amiss with the production line. Suddenly, all the women in a certain section have stopped processing fruits and vegetables and seem to be overly excited, hugging each other at apparently the sharing of some good news.

Judging by the body language, she traces the origin of the news in the direction of none other than Rose, Marcella, Hattie, and Lucile, who all work these days together on the line at the same station. That's something else Fulton would correct. No immediate family members should ever work together.

As Claire walks over to investigate, they all see her coming and try to get back to work as if nothing happened, but she won't have it.

"What?" she says to any of them that will listen. "Tell me, what is going on?"

They are all fully back at work now except for Lucile, who can't stop herself from smiling ear to ear.

"Que se passe-t-il?" Claire says to her.

A huge annoyance to the twins, Hattie, and the rest of the women in Atascadero is when Claire talks to Lucile in French. They work all day to help Lucile learn English, but Claire sat down one weekend with a mail-ordered "How to Learn French" book and memorized the whole thing, believing it would be the most efficient way to communicate with Lucile rather than waiting years for Lucile to learn English.

"Que se passe-t-il?" Claire says again to her. "What is going on?"

Lucile can tell by the body language of the other ladies she isn't supposed to tell Claire, but Lucile just can't help herself.

"Enceinte," Lucile finally says, smiling ear to ear.

"You're pregnant?" Claire says. "Well, congratulations."

Claire turns to Fulton. "And now I have to optimize for that as well," she says.

Fulton is thinking that's just another reason he could never manage an all-female workplace when Lucile continues.

"Nous sommes enceintes," she says.

Claire turns back around to her.

"What do you mean you're all pregnant?" she says.

Claire makes eye contact with Hattie, who waves her hand as if to say, "Not me." But Claire has figured it out now as she looks at her daughters, who are trying to go about their assembly line duties without making any eye contact with her.

Fulton can immediately tell Claire is fit to be tied. He'll never forget the time he was on the receiving end of her rage in St. Louis. He still relives the look on her face at least once a day.

He'll find out later that Claire never tolerated the twins' supporting their husbands' going off to war. She at least made them promise that they would wait to have children until after their husbands returned. Her twins quit college without her approval. They got married without her approval. She asked for one simple thing only to find out like this that they have ignored her wishes yet again.

However, Fulton didn't know all that at this exact moment and misunderstood her pause as she stood watching her girls pretend to ignore her.

"Back to my calculations…," Fulton starts to say when Claire takes the memo out of his hand and rips the pages into hundreds of scraps, which she tosses into the air like confetti before storming off.

The pieces float everywhere and across the factory floor. Fulton spends the next few hours gathering them all up and trying to reassemble them. He is intently focused on his mission, but, on occasion, he notices after Claire has left, the women are back to smiling and talking again. The twins, too.

Apparently, word spreads quickly through Atascadero, given how Mabel soon shows up, still dirty from gardening, to hug the twins and Lucile. Fulton, however, is intent on getting Claire's diagram back to exactly how it was. He eventually completes the puzzle of the shredded memo when he overhears Mabel excited to have not one but three babies to look forward to.

Children are really only good for one thing in Fulton's mind—job security. Eventually, they'll generate mail.

CHAPTER 32

Pretty much all Ed and Kramer do these days is solve the same basic equation over and over. The equation is simple: revenue minus expenses equals profits. Except profits minus the bank loans equals actual profit. This would be fun to add up each day if the number at the very end would be actual profit. Instead, the number at the end for Ed and Kramer is losses.

Cash reserves are the only way to cover losses. If the cash reserves are very, very low, well, then one's new job is pretty much to sit around all day and do math just to try to stay alive.

When Ed, always lost in thought, walks each day from the cannery building to the press building, what he's really walking between are two entities that are growing in revenue but also have serious expenses of labor, paper, fruits, and vegetables, which are not generating near enough profit to cover the real estate bank loans. Every time someone asks for their land deposits back, his cash reserves sink even further.

Ed and Kramer have done the math so many times that Ed basically has it all memorized. One might say they are running on fumes. But Ed knows it is worse than that. They are out of fumes. They are coasting until the laws of gravity eventually cause them to stop altogether.

Ed is pondering this when he nearly runs into the most peculiar-looking man he's ever seen. The man reveals himself to be even more peculiar as he takes off his hat, exposing his wrinkly bald scalp and neck, not to mention his long beak of a vulture nose. The man extends his bony fingers toward Ed for a handshake.

"I'm the lawyer Oscar Willet," he says. "I've been circling around Atascadero, and now is the time for me to finally meet the infamous Mr. E.G. Lewis."

Ed is wondering if he heard him correctly. He's used to people saying famous, not infamous. But he shakes it off.

"Call me Ed. What can I do for you?"

"It's actually what I can do for you. Might there be a place where we can find some shade and converse privately?"

"It's a busy day here, but you can go up to my office in my wife's big white house over there and schedule an appointment with one of my secretaries."

"Your wife's house? Very clever. A smart move indeed, putting assets in her name. But the thing about my line of business is that I don't think you're going to want me to go up there to your office. When your staff sees my business card and learns of my occupation, well, how shall I say it, it really shouldn't, but it can send ripples of unnecessary angst across an organization."

"And what is your profession?" Ed asks.

"I've found there are some simple words in the English language, like cancer or taxes, which immediately invoke an emotional reaction. My occupation, I'm afraid, is on par with those."

"So, what is it you peddle exactly?"

"Bankruptcy."

CHAPTER 33

It's been a long time since Ed has had to call an emergency executive staff meeting. Back in the presales days, these meetings were about strategies to grow deposits and meet deadlines. But the reality of having burned through millions of dollars in bank loans, investments, and deposits over the last three years sets a slightly different tone.

Ed and Kramer have laid out all the math for Mabel, Claire, Hattie, Alphonse, George, the twins, and even Lucile, who continuously nods despite there being no way, Ed assumes, she can fully understand the situation.

"So what that vulture Oscar is suggesting…" Ed starts to say.

"You mean threatening," Claire says.

"However you look at it," Ed continues, "he's proposing we accept a voluntary bankruptcy plan to lighten the pressure of the loan, restructure, and bounce back."

"But doing so would entrust him in leadership until such time as we do 'bounce back,'" Kramer adds. "Also, remember it isn't in his best interest to remediate our situation any time soon. The longer the duration, the longer he is compensated for his services."

"The new wartime *Illustrated Review*, as you all know, is doing great," George says. "Aren't all our different entities separate in the books? Isn't real estate treated separately from the magazine? And separate from the cannery? And the movie theater? And the beach hotel? And the golf course? And the orchards? And the brick factory? And the Community Center? And the Administration Building? And the roads? And the water plant? And the acres and acres of undeveloped land? Isn't real estate really our only problem? Isn't everything separate?"

All eyes go to Kramer, who certainly knows the answer, but he looks to Ed.

"We have meticulous accounting for everything. But, I'm afraid, all the assets and books are commingled," Ed admits. "Except for the personal assets that are in Mabel's name."

Everyone starts to blurt out questions. Anger and confusion rise in the room as everyone tries in their own way to come to terms with the situation.

"Look," Ed implores, cutting them all off, "I'm doing everything I can to keep us afloat."

Alphonse is the only one who doesn't appear to be upset. He's just not been himself since Lt. Malone left. He's always distant these days. Ed does his best to take back control of the meeting.

"You've heard me say this before," he says, "but as talented as we all are, none of us can change the past. The past is irrelevant. It's only the present and the future that matter."

They all let that sink in, except Mabel, who has heard this too many times before.

"Unless you have a bank debt," Mabel said. "That's a decision from the past that always affects the future."

Everyone starts talking again, throwing out questions and ideas. Ed has to retake charge.

"I have a plan to pitch you," he says. "There is another way to raise money that doesn't have a hard and fast payback date, like a bank loan. I've held off doing it, but I don't see any other path at this point."

They wait to hear what he is going to say, but Mabel begins to join Alphonse in also checking out, given she already knows the answer.

"We need to raise more money from investors," Ed says.

Investors. Mabel's least favorite word. Next to the word *mailer*, that is.

"And let me show you a draft of a new mailer Mr. Kramer and I put together," Ed says.

Now Mabel tunes Ed out completely. On occasion, she picks up on him saying phrases like "deeds to pecan trees," "lifetime subscriptions," "endless chain schemes," and later, she'll recall she may have even heard him propose something much bigger, much riskier, and even entirely downright preposterous.

As a result, Mabel isn't mentally in the room any longer. Physically, she is in the room, but mentally she is now tending her garden, thankful to have her own bank account and most thankful to have a deed to her own home.

CHAPTER 34

At the next all-community meeting in Atascadero, Ed takes the stage before an audience of women who, despite having worked all day in either the cannery or the printing press and despite having their sons and brothers and husbands off to war, are full of smiles.

"It's an understatement, to say the least, that the last few months have been a bit, how shall I say, brighter," Ed says, holding up a vial of dark liquid to thunderous applause from the community.

Despite protests from everyone in Ed's inner circle—besides Kramer, that is—the mailers did indeed go out. As always, a fresh batch of cash has come in, giving Ed more cash reserves to stave off Oscar. But the reason this particular mailer was so successful is that it has nothing to do with real estate or Atascadero or agriculture or anything Ed has ever sold before in his career.

The wartime *Illustrated Review* and the cannery were the first two enterprises that had come to Ed's mind since the war started to generate revenue quickly. But in short order, Ed, along with the entire world, learns that war has proven that a certain asset will become the most valuable commodity. Almost more valuable than food or weapons or money. The war effort has quickly realized it needs something far more precious, and it can't get it fast enough. The world suddenly needs oil.

Ed has enough money now from new trusting investors to try his hand at helping the boys overseas power their planes, tanks, and automobiles. Nearly overnight, Ed has used the new investment dollars that came rolling in to buy oil exploration rights at ten locations spread throughout Los Angeles, Montana, and Wyoming. The mailer explains that only one out of the ten wells has to hit to cover all of Atascadero's losses and to create a further annuity for life for all the investors. With those odds, how could anyone lose?

With a renewed focus on transparency, Ed starts to sell subscriptions to the local *Atascadero News* newspaper, in which he publishes the weekly progress on each of his ten wells, including how many inches each well has been drilled over the last week.

In short order, one of the wells in Los Angeles, the only one that had been previously dug deep but had been abandoned, serendipitously spurts out oil for a few days before going dry again. But it is enough of a win that many of the investors sent in even more money, allowing Ed to hold the vile of black crude oil high in the air.

"Isn't it beautiful?" Ed says to the audience. "Once again, Atascadero is doing our part to support our boys. Our mission is supporting their mission."

Again, cheers ring out from the crowd.

"Now I get asked all the time by you all if your land investment gives you an interest in our newest endeavors, including the cannery, the *Illustrated Review*, and even oil exploration," Ed says. "The answer is absolutely. Absolutely I will share it with you once we have the loans paid and we turn a profit. You have my word."

Cheers again ring out from the crowd. He's already said this to all of them in private, but they love hearing it said out loud, and soon they will read his promise in the *Atascadero News,* as well.

"But I know what you most want—that is, other than our boys home safely from war," Ed continues. "You want to be able to build on your properties. Mare, I'm listening. I really am."

In the front row, Mare is nodding in such a way as to say, "We'll see."

"Well, guess what? That time has come."

Now the cheers are really ringing out.

"But not quite what you are thinking," Ed says, to which the crowd settles down again, and Mare appears ready to grab pitchforks. "As you know, there are not enough workers to build everyone a home just yet. We need the war to end for that. But there are enough workers to start to build a garage on each of your properties. We figured out that we can assemble them in a modular fashion in a warehouse in the city center and then simply erect them on-site. This will give you a place to store your belongings. And give you a place to sit and enjoy the views from your property. We'll build them in the order you sign up. It's up to you. We have four tables set up here. Who wants to be the first to build on their property?"

Ed watches with pride as the women, without hesitation, start clambering to the tables to sign up and get an official date and time stamp next to their name on the list. His entire strategy is very simple: if he doesn't know which bet is going to work, then he must place multiple bets.

"It's just a matter of time now," Ed hears himself saying over and over. All day long, he can be heard telling people, "It's just a matter of time."

Just a matter of time is also what bankruptcy lawyer Oscar Willet tells himself as new copies and clippings are sent to him by the mysterious sender. Oscar thought he had timed it just right, but even he underestimated Ed's ability to make the pot of assets magically grow even bigger. Eventually, everyone takes Oscar's deal. That, too, is just a matter of time.

Just a matter of time is what Postal Inspector Fulton tells himself as well upon receiving the same copies and clippings that are sent to his office each month by the same anonymous sender. The latest batch of mailers includes ones that he had not been asked to advise on despite the fact that he visits Claire all the time. Fulton believes this can only mean one of two things: either Claire has kept the mailer a secret from him, or Ed has sent them without Claire's knowledge. It doesn't matter which it is because neither action can be forgiven this time. Fulton has always known it was just a matter of time with Ed.

Just a matter of time is also, sadly, what Mabel tries to keep out of her mind each day as she tends her garden. She also knew it was just a matter of time before her sister Claire would give up going daily to the cannery or the printing press. She is now back to helping Mabel in the garden. Both of them go about their daily chores while trying not to think about it all just being a matter of time.

CHAPTER 35

♦ ♦ ♦

After six months of combat training, Teddy and Larry finally arrive in Europe only to find themselves guarding ammunition supplies on a base in England far from the front lines in France.

Every day they watch new recruits head out to the front lines. They also watch troops return. The difference between the two groups couldn't be more of a juxtaposition. Clean uniforms versus unrecognizable ones. Clear eyes versus distant ones. Chatter versus silence. Luggage versus coffins.

One day at their guard post, they would have never recognized him except they hear someone on a transport call out the name Lt. Malone. They quickly decide Teddy will cover for Larry, allowing Larry to jog over to the transport to confirm it is indeed their friend.

"Lt. Malone," Larry says, "It's me. Larry. Look over there. That's Teddy."

Teddy is waving. Despite their warm welcome, Lt. Malone barely even acknowledges them. To Larry, Lt. Malone looks like the group they see headed back from the front lines, except he is on a transport headed to the front lines along with his men, whom Larry also recognizes from back at Atascadero. None of the soldiers will make eye contact with Larry either. It's an entire transport of soldiers with distant eyes and disheveled uniforms, beards, and hair headed back out again.

"You're headed back out?" Larry says. "I wish we would have known you were on base. What's it like out there? All we ever hear is that it is muddy and freezing."

Lt. Malone doesn't bother to answer. Neither does anyone else.

"We get letters from back home almost every day," Larry says. "We're going to be fathers. Both of us. George, too. Pretty soon now, we think."

Lt. Malone still doesn't react. Some of the other guys at least nod at this news.

"We get letters from Alphonse, too," Teddy says more privately to Lt. Malone. "Asking if we've seen you or heard from you and how you're doing."

The mention of Alphonse's name finally seems to elicit at least a slight reaction from Lt. Malone as he finally turns in Larry's direction.

"Alphonse says you won't return his letters," Larry says. "Want us to relay something to him for you? Anything at all?"

From the guard post, Teddy sees Lt. Malone finally mumble something to Larry as the transport heads back off to the front lines. Larry watches them go and slowly walks back over to Teddy.

"So, what did he say?" Teddy asks.

But Larry isn't himself any longer. Now Larry looks to Teddy like someone from the group returning from the front lines. It's all Teddy can do to get Larry even to make eye contact with him.

"So, what did he say?" Teddy asks again.

"He said, 'What's the point?'"

"That's what he said?" Teddy asks again. "All he said was, 'What's the point?'"

"That's all he said."

The two of them work the rest of their shift, watching troops go by in both directions, trying not to also give up all hope, but now starting to think to themselves as well what a good question that is. *What is the point?*

CHAPTER 36

Despite a fresh batch of cash in the bank from loyal investors, Ed and Kramer still find themselves doing math every day. Except now, they are calculating what is called a burn rate, which, given the current rate they are losing money, is how many months they have left until they have burned through it all and are flat broke again.

Modeling cash flow in this way is a bit of a game. Or, as Ed likes to call it, a game of assumptions. No one can predict the future. But Ed assumes the *Illustrated Review* and the cannery will continue to perform well. Home sales won't. Oil well drilling, despite it still not having had success, should continue, given it is their only real hope. With those assumptions, they can calculate how much money they'll burn each month and, thus, how many months they have left before they run out of their new stockpile of cash.

"Six months at best," Kramer says, doing the calculations always in his head. "At best."

"What if we go from ten wells to twenty wells?" Ed asks.

Kramer's mind adds up a few more figures, rounds, carries a few numbers, and has his new number.

"Three months," he says. "But I don't advise taking such risk."

"And what if home sales take off again?"

Kramer doesn't even bother to run those numbers in his brain. New home sales are not going to happen.

"What if we drill faster? Deeper?" Ed says.

"The laws of physics don't permit us to proceed any faster," Kramer says. "The drill bits break."

"There has to be something," Ed says. "There is always something."

"Send out another mailer," Kramer says.

"But we can't raise more money. We just raised money. If a well hits, we can raise more. If sales take off, we can raise more. Come on, Mr. Kramer, give me something. Some idea."

"If we owned an asset for which we could leverage, we could get additional funds."

"Yes, of course, but we don't. Why would you say that? Ridiculous. You can't just own an asset out of nowhere and get a loan against it."

"That's exactly what Atascadero is."

"You know we can't do a new real estate development during a war. Come on. There's nothing else to develop around here. Except...."

The moment Ed says that out loud, he realizes there is indeed right under his nose a possibility for increasing his assets. More specifically, right next door. He's been so focused on creating something new he forgot about the other way to grow—a merger.

Before Ed can share his thoughts with Kramer, Hattie bursts into his office holding a newspaper. Ed can tell from her face the news isn't just bad. It's tragic. She can't even say it out loud. Ed has to read it for himself. As does Kramer. They immediately see the utter gravity of the situation as the article is about Lt. Malone and his troops.

"Has Alphonse seen this?" Ed asks.

"I don't know," Hattie says. "You and I need to get Claire and go over to the movie theater."

Ed and Hattie can't find Claire, but they do find Mabel. When the three of them arrive at the movie theater, they can hear that Claire is already there, yelling from inside, which causes them to rush even faster into the building.

They find Claire banging on the locked door of the projection room, imploring Alphonse to open the door. She's throwing her body against the door, but it is no use. She can't break through it.

Inside the projection room, Alphonse is indeed holding the tragic newspaper, which reports that Lt. Malone and his entire regiment, all those boys Atascadero has grown to love and support, have died in a gas attack upon returning to the front lines. The entire regiment was enveloped in a gas cloud from which, the article reads, there was no escape even with their masks on. The entire regiment is gone.

Alphonse has known this news privately now for an hour. He's gone through every reaction. Shock. Denial. Hysteria. Bargaining. Reasoning. Now he's reached a point of pure depression as he sits holding the newspaper in one hand and his loaded revolver in his other.

"What's the point?" Alphonse continues to mumble to himself.

"What's the point?" is what Larry and Teddy had relayed to Alphonse just a few days prior in a letter after they saw Lt. Malone.

It's not just that his dear friend Lt. Malone is dead. It's not just that all the other boys in Lt. Malone's command are dead. But who is next? Teddy? Larry? All the others from Atascadero who are bravely serving? All the other sons and brothers and fathers and friends. Even lovers. All of them risking their lives for what? For what?

What's the point?

CHAPTER 37

Claire first met Alphonse at a saloon. Which is entirely cliche, and she dreads the rest of her life when people ask where they met, and she has to say "at a bar." Alphonse has always been willing to concoct for her a better story. He's pitched her very creative ways they could say how they met. But their marriage itself is already fiction. So, in the end, at least saying they met at a saloon is true.

When Claire left St. Louis suddenly with her then 12-year-old twins, she didn't have much of a plan except that she felt they needed a change. She felt that she and the girls had grown entirely dependent on Ed and Mabel, whose business foundation was crumbling at the time.

Claire never wanted to move to St. Louis, to begin with. Her plan was to stay in Memphis and manage Ed's household products line, but Ed wouldn't have it. In fact, he put Howard Nichols—a disgusting man, to say the least—in charge of the Memphis operation just to force her hand. Before that, she had picked out an apartment for herself and the girls. *At least that could be a place to start*, she thought to herself as she boarded the train to Memphis with her twins.

Over the next five years, they did indeed live in that apartment. The girls adjusted to a new school. Claire got a factory job, and, just like always, in no time at all, she was promoted and promoted and promoted until she had entirely reorganized the factory and was basically running the place. Everything was back to normal, including a business owner that eventually couldn't keep his hands off her.

As her girls were going away to college, she shared with her friend and drinking partner, Alphonse, that with the girls leaving she was about to get her life back. However, she lamented that she was about to be forced to find work in a new factory when Alphonse suggested they get married.

Claire definitely saw the advantage. Maybe, just maybe, being married would keep her boss and all the other men away. Being single and never married with kids caused men to think of her as a "good-time gal."

She'd been a regular and a drinking buddy with Alphonse at the saloon for years, and she absolutely adored him. She knew him to be funny, kind, handsome, smart, and caring. He was by all standards a perfect match, and marriage was a wonderful proposition except for one tiny thing. He wasn't her type. And she certainly wasn't his type. She wasn't even the right gender.

But over the next few weeks, he made the argument that the arrangement was perfect for him, as well. Saying he was married could actually help him land better theater jobs, especially ones with family and children's programs. All their challenges, Alphonse argued, had simply to do with a lack of societal conformity. If they could both say they were married, maybe the world would open up to them. And he was right. She eventually agreed, and it worked.

Claire sent the girls off to college in Chicago one morning, had a justice of the peace wedding over lunch, and moved into

Alphonse's two-bedroom apartment that afternoon. That evening they celebrated publicly at the saloon.

In short order, everything changed with wedding rings on their fingers. Her boss and all the other men she interacted with on a daily basis left her alone to do her job. Alphonse got hired to run a new family theater that opened in Memphis. They each had their own rooms in the apartment, they each had someone to split the rent with, and they had been friends for years, so living together was wonderful in terms of companionship.

On occasion, Alphonse slept over somewhere else. On other rare occasions, he asked if she could come home a little later or at a certain time. Those were easy accommodations for her to make, and he offered her the same, but she was content to continue her focus on work and sending some money each month to her girls.

That was that. Claire's life was both efficient and effective. At least until Ed's schemes shook it all up yet again, and the girls had to quit college.

Claire reminisces on all of this as she attends a memorial service for Lt. Malone and his troops on a beautiful day in Atascadero. Almost every day in Atascadero is beautiful, especially today as the entire community has gathered to pay tribute.

Even Mare, whose only visible emotion has been one of sternness, seems to express a look of something else this day. All the women in attendance, which is nearly everyone in town, grieve not only for these boys that died but for all the other boys over in Europe whose fates are still uncertain. Hattie and Lawrence can only imagine what their sons Teddy and Larry must be going through today, not to mention Marcella and Rose.

Claire can't help but admire the very pregnant figures of her girls and Lucile. As some lives are ending, others are beginning. A cycle that has continued for all of mankind's existence.

Claire takes all this in as she feels fortunate to take hold of Alphonse's hand. She, Ed, and Mabel together were strong enough to bust the door open. They were, in the end, able to subdue and comfort Alphonse, at least for now.

She knows that as sad as today is for the community, inevitably these memorials are going to soon become commonplace, given all the other young men from Atascadero who are still fighting. She doesn't know how this community is going to be able to continue to hold it together. But at least she can still hold Alphonse's hand.

◆

As the memorial ends and Ed is walking back by himself alone to his office, he's thinking similar thoughts. Nothing is grimmer than the reality of senseless death. Nothing, that is, until a bony hand taps him on the shoulder, and Ed turns to see none other than the vulture, Oscar Willet, who has yet again paid him an unannounced and inopportune visit.

Ed has come to realize that Oscar must always be lurking in the shadows or circling, as he prefers to say. Somehow he always catches Ed both unexpectedly and alone.

"It's time," the bankruptcy lawyer says.

CHAPTER 38

Oscar feels it best they always meet in private. But in Atascadero, Ed has zero privacy except for one location—his Cadillac convertible parked on the overlook that looks out at the valley.

"This locale will do very nicely," Oscar says.

Everyone Ed has ever taken to the overlook marvels at the view. But it seems to invoke a different reaction from Oscar. He doesn't admire the view as much as he appears to want to devour it.

"It's relatively simple, actually," Oscar says, handing a contract over to Ed. "It gives me the power of attorney to negotiate on your behalf with your banks, investors, and other creditors. We'll operate as if you have formally declared bankruptcy, even though you haven't. Avoiding those costs. And I'll negotiate all new terms with everyone."

The last thing in the world Ed wants to do is read the thick contract he's now holding in his hand as Oscar continues.

"You'll come out of this in a better place. On the best possible terms. Having avoided the public courts. My approach is private and respectful. A gentle landing while still being respectful of your mission out here."

Ed isn't really listening any longer. Instead, he's looking out at all he's built. The valley was raw when he arrived but look at it now. Roads. Buildings. Orchards. Water lines. Sewers. Autos. People. Promises. And it all still has promise.

Ed promised a utopia, and he delivered. Or, at least, he had delivered it right up until powerful men in Europe couldn't get along. The whole world has had to sacrifice as a result.

Ed can't help but think there has to be a better way. He's come too far in life and in his career to just roll over and die today.

"There has to be an alternative," he says. "There has to be."

Oscar hands him another file.

"Here's the alternative," Oscar says. "Flip through it. It's an affidavit of dozens of your investors who are willing to testify against you in court that they have sent you check after check over the years only to receive the promise of additional promises in return that never materialize."

Ed flips through it, confirming indeed that Oscar has collected statement after statement from names Ed certainly recognizes. Most of them are women. All of whom are not just long-time subscribers to his magazines but ones that have sent him volumes of fan mail over the years. Ones who are the first to read his columns and send in recipes, desserts, and much more throughout the years. Ed would always publish their names and responses, including their affirmations for the different investments they've signed up for. Which, he now realizes, gave Oscar an easy way to find his investors.

Oscar hands Ed another file. In it are signed letters of support for Oscar's voluntary bankruptcy plan already signed by all of Ed's bankers and major creditors, which Ed realizes are also easy to track down just by reading the weekly issues of the *Atascadero News*. Ed's insistence on transparency, in the end, made it very easy for Oscar to piece everything together.

"Other than you signing, there's just one thing left to do," Oscar says.

"And what could that possibly be?" Ed asks. "You appear to have already talked to everyone without my permission."

"Everyone but the folks that live in Atascadero and others that have purchased land," Oscar says. "Certainly, I know who they are, but those folks need to hear it from you. They need to hear from you directly that this is the best course of action for them."

"It will decrease their property values," Ed says. "Why would they possibly agree to this?"

"They will if E.G. Lewis tells them to."

"They will also fight it if I tell them to."

"Then, just like the Great War that is raging today, you'll have blood on your hands, sending them into a battle that can't be won. The contract you are holding in your hand isn't an admission of defeat. It's a peace treaty allowing your mission to continue. When you do take the time to read it, you'll see there is something for you in there as well. You'll find you'll come out ahead just fine in the end. Just fine, actually. All you have to do is rally the community behind the plan and not wait too long."

Now Ed finally understands what is going on. Oscar's approach is about a gentle landing by avoiding the courts. But Ed never understood why the owner wouldn't just fight it to the end since they are going to lose everything anyway. But now he understands. Somewhere in the annals of the agreement he is holding must be some kind of kickback for his cooperation.

"I'd estimate that you have a few months left of cash before you run out," Oscar says. "Am I accurate?"

Ed doesn't bother to answer. It appears there is nothing Oscar doesn't already know about the business.

"The sooner you sign," Oscar says, "the sooner we can make any remaining cash work to your personal advantage. But if you wait too long, we have nothing to work with."

All of this is becoming too much for Ed to process. When he had to flee University City in St. Louis, leaving all his investors with nothing, he saw what happens when you wait too long. The prospect of that happening again is certainly unsettling. The mission of Atascadero certainly matters, but so does that of his investors as well.

"My whole career," Oscar says, "I've had to endure the vulgarity of being called a vulture. But that is cruel and unjust, and I couldn't be more the opposite. The agreement you're holding in your hand is not your demise. I'm not a vulture. What I'm offering to you is instead a new lease on life. A way to make it as fair as we can for all parties before it is too late to do so."

CHAPTER 39

A month later, Marcella, Rose, and Lucile all have healthy baby girls within a few weeks of each other. The irony of bringing even more women into Atascadero doesn't escape Ed or the rest of the community.

George couldn't be prouder to be a father. Hattie, Alphonse, and Lawrence couldn't be prouder to be grandparents. Mabel and Ed have a distinct pleasure now of being what Ed calls the "Super Aunt and Uncle" to all of them. Claire, especially once she held the babies for the first time, eventually came around, as well.

Unfortunately, letters sent during wartime often arrive out of order or not at all. But in the cold depths of muddy trenches in which Teddy and Larry now find themselves, having been transferred from guard duty, any piece of mail is a welcome escape.

A month after the babies are born, Teddy and Larry learn the news via letters that arrive out of sequence. It takes them a few weeks to piece it all together as they read about nursing and burping before eventually receiving the initial announcement of the births.

God forbid a letter would end with a mention of the babies having a rash or a cold or a cough, for there would be no telling when they'd next learn of its resolution. All of war is terrible, but the communication challenges now that they are in the trenches make it far worse.

As Atascadero limps along into late 1918, more of Ed's cash reserves burn with each passing day. He has just a few weeks left now. Ed was certain—absolutely certain—that one of the wells would have hit by now. But, alas, they haven't. Thus, every day, at some point, Ed catches himself looking over at Oscar's agreement, which is stacked in the corner of his office. Having it sitting there was initially haunting, but every day it becomes more tempting.

At least his evenings and weekends are filled with joy. Helping to raise three healthy baby girls gives him, and especially Mabel, a purpose and a distraction.

What they all need is for the war to end. America's involvement in the war has helped to tip the scales, and according to all the newspapers, a treaty appears imminent. But it has also generated monthly funeral services for another boy serving overseas. The cause of death is rarely from battle as more boys are dying from sickness in the trenches, including what appears to be a deadly pandemic of influenza sweeping the world. Newspapers routinely report that non-combat deaths greatly exceed combat deaths.

To make up for printing and cannery jobs that will inevitably be lost when the war ends, Ed has recently brokered a deal with the manufacturer of a new kind of train engine to open a plant in Atascadero, which will both create jobs and families who will need housing after the war. He's also completed a deal with a doll manufacturer, who is especially excited to have access to so much female labor as the dolls need to be sewn, assembled, and painted by hand.

His biggest challenge in Atascadero is something that seemed impossible in the oasis of his valley, literally named "Abundance of Water" in Spanish. In this past year, Atascadero experienced both a frost and a drought that inflicted permanent damage to his orchards.

Ed has invested in the most modern water and sewer system in the world, but none of it matters since the creeks that feed it have gone dry. A valley that was once so green is now gray.

He has gotten to know the neighboring communities over the last five years living in California and buying his fruits and vegetables from them to fulfill his cannery contract with the U.S. government. He's since learned that to be successful, one must both irrigate orchards year-round and have heaters at the ready.

Ed instead has miles of water pipes going to homesites that aren't yet sold, much less lived in, and with no water going to his orchards. As a result, those orchards five years in, along with all his Atascadero Seed Company plans, can only be described in the purest form of the word barren.

But all the worries in the world go away when he's holding a baby. Ed has that special skill to make babies laugh. His favorite is to sit them on his lap and hold out his finger as if it is a chain one pulls to flush a toilet. The toddlers learn when they pull on his finger, Ed will make a swirling water noise as he opens his legs and flushes the toddler down to the floor. Over and over again, the girls clamber onto his lap for their turn to pull the chain. It's funny to the kids every time, and it gives all their mothers a little break.

Try as Lawrence may, he often attempts to copy Ed with the kids, but it just isn't the same, and soon all the kids are in line with Ed again. Ed doesn't talk business ever with Lawrence, but now seems as good a time as any.

"How many homes have you built over in Eaglet, Lawrence?" Ed asks.

"Oh, I don't know exactly," Lawrence says. "It's still just little ole Eaglet. Just trying to get by."

"Well, I finally got out there the other day. And by my count, you are nearing one hundred."

"My goodness, you know I would have given you a tour. Let me take you back out there and show you around. It's just a flea on a tick compared to Atascadero."

"Well, you are a hundred completed homes ahead of me."

"Not for long, I'm sure. You'll leapfrog right over me any day once the war ends."

"I never asked in all these years, but who do you bank with?"

"I don't bank with anyone," Lawrence admits. "Gosh, I guess I should, but I just roll the profits from one home into the next and into the next until I've generated enough cash to be my own bank. I'm sure someone who knows how to think big, like you, could have shown me a better way. But slow and steady is all I know. It's just my nature, I guess."

Ed is shocked as he realizes he is bouncing babies next to what might be the only real estate developer in the history of America not to have any debt.

"Lawrence, here's a crazy idea. Brace yourself."

"I'm braced."

"What if Eaglet and Atascadero merged? All my infrastructure here will officially become yours."

Lawrence appears as if he's about to pass out. This is a concept he's clearly never contemplated. Ed can tell Lawrence's mind almost can't even process it.

"Oh my. My oh my. My word. Oh my," Lawrence stutters and stutters and mumbles to himself, trying to come to terms with it all. "I don't even know how to think about that. I…I…need Larry. Larry has a mind for all that. Maybe when Larry gets back from the war. It's Mitchel & Son, as you know. But I was ready for it just to be 'Son' when he returns. Wowzers. What an offer. Amazing. I just…I need Larry…I think."

"Or maybe we work all this out ourselves and surprise Larry upon return so he doesn't have to deal with it?"

"Maybe. Maybe so. Again, wowzers. So much to consider. Maybe that would be less hassle for Larry."

The toddlers are all lined up and waiting patiently while Ed and Lawrence have been talking, but the girls can't take it anymore. So, Ed loads them all together on his lap at once, and they all giggle louder than ever as one of them pulls the fake chain, sweeping them down the toilet together.

CHAPTER 40

◆ ◆ ◆

The most exciting days in Atascadero's history were when trainfuls of women would arrive daily. Now a new form of excitement fills the community each day at the train station as each day another boy returns home safely from war.

With a peace treaty having been signed, boys are returning daily now. But one thing is for sure, none are the same as before they left. They are grateful to be home, but everyone is noticing something about their eyes, especially for the first few weeks they are home. They are so distant. Over time they come around a bit, but maybe never entirely.

Larry certainly isn't the same. Not by a long shot. He has a window seat as the train pulls into the station. His family hasn't spotted him yet, but on the platform, he can see his father, Lawrence, straining hard to spot him through the train windows. He also sees his beautiful bride, Marcella, and who must be their daughter in her arms. Larry is already crying. But it is spotting Rose and Hattie, who are desperately looking for Teddy's face, that most affects him.

As Larry exits the train, he walks up to the entire group, who still hasn't spotted him yet. When they see him, they leap for joy. All of them. Marcella, his dad, Hattie, Rose, Ed, Mabel, Claire, Alphonse, George, Lucile, and even Kramer.

To get to hug his wife after all this time, meet his daughter, shake his dad's hand, and receive hugs from all of them is overwhelming and better than he ever imagined. His return to Atascadero could not be more wonderful were it not for what he knew was about to happen next. As happy as Hattie and Rose are to see him, what they are really looking for is Teddy's face, which they haven't been able to find in the crowd.

Larry takes their hands in his, but he almost doesn't have to say anything as they can see it in his face that something is terribly, terribly wrong. They desperately continue to look around for Teddy, but their worst nightmare materializes as the train porters unload, amongst all the luggage, a casket.

Larry can see the confusion on their faces, for they know that Teddy survived the war and sailed back with him on the ship. They know he was in New York City with Larry. They know he was to be on the same train. So, this makes no sense.

"The day before we boarded in New York City, street vendors were selling these beautiful parasols on a busy corner in Times Square. The woman ahead of us got out her money to pay when a man ran by, pushed her on the ground, took her money, and ran through traffic across the busy street.

"My instinct was to help the woman up. Teddy's instinct was to chase down the thug who robbed her. By the time I had the woman back on her feet, Teddy was smiling at us from the other side of the street. He had already chased the thief down and got the money back.

"From behind him, I could see the man coming back with a vengeful look on his face. I tried. I even ran out in the street, but I couldn't get Teddy's attention before the thug pushed him from behind out in front of a speeding bus. It all just happened so fast. So fast."

The next few minutes, watching them all go through the first few of the seven stages of grief, starting with shock, denial, and anger, including questions about why he hadn't told them sooner, are the hardest for Larry. At one point, someone asks, "How dare he not tell them sooner?" as if he is the one to blame.

He's the one that had to hold the hand of his dying friend in the street who begged him to remind Rose and the baby that he loves them more than anything in the world, to tell them that when Teddy spent all those months in the muddy trenches, he was indeed asking himself, "What's the point?" But his answer was always the same: a peaceful future for his family.

Upon hearing the full story, and with all the attention on Rose and the baby, Ed is the only one whose eyes go to Hattie, who has just lost a son. Ed sees her start to wobble, and he is fortunate to be able to catch her before her head hits the wooden floor of the train station.

It is Ed's face that Hattie last sees before collapsing in grief in his arms. Again, her hero is there to save her.

CHAPTER 41

◆ ◆ ◆

Teddy's funeral, like all military funerals before in Atascadero, is attended by the entire community. The babies are, of course, fussy. But they are also a valuable distraction that everyone needs.

Something about this funeral service feels different than the others. Given the war is over, one can only hope this will be the last soldier to die, and, as such, in many respects, it sets this funeral up to be a memorial of sorts for the entire war.

Something else that makes it particularly painful is the presence of Larry in uniform, which is both a symbol of the soldiers that fought and the soldiers that didn't return home. Exerting an incredible amount of grace, Hattie invites her estranged husband, Ted Sr., up to the front row to sit by her during the funeral.

Ted Sr. had telegrammed ahead that he would be attending in a spirit of peace. He came alone and stayed to himself. George's eyes especially are always on him, and rumors are swirling that George may or may not be armed.

During the service, for a brief moment, Ted attempts to hold his granddaughter until she fights her way out of his grasp and runs over to Ed. As Ed holds the baby, he can't help but think that Teddy survived an entire war only to die a Good Samaritan back on U.S. soil. *What's the point of that?*

Though Ed wants to keep his full attention on memories of Teddy, he can't help but think about his own situation. Tomorrow, he's going to have to break the news to the community that the government, now that the war is over, has canceled the cannery contract. The same is happening with advertising contracts at the wartime *Illustrated Review*. Readers want to move on from the war. Everyone wants to move on.

Ed will at least be able to announce that the Dooley Doll Factory is indeed setting up shop in Atascadero. They have a hot seller called the Scary Ann, which is a little wooden doll that needs a hundred workers to paint and assemble them. It's a unique toy in that a child can simply push a lever and cause the doll's hair to stand up on end. Just like Ed's game of flushing the kids down the toilet, it's shocking and fun every time.

Most jobs, however, will be created when the locomotive plant opens in Atascadero. That deal is moving slower, but especially now that the war is over, Ed is told he'll be able to announce the news shortly. The new plant will not only create jobs but also increase demand for homesites. Manufacturing trains was not Ed's master vision for Atascadero, but at this point, anything will do.

In the end, though, he's out of tricks to fend off the vulture Oscar. Even with the war over, he just can't seem to get the timing of these deals to ever line up properly.

After the service, Hattie, Rose, and the baby see Ted Sr. off at the train station with Ed, George, and even Lawrence carefully watching from a distance. Ted boards without issue, and that appears to be that. With the exception, of course, of trying to figure out how they will all get on with their lives.

Later that afternoon, Ed goes back to his office to do some work when he finds a sealed envelope sitting on his desk. He opens it and scans to the bottom of the letter to see it is signed by none other than Ted Sr., which causes Ed to pause, wondering when and how Ted had slipped into his office and what else Ted had seen while he was in there.

As Ed reads the letter, he quickly loses all the color in his face and slumps into his chair.

CHAPTER 42

◆ ◆ ◆

There have been multiple times over the past few years when Postal Inspector Fulton has considered purchasing a homesite for himself in Atascadero.

Technically, he's based in Seattle, where he has an apartment, but given his entire territory is the West Coast, he's hardly ever there. Most criminal activity involving the mails in his region originates in San Francisco, within the Asian communities, who do love their lotteries. However, increasingly, more and more criminal activity is coming from Los Angeles, especially as the mafia continues to creep west after crackdowns in New York and Chicago.

Though having a family has never and will never interest Fulton, as he gets older, the prospect of retirement is beginning to dawn on him. He's already on pace to receive a generous pension from the Postal Service. Regardless, he's saved up 75 percent of every paycheck he's ever received his entire life.

He's been reluctant to do the math, but he could probably retire whenever he's ready. But he's far from ready. Early in his career, he thought the growth in Nashville and St. Louis was overwhelming in terms of mail crime, but every day the population in California is growing at such an exorbitant rate that each day brings more and more new leads to investigate.

Ironically, the city in which he finds the most comfort is Atascadero. Advising Claire, though unsolicited, on the printing press and cannery has been the highlight whenever he passes through. Atascadero is now the third largest post office in the state of California, and he's been able to advise and organize the operation so successfully here that the best practices he's established are now being used in all new cities across the country. Most of those ideas were Claire's, but a few were his.

But thoughts of retiring entirely leave his mind as Claire and Ed burst into his Atascadero office unannounced, holding the envelope Ed just discovered on his desk.

"Fulton," Ed says, red-faced, "you've back-stabbed us."

"I've done nothing of the kind."

"Read it," Claire says, taking the letter out of Ed's hand and shoving it into Fulton's chest.

There are only two things in life that can really fluster Fulton. One is Claire, and the other is having his personal space invaded. Her hand touching his chest is the culmination of both.

Fulton wants to read the letter. However, he'd prefer to find a mirror. *Did she put a crease in his uniform? Did her hand smear his buttons?*

Seeing the fire in Claire's eyes forces him to try to focus and attempt to read the letter. But it's hard for him. The more he reads, the more it feels like Claire and Ed are getting closer and closer to him. Instinctively, he backs up more and more, but it feels like they are still getting closer.

Now he finds himself just scanning the letter for keywords. But the letter is starting to blur. The room is starting to spin. He's certain there must be a crease on his uniform from her touching it. If they would just back away for a moment, give him some space. Preferably, a chance to completely change his uniform and restart his entire morning routine from scratch, which would only take him an hour and a half or so—it used to take two and a half hours to dress, but he's found some efficiencies, which he's wondering if Claire would find interesting to learn how he's improved his process.

SMACK.

Claire slaps him right across the face.

SMACK.

She does it again.

"Focus," she says. "According to that letter, the Los Angeles federal prosecutor is filing an indictment for mail fraud against Eddie."

Now that snaps Fulton out of it.

"It doesn't surprise me," Fulton says. "It is their decision, not mine. We've gone over this. The days of Postmaster Generals or even postal inspectors handing out fraud orders on their own are gone. Except...."

"Except what?" Claire says, imploring him to continue.

"Except I haven't yet turned over any evidence," Fulton says, walking over to a filing cabinet in his office.

The cabinet is five drawers tall, and Ed and Claire assume Fulton is going to pull out a file, but instead he opens all five drawers, revealing hundreds of file folders in each drawer. The entire cabinet is focused on Ed.

"All of this could be used against you," Fulton says. "All of it. Any of it. I have it all right here, perfectly organized. It would almost be the easiest case for the federal government to win in the history of fraud cases. It's all buttoned up. Black and white."

Now Ed feels the room spinning as he looks around to find a chair to sit in, but the only choice is Fulton's desk chair, which he takes.

Great, Fulton thinks to himself. Not only am I going to have to start my entire morning routine all over again, but I'm also going to have to deep clean my chair and this entire office.

"I'm confused," Claire says. "You didn't turn anything over to the attorney general?"

"I didn't need to," Fulton says. "Every month, an anonymous sender gives me damning clips from your periodicals and mailers. Information I already have, by the way, so my assumption is this person is also sending it to others."

Ed finally realizes that this is how Oscar is getting all his information as well. If it is being sent to Oscar and Fulton, then Ed can assume it was also sent to the federal prosecutor.

"Why haven't you yet made a case to the prosecutor?" Claire asks Fulton.

That is a question Fulton has thought about for some time, especially given his superiors will inevitably ask him this as well. One might assume it is because Fulton likes Ed. But that isn't it. He's never trusted Ed. One might also assume it is because Fulton likes Atascadero, where he spends so much time. A scandal in Atascadero would actually make the homesite even cheaper to buy. But, again, that isn't it. Finally, one might assume Fulton likes Claire. She is the person Fulton most respects and has spent the most time with. But technically, he does not have a friend in the world. Claire would never admit to being his friend. So, Claire isn't it either.

"I haven't yet turned it in because I can't prove you are actually committing fraud," Fulton says. "You have planted orchards. You have built roads, buildings, sewers, and a water plant. You've even dug ten wells. I have personally visited each of them. Even the ones in Wyoming and Montana."

Ed will never cease to find Fulton fascinating. Even Ed hasn't visited all ten of the wells.

"So how can they be close to an indictment?" Claire asks. "What do they know that you don't know?"

"There is nothing I don't know," Fulton says.

Claire believes that probably is true, which now causes her to turn her attention instead to Ed, as does Fulton.

"What do they know that we don't know?" Claire asks Ed.

Ed racks his brain. He's been completely transparent the entire time. He's revealed everything he knows in his publications. It's all laid out for the world to see. There isn't anything else. All he knows, he has shared.

Except for one thing, Ed now realizes. He has shared all he knows. But does he know everything? There is actually one person that knows, on occasion, a bit more than him. Not Mabel. Not Claire. Not Fulton. Not George. Not Alphonse. Definitely not Lawrence. Not even Hattie. But, as Ed thinks about it….

There is one person. A little weasel.

CHAPTER 43

◆ ◆ ◆

Kramer never could quite acclimate to the California sun. Connecticut will always be his climate of choice. His love for the East Coast is one of the reasons he didn't follow Ed to the Midwest years ago. But not the main reason.

Kramer met Ed back in the late 1880s in their days at Trinity College in Hartford, Connecticut. Kramer hadn't really made any friends at school—not that he was trying—when Ed invited him to a party. Back in those days, Ed was going by Edward.

Kramer never got invited to anything. So, this was a big deal. He didn't even know Ed knew him. Everyone knew Ed on campus. No one cared about Kramer, but apparently, Ed did.

The party was off campus at an address that baffled Kramer. For a moment, he wondered if the invite was some sort of hoax as he found himself at an industrial warehouse near the Hartford River. The address led him to a door in a back alleyway, which he hadn't yet knocked on. Just as he was deciding if he should just turn around and go back to his dorm room, the door flew open, and none other than Ed popped his head out and seemed both relieved and excited to find Kramer sheepishly standing there plotting his retreat.

"Mr. Kramer," Ed said, "get yourself in here, my boy. Perfect timing. We're ridiculously outnumbered."

Kramer had no idea what that meant as Ed took him by the arm and basically pulled him through the door into a world Kramer never knew existed.

It took Kramer a moment to scan the room and realize the men were few and far between. It was basically he, Ed, and a few businessmen. The overwhelming majority of the room was filled with women—all of them stunning.

It wasn't entirely surprising that all the women were holding a cocktail. Or even that they all seemed to have a cigar. But it took Kramer a moment to realize something else. They were all wearing diamonds. Diamond necklaces. Diamond earrings. Diamond bracelets. Diamond everything.

"Ladies, meet my friend, Kramer," Ed said. "He's a second cousin to Rockefeller on his mother's side and Carnegie on his father's."

Kramer's expression clearly showed that was, of course, entirely untrue, but the women didn't seem to care. Immediately, he had a woman on each arm as they showed off their diamonds to him.

Kramer hadn't really spoken to a woman since, well, ever. Never. He had no idea what to say or how to act. In no time at all, they got bored with him, and he found himself just standing alone until Ed brought a new group of women over to meet him. Each time, Ed couldn't seem to remember that Kramer was supposed to be a Rockefeller and a Carnegie because as the night went on, Ed also introduced him as a Mellon, Astor, du Pont, Sloan, Hunt, Morgan, and even as part of the up and coming Kennedy family.

A while later, Kramer again found himself alone when a man in his mid-20s, a few years older than him and Ed, handed him a fresh drink and a cigar.

"Edward speaks very highly of you," the man said. "I'm his oldest brother, Robert."

Kramer got a good look at Robert. His eyes resembled Ed's, but Robert was considerably taller, although he shared Ed's pronounced cheekbones. Kramer would learn over time that all four Lewis brothers shared similar eyes and cheekbones despite being of strikingly different heights.

Robert also had what Kramer believed to be the finest mustache he had ever seen. All adult men wore a mustache. Most college boys couldn't yet grow a real one. Kramer certainly couldn't. But Robert's was a wonder, given how it flared at both corners. Kramer had never seen a mustache worn like that before. Handlebar was the best way he could describe it.

"Have you picked out the real winner in the room yet?" Robert asked.

Most people would instinctively look around the room after a comment like that and assume Robert was asking him which of the diamond girls was the prettiest, but Kramer didn't need to look back at the room. He had the room memorized. He knew how many people were in the room. How many were female. How many were male. The total number of drinks. The total number of cigars. The number of dresses that were white versus blue versus black versus the one red dress. The total number of strands of diamonds. The total individual diamonds.

However, Kramer wasn't that interested in any of the women's faces, although the woman in the red dress would immediately get anyone's attention—even women's attention. She was striking. Anyone would say so. He'd later find out her name was Claire.

"The diamonds on the woman in the red dress," Kramer said, still not looking out at the room.

Robert smiled. When he smiled, Kramer noticed Robert's mustache took on a life of its own, almost dancing or even swirling as his lip curled.

"How did you spot it?" Robert asked him. "Red dress? Gorgeous girl?"

"The reflection," Kramer said. "The particular radiance. I admit it is subtle but yet present upon scrutiny. Once cognized, it is ineluctable."

"What?"

"Apologies. Once you see it, you see it."

Robert was impressed. Kramer had indeed spotted the real winner in the room—the only strand of diamonds that was real.

"How about you come work for us?" Robert said. "How about you take on a part-time job while you're in school."

"What is the nature of your role here, exactly?" Kramer said. "What would be demanded of me?"

"Isn't it obvious?" Robert asked.

True, it was very obvious.

"Importing diamonds and cigars?" Kramer asked.

"And on occasion, rubies and pearls and even gold watches," Robert said.

"And on occasion, *real* rubies, pearls, diamonds, and *real* gold watches?" Kramer added.

"On occasion," Robert said. "Yes, real ones too."

Clever, Kramer thought. Very clever. The two of them quickly became fast friends as Kramer joined the family business. In the months that followed, Robert handled the importing, Ed handled the sales, and Kramer lent nuance to the advertising to fend off any legal ambiguities. John—Ed's and Robert's brother, who also attended Trinity College—would never touch the business with a ten-foot pole. George was just a baby. It was a devious uncle on their mother's side who was the real mastermind of the operation. But that's a story for another time.

In short order, Ed recruited over a hundred young women, not just to work in the growing warehouse but also to model the jewelry around town. These women quickly became known as "diamond girls" or "Edward's girls." If a man spoke to one, he quickly realized they were all trained by Ed to say the exact same thing: "You think these diamonds are pretty? You should see the girls down at the warehouse." When they arrived, there'd be a cigar and cocktail waiting for them with their name on it. All they'd have to do is ask for a Mr. E.G. Lewis, but call him Edward. He will see to everything.

Kramer didn't follow Ed to the Midwest to expand the operation. He instead stayed focused on his infatuation with Robert's handlebar mustache and the intrigue of the uncle until an unfortunate incident led to Kramer having to flee Connecticut just as Ed needed some help in California.

The only joy in life Kramer has ever allowed himself is watching the corners of Robert's mouth, hoping he might smile, causing that glorious mustache to dance a little. Kramer thought he might never reach that level of joy again with another man until that is, he met Alphonse.

CHAPTER 44

◆ ◆ ◆

Ed beelines back to the Headquarters House to confront Kramer, arriving to realize that instead of attending Teddy's funeral, Kramer got a whiff of the indictment and spent that time cleaning out his office and desk.

"He's gone," Hattie says, calling out from the other room.

Ed is surprised to hear Hattie's voice. The last thing she should be doing today is visiting the office after her son's funeral, but nonetheless, she's here.

"I saw him for a moment. Mr. Kramer mumbled something about escaping to San Francisco," she says. "And something about a trial. That he should never have attended some kind of diamond party in Connecticut all those years ago."

Ed is not sure what to say or where to start, so he just sits down in a chair next to her. He takes a good long look at her face. Sometimes people look tired. Sometimes they look exhausted. But on the evening of her only son's funeral and having had to mingle with her estranged husband the past few days, she looks something different than tired. She looks downright spent.

"Mr. Kramer also handed me this envelope he'd been served from the federal court in Los Angeles on your behalf," Hattie says. "I had no business reading it, but it was just sitting here. Unsure what to do to occupy my mind, wanting some form of distraction. Anything to do, I guess. I'm sorry, but I read it."

Ed feels terrible for her. He knows he should walk her home. He should hug her. Console her. Hold her. Let her cry. Be there for her. There are a thousand things he should do or say for her benefit. But instead, he reaches for the envelope, pulls out the indictments, and reads through them for himself.

This is not his first time being charged with criminal acts by the federal government. In fact, this is his fifteenth time. But there are more charges in this one than all the others combined due to the accusation of commingling funds and mail fraud associated with Atascadero land sales, the Atascadero Seed Company, the exact depth of oil wells, and even discrepancies pertaining to the total number of pecan trees planted in his orchards.

This time it is not one particular accusation for him to refute. This time it is as if the entire book is being thrown at him. Every promise he's ever made in print since he's been in California is in there. Laundry list after laundry list. But the toughest thing to read is the sheer number of counts against him. When he adds them up in his head, he realizes the repercussions could lead to over twenty years of jail time.

After flipping through it all, one might expect him to join Hattie in looking spent. Except he's fought and won legal battles like this in the past. He knows how it all works. He's spent almost an equal amount of time in his career defending himself in court as he has fundraising and building things.

There's nothing more intimidating than receiving an indictment. But there's nothing more exhilarating than winning fourteen cases in a row. He's up for the fight, but the bigger question is who can he count on to be in his corner this time around.

Apparently, not Kramer. But he knows he can win this thing if just one particular person is willing to support him, the one person who can corroborate his side of the story. Only one person can save him now. And she isn't sitting in the room with him. It's Mabel that Ed really needs right now, who he needs always.

"I think it is time you do something," Hattie says, looking pointedly at him and finally showing some signs of energy. "It's been lingering out there for too long. It's time you consider it."

Ed is not entirely sure what she is referencing.

"The indictment is not the only envelope around here I've opened and read," Hattie says. "I think it is time you signed Oscar's bankruptcy plan."

Ah, that has been sitting in the corner of Ed's office for months. He certainly would have read it as well if he were her.

"The main reason I haven't signed that," Ed says, "is because it only works if all the women in the community sign it as well. Everyone has to go along with it."

"I'm aware," Hattie says.

"I'd need your help to win them over," Ed says. "You and especially Mare. I just didn't know how to ask that of you."

"You've never known how to ask anything of me," Hattie says. "But yet I continue to persist here with you. I'm really stuck in this place now. My granddaughter keeps me here. Not to mention you've merged poor Lawrence and Larry into it all. We're all stuck to you."

Ed has never thought of it like that, but it is true. He'd say connected, not stuck. He'd prefer even to call them all a family.

"At the end of the day, I go where Rose and the baby go," Hattie says. "This is their home. And I'm committed to them having a home. I'm a bit tired of helping you, but I'm stuck.

Regardless, I'll probably still help you no matter what. I suspect we all will. But you already know that, don't you?"

Again, he hates to think of it like that. But he has to admit that may be true.

"Sign Oscar's bankruptcy plan so you can put all your attention toward winning that court case," Hattie says. "Us ladies will see to Atascadero. We'll see to the mission. Only you can see to you."

CHAPTER 45

◆ ◆ ◆

A few weeks later, Ed and Mabel are having breakfast together at a hotel in Los Angeles. It was actually Mabel's idea that she and Ed escape Atascadero for a few weeks. Ed signed the custodianship of Atascadero over to Oscar, and Hattie and Mare now speak for the investors and homeowners. With Kramer still missing, George now speaks for all the business affairs. In Mabel's wisdom, she knew that Ed should not be there to witness all of this, given Oscar is now the man in charge, and not him.

"I have one more lawyer for you to meet with today," Mabel says. "Even though I know you hate interviewing them."

"I could do better on my own," Ed says. "At every trial back in St. Louis, I sat there thinking, why didn't I go to law school? I'm great with a jury."

"You really think you could do better than a trained lawyer?" Mabel says. "Better than Clarence Darrow?"

"That's different. If I could afford him. Okay, maybe he's one who is better than me. Besides Oscar controls all my money now. I don't even know how much you have stored away. I'm not sure what kind of defense lawyer we can even afford."

Ed really has no idea how much money Mabel has. It's a mystery to the Atascadero community, the creditors, Oscar, and even him. It's even been written about in the press. No one knows for sure. And Mabel intends to keep it that way.

"I'll meet exactly one more," Ed says. "But I have a surprise for you, too. Something I want to drive you out to see. In fact, the hotel is bringing our auto around."

Mabel isn't really listening as she spots the familiar and expected face behind Ed.

"Let me drive you somewhere," Ed says. "Now, when is the next lawyer meeting you set up?"

"Right now," she says. "Turn around."

Ed is in the middle of a full bite of eggs and bacon when he turns to see none other than his brother John.

Mabel immediately gets up and gives John a huge hug as they make small talk about his trip out to Los Angeles and such. But Ed doesn't get up. Instead, he turns back to his plate and takes another bite of his breakfast.

This is the third time now in his life that Mabel has requested John's legal help without his permission. The first was in Nashville when he got in a misunderstanding with the Postal Service over selling gold watches that may or may not have actually been gold. It's still debatable in Ed's mind. The second time was in St. Louis over the accuracy of the published subscription count for his *Woman's Magazine*. Today, for the third time, Mabel has the audacity to contact John without his permission.

John joins them at the table.

"Hello, brother," John says. "Again, your sweet Mabel contacted me. I'll never be able to turn her down as long as I live."

Ed doesn't answer. Instead, he takes another bite.

"It's not what you think," Mabel says. "John lives here now. He lives in Los Angeles."

That news does seem to get Ed's attention.

"I took a job with a defense contractor out here who's eyeing expanding into commercial airlines if you can believe it," John says.

Ed does believe commercial airlines are around the corner. But John moving to California is harder to believe.

"I didn't call John in to help us this time," Mabel says. "He lives here now. That is all. I swear. I just thought you'd like to see him."

The hotel concierge approaches the table to let Ed know his auto has been pulled up, washed, and is ready.

"I don't know if I fully believe either of you," Ed says. "Regardless, let's all go for a ride together."

It takes a little more convincing, but John and Mabel eventually agree to ride with Ed to see his surprise. Along the way, Ed listens to John and Mabel catch up on their lives, and it is lovely to see them interact and for them all to be together again. After all, Mabel and John, along with Claire, do just happen to be his favorite people in the world. They are also the best team he's ever worked with, which could lead to another opportunity as Ed drives south of Los Angeles and out toward the ocean.

Ed listens as Mabel asks questions about John's new job, his decision to move his family out of St. Louis, and most importantly, her learning about his strained relationship with his wife, Marguerite, going back to the crash of Ed's last business and her family losing a bunch of money.

"Good news and bad news regarding Marguerite," John says to Mabel. "Good news, we are still married, and she agreed to move out here along with the kids. The bad news is she insists we live in two separate apartments."

John can tell by Mabel's face she's never heard of such a thing.

"It's apparently very California," John says. "She says we are going to try being separated but still married."

"Oh, John," Mabel says. "I'm so sorry to hear that."

"She thinks it could be good for us," John says.

"What do you think?" Mabel asks.

"I think it is better than being out here alone."

Ed is processing their conversation as he drives them down a dirt road to a ranch house out in the middle of nowhere. Even after all these years, Ed still drives insanely fast. He skids to a halt in front of the house, throwing up a cloud of dust in his signature way. Once the dust clears, Mabel and John realize the ranch house overlooks an undeveloped peninsula just south of Los Angeles with a sweeping view of the Pacific Ocean.

Out of the house walks an older man with a cane in one hand and a handkerchief in the other. He doesn't look or dress like a rancher but like a city dweller who is out of place on a ranch. Mabel wonders who he could possibly be but is more surprised to discover that John knows him.

"Frank Vanderlip," John says. "I'll be damned. What a surprise."

"Johnny boy," Frank says, giving him a fantastic and energetic handshake. "I never thought I'd see you in California."

Frank also enthusiastically shakes Ed's and Mabel's hands.

"Did you tell them?" Frank says. "Or is it still our secret?"

"Go for it, Frank," Ed says. "It's all yours to tell."

"Welcome to the Palos Verdes Peninsula," Frank says. "Or, what is soon to be known as…."

But before Frank can finish his sentence, he starts coughing. And coughing. And coughing. More phlegm than anyone might think possible spews out of him and into his handkerchief until it is becoming obvious the handkerchief can't possibly hold it all. Ed and John hand Frank their handkerchiefs, which Frank gladly accepts. The coughing fit goes on for what feels like five minutes until it finally reaches a point where they have to sit Frank down on the porch of his ranch home to catch his breath. Frank eventually motions for Ed to do the talking for him.

"As John knows," Ed says, "Frank was a journalist and a banker who helped us not just with the *Woman's Magazine* but also with our People's Postal Bank before the government assassinated it. Frank was also the Assistant Secretary of the Treasury and hated Senator Platt even more than John and me. Anyway, Frank bought this peninsula we're standing on a while back. On doctor's orders, he comes out here on account of his lungs. The climate out here, how should we say it, Frank…helps empty him out a bit."

Frank nods in agreement but is still too weak to respond.

"After a few weeks, the climate shakes all the snot out of him, and the Frank of old returns," Ed says, putting his hand on Frank's shoulder. "Mabel, Frank admires what we've done in Atascadero, especially right up until the Great War broke out and the economy went sour on us. He wants our help doing the same thing here. It's where we should have built all along. It's close to Los Angeles. It's directly on the ocean. Believe it or not, Frank, all this will merge into Los Angeles someday, just like University City has now blended into St. Louis. And, John, get this, Frank has cut a deal to have UCLA build its new campus here, just like we had Washington University right next to University City. And I even have an idea to build a monorail from here to Los Angeles."

Frank, fighting to smile through his coughs, especially likes that idea as Ed continues.

"Mabel, if I had just listened to you, Palos Verdes is what we should have done instead of developing out in Atascadero, so far away from a big city. You always say I made a mistake passing on San Fernando Valley. This is a chance to make up for that. This is the type of project you always said we should do closer to Los Angeles. This builds on everything we've ever learned, everything we've ever done. This is the one."

Ed is sure both Mabel and John will be ecstatic to hear this latest plan. After all, a development like Palos Verdes could easily right all their wrongs, allow him to purchase Atascadero out of bankruptcy, fix every mistake he'd ever made, make all his investors whole, get them back to their mission, and even help Marguerite's family get their money back and John get his wife back. Surely, John and Mabel can see the potential, it has to be so obvious to them. Frank still can't talk but pats Ed's shoulder in support. Anyone could see it. Frank sees it. Ed basically has his arms out now, expecting an enthusiastic embrace from both his wife and his brother.

But he doesn't get an embrace. Instead, both Mabel and John get back in the auto, indicating they are ready for Ed to drive them back to Los Angeles. Frank tries to get up to persuade them, but he doesn't have the strength. Ed helps him sit back down.

"It's alright, old friend," Ed says. "They'll come around. They always come around. Every project I've ever done started out like this with those two. But this is the one, Frank. This is the one."

CHAPTER 46

◆ ◆ ◆

The entire drive back to Los Angeles, Mabel and John have to listen to Ed basically say the same thing over and over again about the virtues of the Palos Verdes plan.

In the old days, Mabel and John would have helped Ed at least recognize the risks. On his own, they know Ed is incapable of seeing what could go wrong. He gets so hell-bent on the mission that his mind only processes what could go right. But Mabel and John just listen in silence the entire ride as Ed never once brings up a single downside to his new idea.

Back at the hotel, Mabel wishes John well at his new job and life in California. Then she takes the first train back to Atascadero, leaving Ed to his scheming and planning, knowing the last thing on his mind is the only thing that should be on his mind: hiring a professional to defend him in court.

All Mabel wants to do upon her return to Atascadero is check on her home, change her clothes, and join Claire in the garden, which she does, but not before having to listen to the grievances of everyone she runs into on her walk home. Oscar appears to have had a productive week, putting immediate changes into effect.

Lucile, whose English is nearly perfect now, asks if Mabel knows the presses are being sold to Hearst and are to be moved to

San Francisco, and whether Mabel knows that part of the deal is for George to move her and their baby along with it. Mabel doesn't know that, but it doesn't surprise her. Lucile says George is actually excited about the prospect of it all. But oh, how Mabel was going to miss being near their baby and what she assumes will soon be many more.

Marcella also catches Mabel on her walk home and asks if she knows that since Lawrence's Eaglet development is wrapped up in Atascadero now, Oscar is leveraging the equity that Lawrence has patiently built up over the years to pay off a portion of Atascadero's land debt. Marcella said Lawrence and Larry are considering moving and starting over in Sacramento to develop homes up there. Mabel doesn't know that either, but it also doesn't surprise her. But oh, how she is going to miss Marcella and her baby as well.

Then Mare catches Mabel. But, surprisingly, Mare is happy for the first time since Mabel has known her. Mare is elated that Oscar is immediately starting construction on everyone's homes. Oscar, Mare says, at least has his good senses to realize that building homes is where the actual revenue has always been hiding. Now that is something Mabel did know all along, making this the news so far that is the hardest to hear.

Hattie catches Mabel next, mostly just to complain about what it is like to work with Oscar. And to gush on and on about what a dream it was to work with Ed. However, Oscar has decided that Hattie's home is to be one of the first to be built in exchange for her willingness to show it off as a model of what homes in Atascadero can look like. She is also excited to have talked Rose, along with the baby, into moving in with her, sure they would move to Sacramento if she didn't make the offer. At least one baby was going to be staying. Hattie also asks if Mabel knows that

Alphonse left for San Francisco a few days ago to try to find Kramer and get him to return to help Oscar sort out everything. Mabel doesn't know that, but she's certainly appreciative that Alphonse is willing to try.

Other women approach Mabel complaining about their new jobs at the doll factory. The printing press and cannery jobs were more mindless and afforded them all the opportunity to socialize all day with the other ladies. The doll factory necessitates very precise craftsmanship because painting by hand requires precision, focus, and attention to detail. It is taxing work. They want to know if Ed had heard more about the locomotive plant that is coming and what those jobs might be like. But Mabel has no information for them.

Even Postal Inspector Fulton approaches Mabel. He can't get a straight answer from Oscar about the future of the printing press volumes, which the Postal Service needs to know given the number of employees and infrastructure they have built up over the years to keep up with the growth of the wartime *Illustrated Review*. Fulton wants to know if Ed is planning to go back to the *California Illustrated Review* and what might be expected in terms of predicted volume. But that is the last thing Mabel knows anything about. Fulton nearly follows her all the way home going on and on forecasting and modeling and describing the inner workings of the Postal Service and its commitment to ensuring that American commerce is supported in rain, sleet, or snow. Of all the worries in the world, Mabel couldn't care less about inconveniencing Fulton or the government.

She might still be talking with Fulton if millionaire and former Atascadero landowner J.H. hadn't sauntered up to them. He asks if he might be able to come over later and sit on his old porch with her for a spell. He reckoned tonight to be about the best sunset of the year, according to the almanac. She has turned down his same offer for years whenever he shows back up in town, but she thought, *what the heck?* She surprised even herself by saying yes and that he can come over at seven. She'll even sit with him. With a tip of his hat, he said he'd be there.

Finally, Mabel gets back home to find her house and garden in perfect shape, which she was never worried about, given Claire was looking after it. Mabel changes clothes and heads out to the garden to join Claire. The entire train ride from Los Angeles, she's been rehearsing how to tell the story of Palos Verdes to Claire. Only Claire—well, also John—could understand, knowing Ed as well as anyone. Before Mabel can get to that, she is going to have to face the fact that surely Claire knows by now her girls are most likely headed in different directions. Mabel can only imagine the anger in Claire she's about to witness.

However, when she catches up to Claire in the garden, it isn't anger Mabel encounters. It is something else. Mabel's whole life, she's only seen Claire either mad or working diligently on something. Instead, Mabel finds Claire a bit listless. It appears she was harvesting some heads of lettuce, but Mabel notices the heads are cut awkwardly and lying haphazardly on the ground. That's not at all like Claire. And Claire doesn't respond as Mabel greets her, as if Claire can't hear her as she continues to chop away with a knife in directions that make no sense.

For the safety of both of them, Mabel delicately removes the knife from Claire's grasp. Even without a knife, Claire is still making cutting motions and is clearly not herself. Mabel worries that maybe Claire is having a stroke or something until she notices a telegram tucked into Claire's apron.

Mabel takes her sister in her arms and uses her weight to force them both gently down to the ground, holding Claire in a tight embrace to try to get her to snap out of it. Claire at least eventually stops making the cutting motions but still is mumbling and not making any sense.

While still holding onto Claire, Mabel removes the telegram from Claire's apron and reads it for herself. As she reads it, she finds herself to be almost as listless as her sister. Nothing makes sense any longer in Atascadero. Nothing will ever be the same. On top of all the other catastrophes this world keeps throwing at them, the telegram reads that Alphonse has died while looking for Kramer in San Francisco.

CHAPTER 47

◆ ◆ ◆

The entire community is preoccupied with making preparations for Alphonse's funeral. Word spreads quickly that Alphonse suffered a major heart attack in his hotel in San Francisco. No one asked for other details, which is just fine with Mabel as her focus has been on Claire.

It's now three days later, and Claire still hasn't snapped out of it. The doctors can't explain it either. She appears to have disappeared somewhere into the recesses of her mind. Mabel imagines Claire must be lost in solving an algorithm of some kind, attempting to maximize all the decisions ever made to maybe lead to a different outcome for Alphonse. Mabel knows all genius minds will inevitably suffer a downfall. At some point, their complex wires are bound to get crossed. She assumes Claire must be lost down an incredibly complex rabbit hole, trying to make sense of her unfortunate realities.

The rest of the community quickly organizes a celebration of life and a theatrical production worthy of Alphonse. After a few days of planning and under the direction of Mare, an appropriate number of sonnets, songs, and scenes from plays that Alphonse has directed over the years are agreed upon.

However, if Claire can't be mentally present for the event, it isn't going to work. Mabel, the twins, and even Ed have been unsuccessful thus far at getting Claire to snap out of it. It's finally decided there may be only one person who can help. Mabel has been resisting it for days and finally invites Inspector Fulton to join Claire alone in the projection room of the movie theater.

When Fulton arrives, he is beside himself, looking at what has become of the person he most adores. He can't stand to see Claire's disheveled state. But he feels he knows exactly what to do. He might be the only person who knows what to do now that Mabel has left them alone together.

"My understanding," Fulton says to a catatonic Claire, "is that movie theaters pay rent for the reels from distributors based on the number of days in their possession. A distributor can show the film as often as they like while the film is in their possession and make as much money as possible in that timeframe. So, the trick is to get the audience excited in advance, hoping they pay to watch the film as many times as possible from the get-go. The theater must also optimize when to send it along to another town and how to time that perfectly for profits. The risk is having a film in your possession for too long or not long enough."

Fulton lays out a piece of paper in front of Claire where he has outlined a few different timelines and scenarios that highlight a successful movie run versus an unsuccessful one, along with the time it takes to advertise it. He also brings into the equation the complication that when one town is done with a print, they then send it to another town, but the next town doesn't know for sure when it will arrive, which further complicates the current movie distribution process. Not to mention that people may read in the newspaper about a popular film, but then they have no idea when that film will come out in their part of the country, which is a waste of publicity.

This goes on for hours, with Fulton talking out loud and exploring a number of different scenarios. Each time, he eventually finds a weakness in what he's contemplating and crumbles up those thoughts and throws them on the floor to move on to another idea.

A few hours later, Mabel takes the liberty of entering the room to bring them some food and more coffee. She attempts to pick up some of the crumpled paper on the ground, but Fulton implores her to leave it. Apparently, all the wadded pieces of paper on the floor are in some kind of organizational order only he understands. Everything needs to be left where it is so he doesn't attempt a solution again that he has already tried.

Mabel glances at Claire and sees she is still lost in a trance, but Mabel doesn't have any better ideas, so she leaves Fulton to his unorthodox plan.

The hours go on and on until Fulton has crumpled pieces of paper across the entire floor of the office. He's both out of floor space and out of ideas as he has fully exhausted everything he can think of as he sits down next to Claire.

Honestly, he is so wrapped up in the problem he also now feels lost. Every thought that comes to his head, he says out loud to Claire. There's a good chance the next time Mabel comes in that he's going to be just as catatonic himself, and then who is going to save him? He admits his only friend in the world is Claire, and he knows the use of the word "friend" is a stretch.

Then he goes down a rabbit hole of trying to find a more accurate word than "friend" for his relationship with Claire. There are so many other words to consider—acquaintance, companion, colleague, associate, pal, co-worker, teammate, partner, ally, confederate, counterpart. He limits his brain to saying out loud for each of the titles, just ten reasons that the word makes sense and twenty reasons that the word doesn't make sense.

He starts to realize it takes him, on average, fifteen minutes to assess each possible word, and he's on word 20 of the 100 or so similar words for "friend" he's selected now. That equates to hours left of him trying to define their relationship.

Fulton wonders if he'll finish on time to go to work the next morning. He could call in sick, but he's never done that once in his career, and he's not even exactly sure who he would call, and as he's thinking this latest dilemma through, he finally hears what he thinks sounds like "release the same movie all at once across the whole country."

But that would require the expense of numerous prints of the movie rather than theaters just re-using the same copy as they pass it along from theater to theater. The expense of releasing it all at once is why he hadn't considered it. The cost would be outrageous. But, wait, his mind is always stuck on the cost or risk side of the equation. He doesn't have a mind like Ed's that considers the upside.

If movies are all released on the same day across the country, then they can also benefit from one national advertising campaign and reviews all at once. So, all the hype and momentum are in place at the exact same time the movie is available. Could the success of a film cover the cost of multiple prints? One significant hit could easily make up for the failures, right? And could there be a standard release day for a movie, like on a Friday?

Yes, that is the answer. Open a film all at once across the country on the same day. That's it. He finally has the answer. Except, wait. He didn't say that. *Who did?*

Fulton turns to look at Claire, but she is already up on her feet, cleaning up all the crumpled pieces of paper from the floor and throwing them into a wastebasket. Except she's only picking up one at a time. That will take forever.

So, Fulton starts picking them up two at a time. Then she starts doing three at a time. Then he scoops up as many as he can possibly hold at once and drops them into the basket, but some fall to the side and don't make it in.

Then she starts to kick the remaining ones into a larger pile. While she does that, he gets on his hands and knees and scoops her pile into the basket. Until, in no time at all, all the paper has been picked up as fast as two humans have ever cleaned up a room, and the entire office is back to normal.

Fulton is still on the floor looking around to see if they missed anything when Claire takes a knee next to him and accidentally brushes up against him in doing so. Claire immediately braces at her mistake, expecting Fulton to freak out from being touched, but he doesn't. He just sits there.

She gets the idea of gently touching the sleeves of his uniform, being ever so careful not to leave a mark or a crease. Fulton is struggling, but he's bearing it. Then she really pushes her luck as she purposefully touches one of his shiny buttons. He's barely holding on now. Then she goes further and touches all his shiny buttons. Each and every one. Some of them multiple times. He's clearly about to lose it.

Then she sits down in front of him and takes his hands in hers. He's still holding it together, barely, when she gives him a kiss on his cheek. But that is too much. Way too much. She's gone too far. She found his limit. Fulton can't help it anymore. He shakes his hands loose from hers as he wipes and wipes away at the lingering kiss on his cheek. He even wipes his hands together frantically and then pulls out a cloth to attempt to shine his buttons. Claire notices he shines the ones she touched once, only once. But the ones she touched multiple times, he shines them multiple times.

It takes what feels like several minutes until he finally gets a hold of himself, controls his breathing, and can look her back in the eyes. When he does, he finds that she is smiling. She never smiles. Though he resists it, in quick order, he can't help but smile as well. Now he's wondering if they've both gone mad.

"You had the correct word the first time," Claire says. "You and I are friends. That's what we'll always be fortunate to be to one another. The dearest of friends."

CHAPTER 48

Every newspaper from across the country is covering the event. Ed's name is called, and he stands up and walks over to the microphone. In the past, he always had to project his voice in a large room or auditorium full of people. This is his first time using a microphone with speakers, and it is especially necessary given that the Shrine Auditorium in Los Angeles is filled to its 6,300-person capacity.

"Palos Verdes Estates rights all the wrongs," Ed says into the microphone, keeping his mouth the exact distance from it he had practiced with the sound technician. The lights are right. The sound is right. Frank's cough is now under control as he sits on stage behind Ed in full support. Everything is right this time. Mabel wouldn't come to support him. But everything else is right.

"We're starting with homesites," Ed says to the biggest audience he has ever addressed in person. "Beautiful homes. And as we sell out a street, we'll pour the pavement just for that street. The same goes for sewers, water, and electricity. We'll build it as we go. Zero excess. Zero waste."

The audience nods, and Ed can tell he is making perfect sense to them.

"Frank and his team have about lined up UCLA to move here, ensuring jobs, students, and commerce in the area for years to come."

Frank nods his head. Again, it makes perfect sense.

"We'll have a beautiful promenade and city center as soon as one-third of the homes are built. Restaurants. Movie theaters. Parks. Even the May Department Store has agreed to anchor our shopping district when the time is right. Homesites first. Then infrastructure."

Ed has all 6,300 in the audience now nodding in unison. But they start to be able to tell by a sheepish smirk forming on his face that he just can't help himself.

"But I really, really do want to build a monorail to Los Angeles," Ed admits, smiling.

Chuckles ring out from the crowd.

"But homesites first. I've learned my lesson. And I know you've read about me in the papers," he says, invoking a few vocal sighs from the audience. "And you know my trial is about to start, and you know evil powers in the government have been chasing me for years—to no avail, I might add."

A few cheer in support and Ed tips his head to them to acknowledge.

"But I've learned from that too," he says. "All the money raised—all the investment for Palos Verdes—will be held in the Commonwealth Trust. Frank can't touch it. I can't touch it. Only the trustees can authorize expenditures, and only once we reach our stated goal of having raised all the millions."

Again, the audience is with him.

"It's a staggering number that we need to raise," Ed says. "Four times what I've raised in the past. But it can be done, and thanks to Frank, me, and the early investors, we're already at the halfway mark before opening this amazing investment opportunity up to you."

Now Ed loses the audience for a bit, but in a good way, as they all seem to think and talk the opportunity over with whoever is sitting near them. After a moment or two of discussion, Ed can see the heads nodding again, and all eyes and focus are back on him.

"This is the one," Ed says, starting to tear up a bit. "Many of you have been with me since I first bought the *Winner Magazine* all those years ago before we renamed it the *Woman's Magazine*. Before University City. Before Atascadero. Before the *Illustrated Review*. Before the oil wells and pecan trees. Some of you out there may have been with me from the very, very beginning. Some of you may have even bought Bug Chalk from me back in Nashville."

That generates a few laughs from the audience. Ed smiles and wipes away a few tears as he settles himself to finish. He loves his supporters. He always has. Everything about today and about this plan is perfect. Except, of course, that Mabel isn't here. But otherwise, it is perfect.

"All I have ever tried to do my entire life is make a better world, especially for women and their families," Ed says. "Along the journey I learn. I learn and get better. We get better. And boy, have we learned. And boy, have we improved along the way. Palos Verdes Estates is the culmination of our entire careers together. This is the one. Palos Verdes Estates is the one. And I'm proud to know you. And I'm proud to share it with you. I'm telling you, this is the one. Will you say 'this is the one' along with me? What is Palos Verdes?"

The 6,300-person audience joins him in saying, "This is the one."

CHAPTER 49

Ed had to take that stage in the Shrine Auditorium without Mabel in the room. It was the first time in his marriage she wasn't there alongside him. The second time is in the federal courtroom the next day with twenty years of his life at stake.

Instead of sweet Mabel sitting next to him, he has to sit alone. Oscar claims not to have enough money in the Atascadero accounts he now manages for Ed to hire a high-powered defense attorney. John works for a living now, and isn't an option. Ed feels public defense attorneys are worthless, and Ed has refused Mabel's financial help, electing instead to represent himself.

"Keep your precious money," was one of the last things Ed regrettably said to his wife the last time they spoke, which is infrequently these days with her living in Atascadero and him staying in Los Angeles. Ed often reflects that John and Marguerite, though officially separated, are at least in the same city. He doesn't know precisely what Mabel and he are at the moment.

The jury selection goes perfectly from Ed's perspective. It is almost entirely made up of women. He's always been great with female jurors. Newspapers back in the day often argued he was quite possibly the best with them. The trial is off to a beautiful start, in Ed's opinion. Especially since he doesn't like the prosecutor at all, and he assumes the women on the jury can't possibly like him either.

The prosecutor appears gruff. Callous. He is a real grandstander who is more in it for himself than for anyone else. If there is one thing Ed knows about an audience—or a jury or even customers—it is that they are selfish. They are always thinking, "What's in it for me?" Ed knows how to make it about them. This guy never will. He makes it about himself.

But then, just before opening arguments, the prosecutor announces he will not be trying this case personally and that he will instead cede the case to his recently hired assistant prosecutor.

Ed, just like the jury and the rest of the courtroom, looks around to see who that might be. The only other person sitting near the prosecutor is his secretary. Or, so they all have assumed until she stands up.

"Judge," the prosecutor said, "Assistant Prosecutor Anne Mackenzie, not me, will try this case for the government."

The judge nods his approval as Mackenzie stands confidently and addresses the jury and the courtroom. She's wearing a dark gray suit with a tailored long skirt and jacket fitted at the waist along with a white blouse and high neckline. Her red hair is pulled back into a severe bun. She's the most impeccably dressed and professional person in the entire room, but Ed can't help but notice she also exudes a natural warmth and friendliness in her demeanor.

Whereas most male lawyers grandstand, bicker, and treat the jury as if they are young children who can't possibly understand anything that is going on in the courtroom unless it is explained to them, Mackenzie doesn't do any of that. In fact, the only people in the room she focuses on at all are the jurors. More specifically, the female jurors who are in their 50s and slightly older than her, but not by much.

"Gentlemen and ladies of the jury, good morning," Mackenzie says, to which the women in the jury respond 'good morning' right back to her.

"This is a big day for me," she says. "My first ever opening arguments at the federal level. I'm proud to be here. But I'm also saddened to be here. Do you know why I'm saddened? It's because I'm a big fan of Mr. E.G. Lewis over here. I've been a subscriber to his magazines for years. He publicly supported a woman's right to vote before it became common to do so. He was one of the first. I love that about him. I love reading his columns. I love following all his grand plans to make the world a better place and always for women. Women in the home support him. But also, women in the workplace like me support him. I love his mission. I'll even let you in on another little secret. If I were under oath up here, I'd have to admit I might even have a little crush on him myself. And I'm happily married."

This immediately causes all in the room to chuckle. Even the judge. But especially, Ed notices, the women on the jury are smiling now.

"He's kind of what we all wish our husbands were," Mackenzie says. "A dreamer who really knows women. Respects us. A dreamer who gets stuff done. Who builds things. And who invites us to be a part of it and to build it right along with him. When I think of him, I can't help but find him to be dreamy in all forms of the word."

Again, Ed notices all the jurors and especially the women smiling. Same with the entire room. But what Ed fails to notice is that he himself is no longer smiling, having to sit there and watch Mackenzie perfectly use his entire playbook against him.

"But here's why I'm especially saddened," Mackenzie says, now matching Ed's serious look. "Because I really, really wanted everything Ed promised his readers and investors to be true. I really, really, really did. We would have a much, much better world if it were true. But it isn't. The prosecution will show in court that all his promises—his bank that no longer exists, his orchards that never yielded, his oil wells that never sprung, his buildings that were never built, his trusting customers' homes that were never built, the dividends that were never earned, even the pecan trees that were never planted. We'll see a pattern of sweet talk. Dare I even say, dream talk that never ever actually materializes."

On occasion, Mackenzie looks over at Ed, but never with a stern look. Always with a compassionate one. As if she really is rooting for him. As if it pains her to say these things.

"And I don't want it to stop. Look at this attractive little man. I want him to keep on whispering in my ear everything I want to hear for the rest of my life. He's absolutely adorable. I don't want him to stop."

She nods to the jury that it is indeed the case. Then her tone changes.

"But it has to stop. He can no longer hide behind his grand mission. Because you are going to hear testimony from women who have lost their entire life savings to this man. You are going to hear testimony from women who have lost not only money but their marriages and families because of this man. You are going to hear testimony from women who can't stop themselves from giving money to this man. And this jury has to set a precedent that men with golden tongues cannot keep taking from women even if we don't want him to stop. Even if he makes us feel oh so good. Even if we have a crush on him. Sadly, it just can't continue."

She moves even closer to the jury.

"This trial is not about me or us or even about Mr. E.G Lewis. It is about women who are consistently taken advantage of by men. We have to be the ones to stop it no matter what comes out of this man's tempting and pretty little package. We don't want to stop it. But we have to stop it. It pains me, but allow me one favor. Let me show you why it has to stop over the course of this trial."

With that, she makes eye contact one last time with each woman on the jury before also being brave enough to make eye contact with the men on the jury and Ed, as well, before sitting back down in her chair, leaving Ed simply sitting in awe.

He has finally met a lawyer he'd be willing to hire.

CHAPTER 50

It doesn't seem to matter what is said about Ed in the newspapers. The more publicity he gets of any kind, the more money rolls into Palos Verdes.

At best, his own opening arguments were described in the papers as a rambling mess. One headline reads, "Golden Man Loses His Tongue." Ed agrees with all of the articles. Mackenzie caught him off guard. But he knows a trial is a marathon and not a sprint. The prosecution goes first. The defense goes second. He blew his opening arguments, but he'll bounce back. He always does. He'll have his day in court.

After the trial each day, he drops by the Commonwealth Trust to check on the Palos Verdes Estates progress. Most importantly, he knows Frank is pleased. Being in the warm California climate brought his lungs back to normal, but Frank has to race off to New York to see to some other businesses he owns. Ed knows all is fine as Frank and he send telegrams back and forth nearly every day.

But one of the most interesting people Ed will ever meet is waiting for him as he leaves the Trust's office that evening.

"Mr. E.G. Lewis, could I have a word?" a handsome young man says to Ed out in the street.

"No interviews today," Ed says, assuming the man is a reporter. "I'm done for today."

"I'm not a reporter," the man says. "Or not any longer. I'm back from fighting in the war. I'm starting my own newspaper."

"In Los Angeles?" Ed says, starting to walk even faster now. "Good luck. Hearst will eat you for breakfast if you do."

Ed keeps walking, smiling to himself at the thought that this young man probably has worse odds than any endeavor Ed has ever contemplated. Ed would rather take on Senator Platt all over again than Hearst.

But the young man is persistent and is now matching Ed stride for stride, nearly running next to him.

"I have a plan to become not just the number one paper in Los Angeles but also in Miami and in Chicago. And one that shares your mission of supporting women's rights."

"You'd have to have so much money to pull that off," Ed says, laughing. "A ridiculous amount of money. Which you'd never be able to raise. No one would ever invest against Hearst. You'd have to have all the money you need yourself. You'd have to be rich. Not even rich but crazy wealthy."

As Ed says that out loud, the young man is still keeping up with him, which leaves Ed to believe that the young man might actually be extremely wealthy. Ed stops for a moment and looks him over a little closer, and in particular, his teeth.

Ed can always tell if a person actually has wealth by the state of their teeth. Only the wealthiest can afford preventative dental care, and, to Ed's amazement, this young man has the most beautiful set of teeth he's ever seen. The only way to have teeth like that is not just to have money but to be born into multiple generations of money.

"Who are you?" Ed asks.

"Cornelius Vanderbilt IV," he says. "But please call me Neil. Everyone calls me Neil."

"Well, I'll be…" Ed says, starting to walk again. "If you are dumb enough to start a newspaper and compete with Hearst, then you must at least read the papers. And you must know my situation. I can't imagine how I could in any way, shape, or form ever be helpful to you."

"I'd like to rent access to the small press you have left in Atascadero," Neil says. "I know Hearst moved your big one to San Francisco. But you have a small one left that you print the *Atascadero News* on."

"What about it?" Ed asks.

"Hearst has blocked me from using every other press in the state of California, and none of the manufacturers will sell me a press," Neil says. "But you no longer do business with Hearst. You've settled with his banks. He bought your big presses. You're free from him. But you're also in a tough spot with the trial and bankruptcy and all."

Ed stops walking and steals a look at Neil's teeth one more time as Neil continues.

"If you'll allow me," he says. "I just might be your huckleberry."

CHAPTER 51

For the last few weeks, every day is the same at the trial. It's the exact same day over and over again. Today is no different, but yet entirely different at the same time.

"Your honor," Mackenzie says, "I would like to call another investor to the stand."

"This will be the 20th version of similar testimony," the judge says.

"Mr. Lewis has taken money over his career from nearly 20,000 women," Mackenzie says. "We think the jury hearing from twenty of them is a fair number. This will be the last."

"Very well," the judge says.

"I would like to call Mrs. Adele Fahrmeier to the stand," Mackenzie says.

Mrs. Fahrmeier proudly stands and marches up to be sworn in. She's also not afraid to make eye contact with Ed on the way, and he notices right square on her face is that huge and famous mole of hers.

In the last few weeks, Mackenzie has called woman after woman to the stand. All of the testimony is precisely the same and matches her opening statement. She starts with a line of questioning that sets up their mutual appreciation for Ed and their excitement about investing in his business endeavors. And then, she has them say how much money they have invested and the resulting financial ruin it has caused their families.

The first few were especially devastating for Ed to witness. He certainly knows he has thousands of readers who have supported him over the years. He certainly has, on occasion, received nasty letters from them. But every time he would write them back. Every time. Or even send them a pecan from a tree planted in their name to show he is working hard on their behalf. But to see them in person is challenging.

For the first couple of witnesses, when it was his turn to cross-examine them, he thanked them for their support. He reminded them he has always been hard at work, trying desperately to get them a return. A fraudster, he reminds them, skips town. He never did that. His home is still in Atascadero. He's committed to seeing it through for them. He's right here, and he's not going anywhere.

Mackenzie would often object that he wasn't asking any questions but just having a conversation with the women. Ed did the same thing with every witness until the judge stopped him. He figures if Mackenzie can have witnesses who can say the same thing over and over, then so can he.

But Mrs. Fahrmeier is different. She's not just a random reader with hardship in her life. She and Ed have a real history together.

"Mrs. Fahrmeier," Mackenzie says, "how do you know Mr. Lewis?"

She answers in her thick German accent, just like she had done before in one of Ed's previous trials.

"He knocked on my door years ago and sold me mole concealer," Mrs. Fahrmeier says, which gets the exact same reaction it does every time. The room laughs and laughs, given the large mole that is still glaringly visible on her face.

She goes on to talk about sending in money to try to guess the attendance at the 1904 World's Fair, which was a gimmick in one of Ed's magazines. She tells the courtroom about investing in University City real estate. Investing in Ed's national bank. Investing in Atascadero. Investing in the oil wells. Investing in the flower seed company. Investing in all of Ed's schemes.

"Have you ever received anything back from Mr. Lewis from your investments? Anything at all."

"One time, he sent me some pecans from a tree planted in my name. They were delicious."

That makes the entire room laugh a little. Ed certainly smiles.

"But you haven't yet invested in Palos Verdes, have you?" Mackenzie says.

"I have not," she says.

"Is it because your husband recently passed, and without him working on the farm and having given all your life savings to Mr. Lewis, you had to default with your bank, and you're about to lose your home?"

"No, it isn't because of that."

"Is it because your children barely will talk to you since you've sent money after money to Mr. E.G. Lewis through the mail over the years?"

"No, it isn't that."

"Is it that you don't trust him anymore? That you would never invest in him ever again despite having burned through your life savings?"

"No, it isn't that."

"What is it then, Mrs. Fahrmeier? Why haven't you invested in Palos Verdes?

"Because I don't have any money," she says.

Murmurs rise from the audience, but Mrs. Fahrmeier isn't finished.

"But if anyone would loan me some, I'd invest it in a heartbeat and pay you back. Eddie has a real winner this time. He's learned his lessons. We have to help him get all those people's money back. Mine too. And get him back to his mission. We have to help him. Palos Verdes is the one. I just need someone to loan me some money."

"No further questions, your honor," Mackenzie says. "Go ahead, Mr. Lewis. She's all yours now."

Mackenzie takes her seat and motions for Ed to ask Mrs. Fahrmeier anything he would like. It is obvious Mrs. Fahrmeier is excited to talk to him. She can't wait, actually. She's dying for him to ask her anything.

"I'm afraid I have no further questions at this time," Ed says, but she's desperate to talk to him.

"Eddie, I think I can get my niece to lend me some money," Mrs. Fahrmeier says. "My kids won't give me anymore. But I think my niece will. The government paid for all my travel out here. I'm hoping they'll let me stop in Kansas City on the way home and hit up my niece. She too has invested before …in the pecan trees. I think she'd do it again. Her friends might as well."

"No further questions, your honor," Ed says again.

Mrs. Fahrmeier starts to protest, but the judge insists she must remove herself from the witness stand. After more debate, she finally does leave, but not before sneaking in a hug with Ed as she walks by.

"Can I stay here for a bit?" she asks Ed. "I want to support you."

Before Ed can answer, Mackenzie leaps up and takes Mrs. Fahrmeier's hand.

"Absolutely," Mackenzie says. "Here, we'll make room for you right in the front row so you can see Eddie. Our pleasure."

Mackenzie finds a seat for Mrs. Fahrmeier in the front row, where the jury can perfectly see her the rest of the afternoon.

"Judge," Mackenzie says, "true to my word, I'm not going to call any other investors to the stand. Mrs. Fahrmeier represents just fine the thousands of women who continue to support Mr. Lewis despite all his broken promises."

"Objection," Ed says.

"Sustained," the judge says. "Move on, Mrs. Mackenzie."

"Our final witness is, I admit, someone not originally on our list," Mackenzie says, "but someone I feel the court should hear from before the prosecution rests."

"And who is that?" the judge asks.

"Yes, who is that?" Ed says, thinking *who could possibly be a better final witness than what just took place?*

"The prosecution would like to call Mr. Kramer to the stand," Mackenzie says.

In the back of the room, Kramer stands, looking as weaselly as ever.

"Objection," Ed says.

"On what grounds?" the judge asks.

"He, uh, I don't know," Ed says. "Objection."

"Your honor, Mr. Kramer was there for all of it," Mackenzie says. "He can testify to Mr. Lewis's true intentions, and the jury deserves to hear that."

"But he isn't on the witness list," Ed says. "I haven't prepared for this witness."

"You haven't really prepared for any witness," the judge says to some laughter in the courtroom. "But I'll give you a few days to prepare. We'll resume next week with Mr. Kramer's testimony. This court is adjourned until then."

What Ed needs most right now is not a break. Or even a lawyer who actually knows what they are doing. Or even his brother John. What he most needs in the world is his wife. He needs his Mabel.

CHAPTER 52

◆ ◆ ◆

Ed knows all of Atascadero is reading about the trial in the newspapers, so he isn't sure what to expect as he returns home for the long weekend.

Many things are the same in Atascadero. He still has no anonymity when walking around town. Everyone knows him, and, to his relief, they appear happy to see him. He receives many well wishes. Folks appear to be rooting for him. Others are excited to talk to him about their new homes that are being built. They are having fun picking out flooring, bathroom fixtures, paint colors, and more. They are full of excitement.

Of course, Mare bends his ear about not enjoying working on the doll factory production line and demands an update on the locomotive factory, which, as far as Ed knows, is all on track.

In the back of Ed's mind, he's hoping the timing is such that it hits after Palos Verdes is a success and after he's bought back his interest in Atascadero because then the boon of the new plant will benefit him and not Oscar as it brings more workers and homes to the region. But he keeps the timing of it all to himself.

Ed finishes a bit of business at the *Atascadero News* and is on his way to see Mabel when he is pleasantly surprised to run into his brother George, who he thought had already left for San Francisco, given the presses have sold and moved.

George is also happy to see him, and instead of shaking hands, they immediately hug, which is something they've never really done before.

"I'm so sorry about everything," Ed says. "We're going to get you and Lucile and your family back here quickly. I promise. Atascadero is going to come back bigger and stronger."

Ed tries to update George on Palos Verdes, but George cuts him off.

"We like San Francisco," George says. "We're doing fine. I'm learning new things every day from Hearst and his people. I'm back to having national accounts again. I'm the only one that can really work a rotogravure press. Readers love all the photos. Everyone agrees that is the future. We've found a new home, and we're happy. Don't worry about us for a moment. Focus on you."

George couldn't possibly mean that, Ed thinks. He's just being nice. Before Ed can protest, George pulls him aside privately with a serious look on his face.

"Brother, it's not an accident I'm here today," he says. "I'm here to warn you. Hearst knows about Vanderbilt and borrowing the *Atascadero News* press. Don't go through with it. Whatever your deal is with Vanderbilt, cancel it. You know better than to mess with Hearst. I'm imploring you to stop."

"Well, George, I…"

"Just stop. Stop. Stop. Stop," George says, starting to raise his voice a little. "If Hearst knew I was here, I'd be fired, and I'd never work again in the industry. He wouldn't think twice about that. Just stop. I implore you."

"Okay. Okay, George. I hear you, okay."

"I'm risking my livelihood here. Just stop all your mission nonsense. It's a lost battle."

George is trying to calm himself down, but he's still worked up.

"Go see Mabel," George says. "You need to be with family. I have to go back to San Francisco right now. Just…I don't know. I don't even know if you know how to enjoy a weekend. But try to enjoy life. Try to enjoy something. Lock all your crazy ideas in a box for the weekend and actually live life for a change. The world is fine without you."

"George, I've got this," Ed says. "I've been in many worse situations. This is nothing. We'll win this fight."

With that George has nothing else to say to his brother. He can tell he's not making any kind of a difference in Ed's thinking. George gives his big brother one last hug and heads off to the train station.

As Ed is walking home, he can't imagine how Hearst could possibly know about Vanderbilt. *How do the uber-rich always know everything in advance?* Although, come to think of it, Pulitzer used to publish the news before it even happened. Ed certainly will give George's warning some serious attention, but now he needs to focus all his efforts on Mabel.

He approaches the garden hoping to surprise her but instead finds Claire. He assumes she must have seen or heard him walking up, but she stays head down on her planting and harvesting as he approaches. He hasn't spoken to her since Alphonse passed away. It's wonderful to see her out and healthy again. Before he can decide what to say, Claire makes it easy on him.

"Be smart about this weekend," she says to him. "Choose your words wisely with my sister the entire time. Every single word. If you don't know what to say, then just listen."

Ed isn't sure what she means, and she can tell. She makes it even simpler for him.

"If I had an extra borrowed moment with Alphonse," Claire says, "the last thing I'd want to hear about is any future schemes or any form of promises or missions."

Ed is starting to understand as Claire continues.

"In fact, since you can never help yourself, I'll let you promise me something."

"And what is that?" Ed says.

"Promise not to promise her anything," Claire says. "Be in the moment for once in your life."

Be in the moment, ha. Ed thinks maybe if he got to tend the garden all day and wasn't responsible for all the women in town and all the investors he could be in the moment too.

"Just how do you suggest I be in the moment?" Ed asks.

"Start by just listening to her, not me," Claire says.

CHAPTER 53

Under Mabel's name on the room reservation, a private suite for her and Ed is waiting for them at The Cloisters Hotel on Atascadero Beach.

For the first time in their marriage, Mabel does the planning and the driving instead of him. At a leisurely pace, she drives him around town in their Cadillac convertible, where every single person they pass waves enthusiastically to Ed. She drives him to the overlook, where they reminisce on the first time they laid eyes on Atascadero during a visit with Hearst and his wife, Millicent, all those years ago. Finally, she drives him on the one-lane highway Ed insisted on building that connects Atascadero to the beach. In the morning, it runs one way to the beach. In the afternoon, it runs one way back to town.

When they arrive at The Cloisters Hotel, he'd misunderstood and thought the two of them spending time alone in the private suite was Mabel's big idea for the weekend, but it isn't. She instead immediately drops off their luggage. Her big idea for the weekend is apparently a stroll, just the two of them, out near the ocean, away from everyone. No humans. No trial. Definitely, no Palos Verdes Estates updates. Just the two of them.

To Ed's surprise, her plan is lovely. He barely says a word. She does all the talking. She catches him up on the hopes and dreams of the twins, of the early personalities forming in their babies, of Larry's and Lawrence's housing development plans in Sacramento, along with their new business name—Mitchel & Dad. She tells him how George and Lucile are loving San Francisco and that Rose has been on a few dates with a young construction worker that served with Teddy and Larry in the war, and the babies are really smart, just like their mothers. She even updates him on Fulton, who isn't around much now that the presses are gone and the mail volume is lower, but he still has lunch with Claire at Mabel's house whenever he passes through. Mabel tells Ed about all the ridiculous conversations Fulton and Claire have together. Often Mabel just finds herself shaking her head at the two of them and at what might be the most unique friendship in the world.

Mabel goes on that there are a lot of rumors now that Hearst's castle is built and about all the celebrities that visit, even Charlie Chaplin. Sometimes these actors and actresses end up making appearances in Atascadero before their movies are shown.

Apparently, Claire is keeping busy by turning the theater into a nightclub most weekends to give the male construction workers and female factory workers something to do. Claire also is continuing something Alphonse had been doing the entire time, which is, based on a certain private signal those in the know spread around town by the way they tuck a certain magazine under their arm, she opens up the theater late on certain prescribed Monday evenings for a certain type of clientele.

Mabel also asks if Ed has noticed that the ads for Atascadero have changed in national periodicals since Oscar has taken over. Ed didn't even realize they were still running ads. The new ads are designed to attract widowed men to move out here, especially professionals such as doctors and dentists. Mare got in Oscar's ear that there are too many women and not enough eligible men. It hasn't yet led to any dating prospects for Mare, but even Oscar has learned it is best to listen to her.

Ed comes to realize what living in the moment actually means. It means enjoying the people around you. Enjoying your family. Enjoying your community. Enjoying what you have today. It has nothing to do with jobs or careers or buildings or developments or money or the future. It has to do with people and relationships in the present, including even taking the time to stroll and actually listen to your spouse.

To his greatest surprise, being in the moment even makes their eventual return to that private suite more meaningful as well.

CHAPTER 54

◆ ◆ ◆

The following Monday, Kramer is very damaging on the witness stand, but not in the way Ed had feared.

Ed was worried that weasel was going to lie and say outright that Ed's intent the entire time was to defraud his investors and that the entire mission was a joke. The government had coerced his old business partner Howard Nichols to basically say just that in his earlier trials in Washington, D.C.

Kramer never goes that far. But, given his love for numbers and counting things, Mackenzie gets him to go over in great detail the depths of the oil wells that Ed promised in print versus the actual depths of the oil wells. In most cases, Kramer says they are accurate, but in some cases, there are discrepancies.

He testifies that Ed instructed him to print that the wells were different depths than they actually were because they surely would be at that printed depth by the time the mailers were delivered. However, in several cases, there were production delays or reasons they chose not to dig any deeper, which caused the variances.

Kramer also testifies to the total number of *Illustrated Review* lifetime subscribers and the promise that each was to receive profits from their own pecan trees to be planted and accounted for in their name. Kramer knows by heart the number of subscribers and the number of planted trees. He also knows the exact date when the number of subscribers began to outpace the trees that were planted.

"Why weren't those trees planted?" Mackenzie asks him.

"Limited fiscal resources prevented us from planting them," Kramer answers.

"But you collected money from the subscriptions. Where did those monies go?"

"Into our bank account."

"Then why didn't you plant the trees? You had the money?"

"All the monies for everything we managed, all of our enterprises, all the monies were…," Kramer chokes, trying to finish, but eventually he does. "All the monies were commingled."

"Co-mingled," Mackenzie repeats with emphasis for the jury. "And speaking of co-mingled, Mrs. Fahrmeier testified that she was sent proof of her pecan trees in the mail. Actual pecans were sent to her?"

"That is correct," Kramer said. "To assuage the doubts of the skeptical and the anxieties of the apprehensive, pecans were dispatched liberally."

"But where did the pecans actually come from?"

"From a bag in the office," Kramer says.

"A bag?"

"From the same bag, yes."

That was the moment when Ed could tell he had lost the jury. He could see it in their eyes. Mackenzie has saved the best for the end. He really did admire her.

"Sorry, one more question," Mackenzie said. "So, the pecans were commingled as well?

"Not exactly."

"I don't understand. Where did you get that bag of pecans, Mr. Kramer?"

"I'd rather not say."

"Judge?" Mackenzie says.

"Answer the question," the judge says.

All eyes are on Kramer, especially those of the jury, as he is forced to answer.

"Ed purchased the bag at a market," Kramer says. "Due to the drought and freeze, we're still yet, as of today, to have an achieved an actual pecan harvest."

That admission leads to audible gasps from the audience.

"Some mission." Mackenzie says to full effect for all the jurors to hear.

After a few moments she turns to Ed and says directly, "The prosecution rests its case, unless Mr. Lewis would like to ask Mr. Kramer any questions?"

Ed does not. He simply waves his hand, and that is the end of Mr. Kramer in his life. That is that.

"We'll hear the defense's side of the story starting tomorrow then," the judge says. "Court adjourned until then."

Finally, Ed will have his chance tomorrow to defend himself. Finally, he thinks to himself. Except for one problem. The only person he could ever trust to put on the stand is himself. But how would he ask himself questions? And what questions might Mackenzie have in store for him? Everything he's read says never to put the defendant on the stand.

It'll work out, he tells himself. It always works out. *It has to work out.*

CHAPTER 55

The newspapers have covered each day of the trial, but today the courtroom is especially lively given the floor is finally handed to the defense. Not just to the defense but to the actual defendant.

"What witness would you like to call?" the judge asks.

"None," Ed says.

"None?" the judge asks. "So, the defense rests?"

"It does," Ed says. "The defense rests."

All the jaws in the room drop, including that of the jury. Including that of Mackenzie.

"In that case, we'll move on to closing arguments," the judge says. "Mrs. Mackenzie, the floor is yours."

"Your honor, I wasn't prepared for this today," she says.

"I imagine she can make it work," Ed says. "Why waste a day of taxpayers' money?"

"I agree," the judge says. "The floor is yours, Mrs. Mackenzie."

For the first time during the trial, Mackenzie shoots Ed a look of admiration. She gathers her notes, tucks behind her ear a stray strand of red hair that has escaped her tight bun, and stands to address the jury.

"I still like him," Mackenzie says. "I really do. He's charming. He's smart. He's a fast learner. He's just turned the tables on me, and now I'm up here unprepared. I admire him. He really is my kind of guy."

She nods again in genuine admiration, to which Ed accepts with a nod back of his own for her.

"But we've proven over the last few weeks that Mr. Lewis simply can't be trusted. Look at the effect he's had on Mrs. Fahrmeier and tens of thousands of women just like her. It's actually beyond charming. It's hypnotic. It's dangerous. One look at Medusa, and men turn to stone. One look at Eddie, and women empty their pocketbooks."

This causes some rumbles in the courtroom.

"There are many, many E.G. Lewises in this country. And it seems like they are all headed to California these days. All of them. We have to stop Eddie. But we also need to stop all the rest of them. The testimony in this trial has shown his true nature. You'll never see it or hear it from him. Never. To the day he dies, he'll never ever say it out loud. Nor will his supporters. Nor will anyone in Atascadero. It will be all about 'the mission.' But in his heart of hearts, he knows he doesn't actually have to come through with wells or homes or pecan trees. All he has to do is make promises. The promise of promise. Ladies and gentlemen of the jury, we not only have to protect the women he promises. We also need to protect Eddie from his own promises. We need to protect him from himself."

With that, she sits down.

Finally, it is Ed's turn. Finally, he gets the last word as he stands up for the world to see. But the world doesn't matter right now. Neither does the judge. Neither does Mackenzie. Neither do the reporters. Neither do his supporters. All that matters is the jury and their impression of him. And that they believe in the mission.

Before he says a word, the main door to the courtroom opens. Ed turns to look, as does the entire room, to see that, for the first time in the trial, Mabel has arrived to support him.

Of all the times Ed has said he could never love his wife more than he already does, today is the day he really couldn't love her more as she makes her way down the aisle.

He steps out to greet her, and she gives him the warmest hug and the biggest kiss he's ever received in their time together on Earth. She takes a seat in the front row for the world to see, and especially for the jury to see, as Ed takes a deep breath and gets back to his closing arguments.

"Ladies and gentlemen of the jury, my fate is in your hands," he says. "In a moment, I'm going to stop talking, and you're going to start deliberating amongst yourselves. You don't need to discuss if I got the depth of a well exactly right in one of my mailers or if I published the right number of pecan trees on the right date. That's all ticky-tacky. You have to deliberate whether or not I committed fraud. Whether or not I 'performed a deception for financial gain.' I ask you to consider what 'deception' did the prosecution really prove? And for what 'gain'?"

Ed pauses to let that sink in before deciding just to come clean.

"Want to know the truth? God's honest truth? I'm broke. If I had money, you'd be hearing from a first-rate lawyer like Mrs. Mackenzie defending me right now. There is no gain. I don't even have control of Atascadero's assets any longer. Zero access. I have nothing. There is no gain. It was never about gain for me."

He pauses for effect, making it clear he's being as honest as he possibly can be.

"And on the deception side, who commits fraud and then stays in town? I'm still right here in California. People who commit fraud take your money and run. I still live in Atascadero. My lovely wife lives in Atascadero. We're still here. Look at us. We live with the same community of people who invested in us. They wave at us every day. We wave back. We've gone nowhere. We've answered every letter ever written to us. We've met with any investor who has asked to meet with us. There is no deception, and there is no gain. I've committed no fraud."

Again, Ed pauses for effect as he moves even closer to the jury.

"If it's not fraud, then what is it? It's just timing. The wells could still hit at any moment, even after this trial is over. The pecan trees could still harvest the next season. Palos Verdes Estates gets closer every day to its fundraising goal. It's just a matter of timing. I couldn't control when the Great War started or ended nor its effect on real estate sales. I couldn't predict a drought or a freeze. All I ever did was put the mission first and put my investors in a position for a chance to win. A chance to win, but I can't guarantee the win. They know that. Although I still do think we will win. It's just a timing thing. Maybe a little bad luck so far, but that never lasts forever."

Now Ed moves closer to Mackenzie.

"But what you heard consistently from everyone who testified is that—except for returning their investment just yet—I did what I said I was going to do. I stuck with it. I'll continue to stick with it. And you could tell that is true for everyone Mrs. Mackenzie paid to haul up here. All the evidence shows is that I fight every day for my investors. Every day."

Now Ed moves closer to Mabel.

"My wife is here today because she sticks with me. And I stick with her. And we've both stuck with Atascadero. We always will. That town is very special to us, and so are the people in it. We were not blessed with having our own kids. That town is our family."

Ed shares a moment together with Mabel before he walks back toward the jury.

"I just need the tiniest of favors from you. From this jury. Stick with me. Don't give up on me because all the witnesses have proven time and time again that I refuse to give up on them. I'm not going anywhere, except I can't help my investors and I can't achieve our great mission—building a model community—if you don't help me. It's not just my fate that is in your hands. Their fate is also in your hands. All the women who testified are counting not just on me but on you. I know you've been listening, and I know you'll do what's right for them. They have put their trust in you."

Ed starts to sit down next to Mabel when he thinks of one last thing to say.

"You've seen my heart of hearts throughout this trial and throughout my career. I just need you to have a little trust in me."

After Ed rests, the judge releases the jury to the deliberation room. Ed takes Mabel's hand in his. Now he just has to wait and see who trusts whom.

CHAPTER 56

◆ ◆ ◆

Some juries deliberate for fifteen minutes. Some take weeks. So far, this jury has been deliberating for three days with no end in sight.

All the newspapers suggest a long deliberation is a positive sign for Ed because it implies the jury has doubts. In criminal cases, juries have to be unanimous, so he only has to convince one juror of his innocence. From the very start, he was more than confident he could do that with or without formal legal training.

His hotel room in Los Angeles also serves as his de facto office for the Palos Verdes project. It is common for someone to knock on his door, just as is happening now. It's also common for Ed to throw the door open, as he's done hundreds of times before, without asking who is there. He does just that and throws the door open to find someone he would never expect to visit him. It's none other than Hearst himself.

"Come in, please," Ed says. "Welcome. Welcome. By all means, please, come in. What an honor and a surprise. Can I fix you a drink or something?"

"This will be quick," Hearst says, stepping into the room. "You're going to read some things in my paper tomorrow, and I'd rather you first hear them from me."

Ed's not sure what to say except to motion for Hearst to go on.

"I'm sorry to say that Frank Vanderlip has died. His tuberculosis finally caught up to him."

Ed takes a seat. That is terrible news on a number of levels, of course. Terrible news.

"As you know, upon his death, the Palos Verdes trust has the right to hire a new promoter."

Ed nods that indeed they do, but he's confident they wouldn't do that to him, given how well the fundraising is going.

"Did you do any background on any of it? Any background at all?" Hearst asks.

"Background on what?"

"Or did you just jump right into it? Did you do any background on Atascadero even? Or did you just fall in love with it the day I showed it to you?"

"Of course I did the background. I did plenty."

"What does Atascadero mean?"

"An abundance of water."

"It means the opposite. Ask any Spanish speaker. And where was UCLA to be located before all your hype about Palos Verdes?"

"I'm not sure."

"Right next to my Beverly Hills development. Right next to my investment, where it will be moving back to. And, who is Cornelius Vanderbilt IV about to compete with?"

"You, but I told him no. I didn't go through with that."

"You told him no after George warned you. But before that, you told him yes, which gave him enough confidence to line up advertisers and eventually to pay another printer here in Los Angeles, which he did and, in the end, didn't need you anyway."

It's clear by Ed's face he didn't know what Vanderbilt was up to. Or about anything else Hearst has said so far.

"By the way, just because one's last name is Vanderbilt doesn't mean anything. Did you know Neil's father, Vanderbilt III, was kicked out of the family fortune by Vanderbilt II for marrying the wrong class of girl? Did you know III's younger brother, who inherited all the money instead, was kind enough to give Neil's father just a few million to live on? And then, did you know Neil's father kicked his own son, the fourth, out of the little fortune they had left? Why? For fighting in the war when they told Neil not to. For being a journalist when they told Neil not to. And for starting a newspaper when they told Neil not to."

Ed didn't know any of that. Now he's thinking quickly, trying to come up with something to say, but Hearst is faster.

"And who gave you extra printing business during the war?"

"You did."

"And who bought your printers and even gave your brother a job?"

"You did."

"And who gave you the loan for Atascadero when no one else would?"

"You did."

"And who, along with Pulitzer, stood up for you in D.C. against Senator Platt all those years ago?"

"You did."

"And who told you to focus on making real money for investors and quit all your stupid-ass mission nonsense?"

Now that one pisses Ed off, and he refuses to answer. Hearst couldn't care less as he continues.

"And who, before coming over here tonight, persuaded the Palos Verdes Trust to kick you out as promoter?"

"Don't tell me you did?"

"I did. You're damn right I did. You're out. And your locomotive plant is over as well. Thanks to a special investigation by one of my papers, the owner of that company was just indicted for fraud. There's a lot of fraud going around, apparently."

Ed can't take any more bad news. That's everything. Literally, everything he's been working on. All of it is gone.

"Why would you do this? I'm nothing compared to you. I'm small potatoes. I can't even grow a single potato. I was just trying to make ends meet. I was trying to help my investors. Why would you do this to me after all our history together?"

"Whenever people luck into the inner circle of the rich elite, it's just a matter of time before they start looking for ways to get something out of us, and then they can't help but try to get more. It happens every time. I'll never have a true friend in the world. I never will. That's my curse. Which is why I always have to do the background work."

Hearst pauses to reflect on that reality before continuing.

"Any one of your infractions against me would be enough for me to immediately write you off, especially after all our time together. But when I put all your infractions together, well, that earns you a termination notice from me in person."

Hearst has said his piece as he starts to leave. Before he can reach the door, Ed thinks of one pressing question to ask.

"What about my trial and the bankruptcy? I take it you are behind that as well?"

Now this causes Hearst to pause for a moment and control his temper before responding.

"No," he says. "But that's also something you never did any background on either. By all accounts, it appears you're at least going to escape those. My legal experts say you are looking good on the bankruptcy and the trial."

That at least gives Ed some relief.

"But know this," Hearst continues. "If I were behind those, you'd already be in jail, and even all those assets in your wife's name wouldn't be protected. So, no, that wasn't me. If you would actually do some background for a change, you could easily figure out who is actually behind that, but it doesn't really matter."

Hearst is halfway out the door now, but he stops to finish a final thought.

"It doesn't matter because all of this is actually your own doing. The sooner you admit that, the better. It's all on you. It's always actually been on you and you alone. You continually conspire against yourself. Every time you rush into something. You do it to yourself."

Hearst has one last parting shot.

"Want to expose the real villain in your story?" he says, "Just find a mirror."

CHAPTER 57

It takes another two weeks before Ed is summoned back to court when the jury finally reaches a verdict.

Over those two weeks, all of Ed's projects fully unraveled and played out publicly in the news. So much so that the judge had to sequester the jury to avoid their reading about it. He also instructed the jury to use only the evidence that was presented in court, even if they had heard or read something outside of the courtroom. The judge controlled everything about the jury, even what they ate and where they slept the past few weeks, so Ed can only hope they were fully sequestered and followed the judge's orders.

However, Ed read the papers where all his business dealings unraveled publicly, including a damning five-part exposé in *Sunset Magazine* entitled "The Champion Borrower of Them All," suggesting Ed has lost more than $30 million from investors over the course of his career without a single success. In better news, Ed also read what Hearst had confirmed—that, basically, every legal expert in the United States is of the opinion that he will be found innocent. At least he has that going for him.

Over the last few weeks, Ed has had many late-night conversations with Mabel, who agreed to stay in Los Angeles with him after the visit from Hearst. He never wants to be alone ever again in their marriage.

They talked about the time they spent together on the beach. He listened to updates about the twins. The babies. About Atascadero. About their community. He loves every moment with Mabel. Ed has vowed to her that it is finally time that he turns a new leaf and focuses on what is important in life. He promises he will. All he needs is an innocent verdict. He promises, and he means it.

"Have you reached a verdict?" the judge asks the jury.

"We have," says the foreman.

There are only three men on the jury, and, of course, Ed thinks, one of them was selected as the foreman.

The bailiff hands the written verdict to the judge, who reads it and hands it back to be delivered to the foreman.

Ed has seen this scene play out fourteen times in his past and has learned that no matter what is said, he is simply to listen for the words "not guilty."

"On all counts of fraud against Mr. E.G. Lewis, this jury of his peers unanimously finds the defendant to be guilty. Guilty on all charges."

Did he hear that correctly?

Ed looks at Mabel's face, and he can tell immediately she didn't hear the correct words either. He looks at the faces of the jury, but they won't look at him. They've always looked at him in the past. None of them make eye contact with him.

While trying to figure out what he heard, he'll remember later the judge continuing on and saying something about him being sentenced for up to twenty years and having to report within ninety days to a federal penitentiary in the state of Washington. Also, something about the possibility of parole much sooner.

Something else about him being denied the use of the mails for promotional purposes for life. *For life.*

Then Ed turns to see Mrs. Mackenzie being congratulated by her team. Reporters are now taking photos and asking questions despite the judge telling them to back off while trying to restore order.

Ed hears Hearst's voice in his head saying all of it was on him. He alone is to blame. He conspires against himself. He's the real villain. Then he remembers Hattie might be in the courtroom. He has something important to say to her, and he wants to double-check her face to see if she heard the same verdict he had, but when he turns to find her, the room seems to spin and spin and spin. Then he remembers Hattie isn't in the courtroom. She never was. Neither is Claire. Neither are the twins. Neither is John. Neither is George. No one is there for him except Mabel.

He realizes that only Mabel matters anyway. But the room is really spinning now. Oh, wow, it is spinning. He's trying to find her. Mabel was just there next to him. He reaches out for her. She was just there a moment ago. Spinning. Spinning.

For the rest of his life, he'll never forget what actually being declared guilty feels like when the room finally stops spinning as his face slams against the courtroom floor.

Act III:
The Man in the Mirror

CHAPTER 58

◆ ◆ ◆

Betty finds it therapeutic to watch wood burn in her fireplace. She enjoys seeing log after log ignite, glow, ember, and eventually disappear, which eases her complete and utter boredom being stuck on McNeil Island off the coast of Seattle, waiting on her husband to come home.

Betty has herself arranged perfectly under her favorite blanket in her favorite chair. The last log in her living room fireplace burns down as she's about to turn in for the night.

Now that she's reached middle age, she is annoyed by feeling cold one minute and hot the next. She's debating with herself about just sleeping in the living room versus making the long dark walk upstairs to the bedroom when she hears a knock on her front door.

The knock just adds to her annoyance, especially given that she's not entirely presentable at this hour, only wearing a nightgown, robe, and slippers with her hair up for the night. She's considering ignoring the knock, but it incessantly continues to pound over and over.

"Step back from the door," Betty finally says. "Step back ten paces, and I'll open it."

"Of course. Yes, ma'am," comes a man's voice that she doesn't recognize. "My deepest apologies."

Betty eventually opens the door and is now holding a loaded shotgun curled under her arm. She looks out to discover Ed shivering on her front walk ten paces back from her doorstep.

Betty can't help but wonder why this tiny little man isn't wearing a winter coat or hat, given the biting cold of tonight's Seattle coast winter. She can tell Ed must have gotten a good look at her shotgun as he takes even a few more steps backward, slowly holding his suitcase up as if it were a shield.

"I'm so sorry to disturb you," Ed says. "May I please speak to the warden? Your husband, I presume? It's just that the guards at the prison won't let me in. They say they don't have the proper paperwork or something to admit me. They say they have no record of me being due to report."

"My husband isn't home," she says. "The guards know that. Those idiots sent you over here to me?"

"No, no. I, well. I just figured the big house next door must be the warden's. They didn't send me here."

"You'll need to come back tomorrow. My husband is not scheduled to return until then."

She starts to close the door, but before doing so, she takes a final look at Ed. She can tell he is visibly dejected upon hearing that the warden isn't home. She notices him looking around, probably trying to decide his next course of action. Eventually, she sees him just sit on his suitcase in exasperation.

All she wants to do is close her door, return to her blanket, finish watching her last log smolder out, and go back to simpler times when tonight's biggest dilemma was deciding whether to sleep downstairs or upstairs. However, she now knows she isn't going to find any peace in that, wondering if, instead, in the morning, she's going to find this little man frozen in her front yard.

"Who comes all the way to the island without a coat or hat?" she says out loud to herself, still about to close the door.

"Someone from California who didn't think it all the way through," Ed says. "The same someone who didn't think a lot of things all the way through."

She notices he's still sitting on his suitcase dejected. He's starting to remind her of something, a stray kitten, maybe. He's just so helpless. She can almost imagine him about to start purring.

"What am I to do?" Betty says, still holding her shotgun. "Let an inmate into my home in the middle of the night? Or would you expect that I'd go put on my coat and march you to the prison, maybe even at gunpoint, and demand the guards take you in?"

"Ironically, that's what I've been trying to avoid," Ed says. "The federal marshal was scheduled to bring me here officially from Atascadero by train tomorrow, but I was told I'd be handcuffed and shackled the whole way. I just couldn't face the humiliation of all that, so I thought I'd get myself up here on my own a day early and just report in."

Begrudgingly, he now stands up from sitting on his suitcase.

"I'm deeply sorry to have troubled you this evening," he says. "Everyone knows it is hard to get out of prison, but I thought it would be far easier to report in. I'll head back over there to the front gates. Maybe I can at least talk the guards into giving me a blanket or a little food or something."

He picks up his suitcase and starts to walk back toward the prison, but Betty knows the guards, and she knows how the system works. The night guards especially will literally let him freeze to death while they play cards inside, probably taking bets on how long he'll last out in the cold.

"If I were to take pity on you," Betty says. "You'll first have to answer two questions for me. What's your name, and what were you convicted of?"

Ed stops walking and turns toward her.

"My name is Mr. E.G. Lewis," he says. "But you can call me Edward or Eddie or Ed. Given I find myself yet again living in a new town, I haven't decided yet what I'll go by here."

But he can't will himself to answer her second question about why he was convicted. Back home, everyone knows, so he's never had to actually admit it. On his own, he would love to answer he's been convicted simply of bad timing. Or maybe even of bad luck. Or good fortune that hasn't yet materialized. Or he'd really love to answer that he's guilty of upsetting powerful men who have conspired against him his whole career.

He knows he'll never be able to bring himself to say the word for which he was actually convicted. He just can't utter the word. He'd prefer to freeze to death rather than ever admit to having been convicted of fraud against his own beloved customers.

He just can't bring himself to answer her second question. Thus, he turns to head back to the prison, missing seeing the big smile that suddenly forms on Betty's face.

"*The* Mr. E.G. Lewis?" she says, lowering her shotgun. "I've been a subscriber to your magazines for years. Your whole trial in Los Angeles was rigged and unfair. Why didn't you say who you were sooner? Get on in here by the fire. I can't have you freeze to death out here, E.G."

With that, Ed now knows what name he'll go by in his new town. In no time at all, Betty sets another chair by the fireplace for him, throws a few more logs on the fire, gets him a blanket, makes him a plate of food, and even lends him her husband's robe and slippers, which are three sizes too large.

"I've read all of your columns through the years," she says. "I even paid for a guess in the World's Fair Contest back in the day. Just missed it by a few hundred attendees. I would have sent in investments for your recent businesses too, but my husband wouldn't let me."

She shakes her head, thinking about her husband.

"Walter has no imagination," she says. "Zero creativity. Even he would admit to being a dullard. In fact, he's at the Pacific Northwest Region's annual penitentiary meetings right now. Wives are invited to the big dinner on the last night, which is tonight, but I just couldn't bear to go again this year. They hand out awards and such at that dinner, and he never wins one. Never once in all these years out here. And he shouldn't. He never risks doing anything different at the prison but then expects to win something. Walter gets so dejected. I just couldn't witness that again."

"What types of awards do they hand out?" Ed asks.

"I barely pay attention. I don't know. Staying under budget, maybe. Creative programming, maybe. Percentage of incidents per prison population. Maybe something about prison newspapers, which, surprisingly, they all have. There are dozens of categories, and he's never come close to winning any category, nor will he ever."

Ed never knew wardens or jails could win awards. But, then again, Ed has never been near a prison. Before the final logs burn out, Ed asks Betty all kinds of questions about Walter himself, prison life, life on the island, the nearby community, her hopes and dreams, how she met Walter, what the guards are like, what the prisoners are like, and more. He listens intently as Betty goes on and on, answering all his questions. They not only have a lovely conversation, but Ed now feels he has a new friend in the warden's wife.

Ever since the trial, Ed's been scared to death of the eventual date on which he'd have to report to prison. He assumed he'd spend his first night on the island in a tiny cell behind thick bars, worrying about the true intentions of a lurking cellmate.

He had hoped that by checking in a day early, he would eventually be let out a day early. But tonight still seems very worth it in the end. Over time, maybe he can still talk them into letting tonight count, just like he was able to talk the guards into revealing which house was the warden's while avoiding taking them up on their offer to spend the night on a metal cot in the prison's drafty front office.

He certainly is cozy, especially since Betty has set him up in the guest bedroom for the night and lent him a pair of the warden's surprisingly warm flannel pajamas.

CHAPTER 59

♦ ♦ ♦

The following morning Ed is in the middle of a dream where he finds himself back on stage selling shares for Palos Verdes and speaking into the microphone in front of thousands of people.

He wants to thank the audience and the board of trustees for giving him another chance, except the microphone keeps moving around and even poking him in the face. Each time it hits him harder and harder until he finally wakes up to realize he is, indeed, in real life, being poked in the face.

"E.G., you son-of-a-bitch," Walter says, shoving a loaded shotgun right into Ed's jaw.

Ed can immediately see why the warden's robe is so big. Walter is a bear of a man. Ed wonders why Walter even bothers with a gun. He could probably snap Ed in half with one hand.

"Boys, take him in. And get my damn clothes off him."

Ed realizes now the perimeter of the room is full of the prison guards he met last night, and they too have their guns out. Following orders, the guards yank him out of bed, strip Walter's pajamas off him, shackle him, and drag him down the stairs of the warden's home and out into the street in the frigid cold. On the way out, Ed thinks he may have heard Betty protesting on his behalf to an enraged Walter, but Ed is now distracted by the townspeople, who must live on the island and are now lining up to watch as Ed is dragged through the cold streets in his underwear.

He sure is fast-tracked into the prison this time. The guards march him half-naked past inmates wearing gray jumpsuits through what feels like every corridor of the entire prison for no reason other than to further humiliate him.

Eventually, Ed is stripped down fully naked. Head shaved. Hosed off. Deloused. Forced into a gray jumpsuit of his own. Finally tossed into a solitary detention cell with no light, no sound, no blanket, and certainly no pajamas.

It's hard for Ed to know for sure how long he's been in the dark and damp room. He's bruised and battered. Everything hurts. To add insult to injury, the most terrible gray-ish looking food he's ever tasted arrives through a slot in his door. Without much light or a sense of time, he can't tell if the food is delivered twice or three times a day or at what hour.

When the food is delivered, he tries talking to whoever is on the other side of the door, but they ignore him. Then he tries shouting. Even screaming. One time he puts his foot to block the slot so the food can't be pushed in. No one cares. All that happens is he doesn't get any food.

The room does have a latrine toilet, which is easy to find, given its foul smell. Mostly he lies in the far corner, away from it. Sometimes he sits on the latrine. Sometimes he leans against the wall. Sometimes he paces in a tiny circle. For all he knows, he has been in there for days, or is it weeks, when out of nowhere, the door finally opens, and blinding light pours in. Two guards, without saying a word, drag him out of his cell only for him to be stripped down again, hosed off, shaved, and given a fresh jumpsuit.

Ed kicks and screams as they take him back to his cell. He just can't bear to go back. At all costs, he fights and fights as much as his little frame allows until he realizes maybe they aren't taking him back. Instead, they drag him down another corridor and throw him into some kind of large storage room that is stacked with dozens and dozens of mailbags that have U.S. Postal Service stamped on them.

The guards leave him alone in the storage room with the door open. Ed is starting to wonder if he's hallucinating. Or if this is some kind of test to see if he'll open the bags or walk out into the hallway or run or hide. He's trying to decide on his next step when he hears a familiar but agitated voice in the hallway with what sounds like multiple people marching toward the storage room.

"The First Amendment of the United States Constitution entitles prisoners to receive and to send mail," Inspector Fulton says. "E.G. Lewis has that right."

Ed has never been so happy to hear a familiar voice as Fulton comes into view with Walter right on his heels.

"Not at this volume," the warden says.

"The volume of mail is immaterial. It's a constitutional right," Fulton says until stopping in his tracks as he spies Ed for the first time.

Over the twenty years Fulton has known Ed, he has only ever seen him large and in charge, confidently wearing a three-piece suit. Fulton is startled to find Ed not just in a gray jumpsuit but also slumped on the floor with his head shaved.

Fulton is in such shock witnessing Ed in this state, and he doesn't even react when Ed basically leaps into his arms, giving him a hug so tight that it undoubtedly has now creased his entire postal uniform.

Walter ignores all of this as he walks into the storage room and motions at what appears to be endless bags of mail stacked in every corner of the room.

"My instinct is just to burn it all," Walter says. "Why should the taxpayers have to deal with this nonsense? How can we be expected to provide storage, etc.? It would be the full-time job of multiple people just to inspect and censor it all, which is also part of the First Amendment, as you know. The prison has the right to inspect it all for contraband and such."

"Here's what you're going to find," Fulton says, opening one of the bags and dumping the contents onto a table.

Out pours letter after letter addressed to Mr. E.G. Lewis at the penitentiary. Fulton rummages through, selects one of the nearly identical envelopes, and hands it to Walter to open. Walter does just that to reveal not just a letter inside but also a stack of one-dollar bills and some assorted coins.

Ed is starting to get some color back in his face now. He's beginning to stand taller. It's now dawning on him that not only is all the mail addressed to him, but what it really means is that he's no longer alone. He's suddenly surrounded by friends and supporters.

Walter, still holding the cash and coins, reads the letter out loud.

"E.G., it's just terrible what the feds have done to you. Stay strong in prison. Don't let them break you. Stay on mission. You'll be out in no time. Here's some money I was able to get the ladies in my quilting club to scrounge together toward your prison cause. We need you rested and ready to get out soon and come back stronger than ever to fight for our investment returns. Be well. Send our love to that sweet Mabel of yours. Write to us when you can. Sincerely, Julia Foster and the Statesboro, Georgia, Quilting Club."

Walter rummages through more of the letters lying on the table, realizing they are all the same. He can feel that they are all filled with assorted cash and coins. He turns and addresses Fulton straight on.

"But the judge banned E.G. from the mails for life," Walter says.

"He is 'denied the use of the mails for promotional purposes'," Fulton corrects. "But the example you are holding is not a solicited investment. If any of the letters contain investments, they must be returned. Each letter needs to be checked, but they are most likely unsolicited donations. Eddie's correspondence back has to be inspected, as well. If he writes back 'thank you,' that is one thing. If he writes back 'send more,' that is another."

"So, we are required to spend taxpayer money processing all of this mail in both directions? Including his response?" Walter says. "Surely this can't be the intent of the First Amendment."

"It is absolutely the intent," Fulton says. "It's just, in this instance, an abnormality of volume."

Walter is beside himself when Ed finally gets the courage to join in on the conversation.

"Charge me to process it," Ed says.

Walter's first instinct is to slap Ed across the face for daring to speak, but then he recognizes the wisdom of the suggestion.

"It's debatable," Fulton says, "but it is often argued in court that the 14th Amendment allows for just that. 'Able-bodied federal inmates must all work unless they are earning an education.' But by the 'grace of the state,' they can earn a modest wage, and the prison can profit off the labor if a customer is willing to pay for it."

Walter knows all that. In fact, some of the more progressive prisons in his region have recently been doing just that. He even had to watch some of them hoist awards at the recent dinner his wife wouldn't attend. Apparently, she'd prefer to room and board an inmate in Walter's own home than attend the annual banquet with him.

"I'll be your customer," Ed says. "I'll pay the prison to have prisoners process and respond to the mail under the watchful eye of guards."

Ed can tell by Walter's face that the idea isn't entirely preposterous.

"Inspector Fulton," Ed says. "How much money do you estimate is in these bags?"

Now that's a fun math problem for Fulton. His mind races as he takes out his notebook and gauges the thickness of the envelope that was just opened compared to the others he can see laid out on the table. He multiples that by how many letters fit in a large mailbag times the number of bags in the room times the fact that he knows letters are still rolling in from across the country to eventually reach a final tally number.

"More than plenty," Fulton says, showing the final figure with lots of trailing zeros to Walter.

Ed can tell from Walter's expression that it is indeed a figure worthy of consideration.

"E.G. Lewis, you're no less of a son-of-a-bitch," Walter says, maybe starting to lighten up just a bit. "But you sure are an enterprising one. I'll give you that."

CHAPTER 60

◆ ◆ ◆

A few months later, Ed checks his hair in a mirror on the wall. It's growing back nicely now.

These days, Ed wakes up in a much more spacious cell with natural light, along with a sink, a toilet with a lid, a more comfortable bed with covers, a mattress, and even bed springs. Ed dresses in his jumpsuit.

The cell doors on the floor all open at the same time as Ed funnels out with the larger prison population into the mess hall for breakfast. Along the way, he's greeted with "Morning, E.G." by everyone he encounters. Not just every single inmate but each and every guard, as well.

Over and over, he hears "Morning, E.G.," or "Greetings, E.G.," or "Sleep well, E.G.?" And he greets them all back by first name, including the guards.

A few of the inmates were kind enough to have already gone through the breakfast line and made him a plate of food, which is waiting for him at his usual table. He thanks them, takes a quick bite or two, and continues to walk through the cafeteria, receiving more well wishes as the guards graciously part ways, allowing him to walk through any corridor unrestricted.

Normally locked doors are opened for him as he makes his way to a processing room where dozens of inmates are already hard at work this morning, opening mail, sorting money into piles, reading over letters, and responding to others. The inmate workers are all smiles as they see Ed, and so is a guard who can't wait to show Ed something that just arrived in a box.

"Got another cherry pie today," the guard says.

Ed takes a closer look and gets a big whiff of it.

"Smells delicious," Ed says to the guard. "Why don't you take it home tonight to Angela and the kids."

The guard is excited to do so as he boxes it back up. Ed pats him on the shoulder and continues to make his way through the prison.

Whenever Ed comes to a locked door, someone jumps up to unlock it for him and to wish him well.

Eventually, Ed makes his way through the long corridors to the administration offices where he greets secretaries and nurses who are normally protected by extra layers of security, but not for Ed.

As he passes the warden's secretary, he takes a quick moment to get her attention.

"So, how did Jimmy do last night in his little league game?" Ed asks her.

"Two doubles and a home run," she says proudly.

"Next stop Yankee Stadium," Ed says, opening the door to the warden's office on his own. "Babe Ruth had better watch out."

She's all smiles as Ed enters Walter's office.

Upon seeing Ed, Walter immediately pops up from his desk to offer him a fresh cup of coffee. Walter is a beast of a man, but he can also be reduced to nothing more than a teddy bear, especially if you get him talking about coffee, which he pays to have specially imported to Seattle and then driven by boat over to the island. Walter is on pins and needles to see what Ed thinks of this newest brew as he takes a sip.

"This is the best one yet, Warden," Ed says to Walter's delight.

"Brazilian," Walter replies. "It's not just the taste, is it?"

"No, it's also the aroma."

"It really is. Spectacular."

"What did Betty think this morning?"

"She wants to know what you think when I get home tonight. But she likes it."

"Tell her I do, too. Good stuff. Hey, I have an idea for you. Mind if I sit?"

"Of course, E.G. Finish your cup. What can I do for you?"

"I think the processing is going really well, do you agree?"

"Great. It's going great."

"Yes, Inspector Fulton agrees as well. Every time he drops by, however, he tries to improve the process, but I keep telling him the guys here don't want to work faster. They are worried they are going to run out of letters and have to go back to janitorial or cafeteria duties. Or worse."

"If you need them to go faster, I'll make it happen," Walter says, starting to stand.

"No, no, not at all," Ed says as Walter sits back down. "It's just that in talking with the guys in the processing room, as you know, very few of them are in here for violent offenses. Most are business professionals like me. Lawyers, accountants, bankers, insurance men, and salesmen, who all have encountered some form of...."

Ed pauses, searching for the word because he still cannot and will not ever say the word 'fraud.' Walter helps him out.

"Some form of financial misunderstanding?" Walter says.

"Exactly," Ed says. "And while they certainly prefer processing the mail over other forms of labor, we've got a nice rotational process going now. Everyone gets a turn in the processing room, but there are so many other paid jobs they could be doing."

"Like what?" Walter asks.

"Like what they are actually trained to do. Lawyering, accounting, insuring, selling. Some of them grew up on farms even. They know how to tend to fruits and vegetables."

"What are you suggesting?" Walter asks.

"I know you're a part of the local businessman rotary club and such," Ed says. "What if you asked the professionals in your circles if they need any help? You've got this underutilized labor force here. They'd work for nothing—they already work for nothing—just to get a chance to properly use their minds. Basically, they'd work in exchange for dignity. You literally have a gold mine of skilled labor here."

"I don't know," Walter says. "I don't know."

"What's your mission here, Warden?" Ed asks.

"My mission?"

"Is it to make sure the inmates peacefully do their time or is it to rehabilitate them? Pick one."

"Well, I mean," Walter stumbles to answer. "I mean. I guess."

"How many recorded incidents have there been since men have been processing mail?"

Walter hasn't really thought about that. That's a good question. He starts to rifle through some papers on his desk when he realizes he's been so caught up in watching the processing unfold that, come to think of it, there haven't really been any incidents, especially since, at Ed's request, the warden started allowing men to rotate getting to work in the processing room.

"But I don't know how I'd market the services," Walter says. "I've never worked in industry. I don't know exactly what businessmen need. Or even exactly what we have to offer. I could get on the agenda at the next Rotary Club meeting, but I wouldn't know what to say."

Ed lets Walter ponder this for a moment before offering a tiny suggestion.

"I know someone who knows how to talk to a room full of businessmen," Ed says.

"Who is that?"

"He's sitting right here enjoying your imported coffee. Give me a shot at it. What do you have to lose?"

CHAPTER 61

A year later, Ed checks his look in a larger full-length mirror, combing his hair, which has fully grown back. He's fortunate to wake up in a newer, larger cell to even more natural light. He fastens the buttons on his freshly pressed three-piece suit and works to get his tie just right.

As he does every day, he greets everyone he encounters walking through the prison corridors. He notices that breakfast this morning looks decidedly different than it used to. Before, all the food was the same dull gray, but it is now vibrant in color, texture, smell, and taste. One of the cooks gets Ed's attention.

"E.G., give this a try. What do you think?" he says.

Ed tastes some gravy designed to go over fresh biscuits.

"So good," Ed says. "Maybe a little salty? I don't know. What do you think?"

"I think you're right. I'll try it again for tomorrow."

"Good stuff, though," Ed says. "Keep it up."

The cook thanks him but is anxious to run off and make some tweaks. Ed pats him on the back as he continues his way through the prison, with every door still opening for him. Eventually, he is allowed to easily walk through the final series of locked doors leading outside into the bright sunlight.

On some land adjacent to the prison, Ed checks in on some prisoners tending a recently designed seven-acre garden, which is now harvesting its first fruits and vegetables. Everyone gives him a thumbs up as they load up produce to take to the cafeteria.

At the very front gate, Ed nods to the guards, who smile as they open the bars, allowing Ed to walk out alone onto the street in complete freedom. He doesn't get far as he's already greeting townspeople along the way who have come to know him over the past year.

Betty, the warden's wife, goes out of her way to cross the street to talk to him.

"You free this Sunday night?" she says. "Walter and I are thinking of taking our new boat out. Want to join us for dinner?"

"Absolutely," Ed says. "In normal conditions I'd offer to bring a bottle of wine, but that's one thing, as you know, I'll never be allowed in here.

"I'll pick up a red," she says. "See you Sunday."

Ed waves goodbye to Betty and enters a modest office building just off the town square where other inmates, also wearing suits, are already busy this morning working away at their desks and meeting with clients.

A guard is stationed there as well, but he mostly just sits off to the side, reading the newspaper. Ed greets him, and the guard is kind enough to share a newspaper he's already read. Ed makes some small talk and carries the newspaper down the hallway.

He greets a few secretaries along the way. The warden's own secretary now works for Ed. She appears to have something urgent to tell him, but he insists on saying something first.

"Tell me Jimmy found himself a Babe Ruth in that pack of cards I sent home with you last night," Ed says.

"He didn't," she says.

"It's just a matter of time," Ed says. "Odds are one of these days, one of the packs will have one. Just have to keep trying. You can't have bad luck every time."

"Speaking of luck or even surprises," she says, smiling as she motions into Ed's office. "You are not going to believe this, but of all people, your wife is here."

Through the blinds in the window to his office, Ed can indeed see a silhouette of Mabel. As confident as he has been lately, almost feeling like his old self, he nearly loses his balance, never expecting Mabel would visit him.

In fact, Ed and Mabel had agreed that she would not visit him in prison. He didn't want her to ever see him in a jumpsuit or behind bars. He just wanted to do his time as exceptionally as he could and to be paroled as fast as possible and put all of this behind him. Now that she has decided to visit, she'll at least find him wearing a suit.

To say their relationship has been strained is an understatement. She barely writes him or acknowledges his letters. Claire never writes him. The twins do, but their letters never mention Mabel. One time he pressed Fulton for some information, but Fulton is a steel trap. It's obvious Fulton knows something, but he won't reveal a thing. Ed assumes Claire probably has him under some kind of strict orders.

After a deep breath, Ed finds the courage to open the door.

"Dearest," he says, throwing his arms out, only to find the woman in his office isn't Mabel.

Instead, Hattie immediately stands up and throws her arms around him.

"You look so great," she says. "I didn't know what to expect, but I should have assumed I'd find you in charge of this place. And here you are."

◆

After getting over the misunderstanding that Hattie is not Mabel, Ed has his secretary cancel his appointments for the rest of the morning as he goes for a stroll with Hattie around the island.

She fills him in on all the gossip back home. She's about done helping Oscar settle all the assets. Rose is now engaged to the construction worker Teddy befriended in the war. Larry, Marcela, and Lawrence are doing well in Sacramento building houses. Mare is still Mare. Claire is busy with the movie and dance hall on the weekends. Hearst fired George for tipping off Ed about Vanderbilt, but John quickly helped George get a good job with the defense contractor in Los Angeles. Homes are still being built rapidly in Atascadero. All in all, things are great.

She also mentions she brought the thing he had requested in his letter, which she left subtly in a suitcase behind the desk in his office while she was waiting for him.

"How about Oscar?" Ed says. "Any word on the final bankruptcy payout I'll be receiving?"

"He's still calculating it," she says.

Ed has an estimate in his head of what he expects it to be. As long as it is in that range, his plans for when he gets out should easily come together.

"Is there anything else at all you need, Ed?" Hattie asks, taking his hands in hers. "Anything at all as long as I'm here and in the flesh?"

He's not exactly sure what she might be implying, but there is one more thing he does need. A piece of information from her. They talked about everyone back home except for one pressing subject: Mabel. Ed can tell Hattie is reluctant to say much, but he hounds her anyway.

"Tell me about her," Ed says. "Let me guess. She's happy. Gardening with Claire. Playing with babies. Volunteering. Tell me she's happy. I get that she doesn't want to visit, but tell me she's at least finding some peace."

Hattie just nods that all those things are generally true, but Ed can sense there is something else.

"What is it?" Ed asks. "You have to tell me."

"It's nothing. She's also been doing a little traveling, is all."

"Really. Like where? Sacramento to see Marcella?"

"Yes, but also, well, south."

"What? Really? Why?"

"It's just rumors. Somebody thought they saw a train ticket. Just rumors. San Diego, maybe."

"Rumors of what?"

"I didn't come here for any of that. That's between you and Mabel. I just wanted to make sure you are doing well, and clearly, you are. And again, I'm straight up asking if I could do *anything* for you before I go?"

She'll never understand how he still, after all these years, never seems to pick up on her increasingly overt hints. Hattie isn't getting near the reaction she was hoping for. She can tell Ed's mind is still stuck on something she said a while ago.

"San Diego," Ed says. "We don't know anyone down there…except…wait."

Hattie can tell Ed has now figured it out on his own, and he suddenly remembers who it was he knows has a home in San Diego. None other than that rat bastard J.H. whom Ed made a millionaire.

CHAPTER 62

♦ ♦ ♦

Two years later, Ed has multiple three-piece suits to choose from as he holds them up to his body in his full-length mirror. Nothing much has changed except his hair is starting to thin out a bit. He assumed he was on a path to being fortunate enough to have a thick head of hair for life, but, alas, it is now appearing his fortunes are disappearing in that arena.

He always keeps his notebook of business and invention ideas nearby and quickly jots down "research hair elixir." That's definitely a market to take a look at when he gets out of jail, along with the 150 other ideas he's written down.

As he walks through the prison, it takes him a few corridors to realize something: he hasn't yet seen a living soul this morning. No inmates. No guards.

He really knows something is wrong when he enters a completely empty cafeteria. He has a passing thought about the recently popular Rapture Movement he's been reading about, wondering for a moment if everyone was so fortunate to ascend to heaven, leaving him to wander the empty halls of the prison for the rest of his life.

Trying not to freak himself out, he simply continues his morning routine and opens the door to the large processing room.

"SURPRISE" rings out from the room, where Ed finds all the prisoners and guards assembled.

In short order, everyone is shaking his hand. They are all so happy. He is so confused. He knows it is not his birthday or anything. Even Betty is there, along with his secretary and all the other secretaries and nurses. They all give him hugs. He has absolutely no idea what is going on when the warden gives him the biggest bear hug of all. Walter literally lifts Ed in the air without even realizing his own strength. Ed is nearly swallowed up in his arms.

After all the hugs, the room settles down as if they all want Ed to make a speech, but he still has no idea what is going on when Walter finally takes command of the room.

"E.G., I have two surprises for you today," Walter says. "The first is this."

He motions to Betty, who retrieves a large trophy cup she has been hiding on the floor behind her. She proudly hands it to Walter, who even more proudly hands it to Ed. Ed barely has time to read the inscription on the trophy as Walter continues his announcement.

"I'm proud to say McNeil Island Penitentiary has won the top award in the Pacific Western region, which now qualifies us to compete at the national level," Walter says. "Read the inscription, E.G. What does it say?"

"Prison of the Year," Ed reads to thunderous applause from all the inmates and guards. Ed is finally catching on that Walter has not just received an award but the top award in his field. Betty is elated for her husband.

"But I have bigger news," Walter says, getting out a piece of paper to read. "This is hot off the presses. 'Mr. E.G. Lewis is hereby awarded early parole for exemplary behavior.' It's going to take a few days to process, but you are free to go live your life."

Ed knew this was a possibility, but he'd been led to believe it could be another few years, at best. He had researched that parole is less frequent and takes longer to earn at the federal level. This basically never happens.

The inmates and guards cheer even louder at Ed's news of parole. The last thing Ed wants to do in front of this audience is tear up. But he can't help himself. The more he can't control himself, the more the inmates and guards cheer and congratulate him. The secretaries and nurses are starting to tear up, too.

Betty gives him a handkerchief and helps get him to a presentable place, as it's clear he's not going to be leaving this room until he makes a speech of some kind. Ed collects himself the best he can.

"I'm usually not at a loss for words," Ed says, to laughter from the crowd. "But my only real thought here is to thank you. We've all been handed some unfortunate luck to be here, and I want to thank you all for helping me get through my time."

"Are you kidding," one of the inmates shouts out. "You're the one who helped us."

The crowd roars again in support, which causes Ed to tear up even more.

"I mean what I'm about to say right now," Ed says. "Each and every one of you men here, when you get out, you come see me in Atascadero. I'll have a job waiting for you. You can count on your life being back on track when you get out. You come see me. We'll start over together."

Walter was actually starting to get worried that outside the prison walls, the town folks might start to worry a riot is going on, given the thunderous applause. The warden is especially starting to worry a little as some of the men pick Ed up and literally pass him around the room on their shoulders in celebration.

It is one thing the way Ed had helped to transform the prison, but it is another to promise all of these men gainful employment. The thing that most worries them is whether they'll ever be able to get a job or their lives back again. Walter just witnessed Ed promise them all those things.

As Ed is being passed over the crowd, he's also thinking about getting his own job back and his own life back. He has a debt to collect from Oscar to jumpstart his career. More importantly, he's going to have to work a bit harder, it seems, to win back his wife.

CHAPTER 63

◆ ◆ ◆

Ed looks himself over in the reflection of the train window one last time before stepping out onto the platform in Atascadero.

As wonderful as Ed's prison send-off had been, it is dwarfed by Ed's return home. He steps off the train to find the entire town waiting for him. "Welcome Home" banners are hung everywhere. The Atascadero High School band is playing an energetic march song. A red carpet has literally been rolled out for him.

Ed is greeted by the twins, their much older daughters, Larry, Lawrence, George, Lucile, and their additional kids. Hattie wraps him in a huge embrace. He gets a solid head nod from Mare. Off to the side, behind the crowd, Ed spies Fulton, who also acknowledges him with a lift of an eyebrow. Even Claire gives him a half hug for all to see.

Everyone is there except, that is, for Mabel.

Eventually, the crowd settles down, and it is obvious they want Ed to say a few words, for which he has prepared.

"Thank you for this warm reception," Ed says. "This unfortunate chapter is behind us now. I'm back. Back on mission. I vow to you I will right the wrongs. You have my word. I love Atascadero. I'm here for good. Sure, I was gone for a while, but I never really left. I'm always here for you. I'm going to make it up to you. This is my home, and you are my family."

Ed shakes every hand and talks to every single resident until the crowd winds down. Oscar has sold off all his Cadillacs as part of the liquidation process, but the real estate development has one left, which Hattie uses to drive him to the office which Oscar has made his headquarters the last few years.

Hattie explains on the drive that except for the fact that many homes have been built, everything else about Atascadero is how Ed left it. Besides all the infrastructure, only three other buildings were built. The Community Center is still used for that purpose and for church services. The four-story administration building was sold to a boy's military academy out of Portland, Oregon. They only use it in the summer as a remote campus. The boys are housed there and go to summer school while exploring the mountains and canyons nearby. And the printing press building is currently vacant.

Ed has grand plans for each of those buildings as he enters Oscar's office, which is stacked with packed boxes and such. Oscar looks the same with his bald head and skinny legs and arms. Ed shakes his still bony vulture hands, except Ed notices Oscar's belly is considerably larger now.

"You've certainly had quite a feast here, haven't you?" Ed says.

"We certainly have returned as many assets to shareholders as possible," Oscar says. "I'm proud to say all debts are settled."

"Except for one," Ed says. "I'll take my check now if you don't mind."

"What check?"

"My portion," Ed says. "For going along with the arrangement. My cut."

"Oh my," Oscar says. "Have you been holding out hope this whole time for some kind of payout at the end? How tragic. This whole time in prison?"

"You owe me. I'm here to collect before you leave," Ed says. "Per our agreement."

"You must realize you ruined that chance years ago when you let all the cash reserves go down to zero," Oscar says. "You missed the chance I gave you. I settled pennies on the dollar with all your shareholders on your behalf. You don't get a check. You get something better. You are debt free. You have a completely fresh start. That's what you get. That's what I've done for you here."

"We had a deal," Ed says. "It's in writing. I'm going to hire lawyers to go through all your books and sort this out."

"If you can afford lawyers, you are welcome," Oscar says. "But if I were you, I'd focus on your future. Why dwell in the past? You can't change that."

Ed has been counting on that check. His promises to all the inmates were based on that check. The promises he just made in his speech at the train station were based on that check. What he'd most like to do is punch the vulture right in his fat gut, but the last thing Ed needs right now is to get in any more trouble.

Without asking permission, Ed gets in the Cadillac and drives off, forgetting about Hattie and leaving her standing there with Oscar.

On the long highway drive to the beach, in a failed attempt to clear his mind, Ed remains livid, realizing he has limited options. He certainly was counting on having the capital from Oscar to fuel his new master plan to save the mission. But he'll figure something out. The more he thinks about it, having Oscar out of town and out of his life and being completely debt-free might be enough of a blessing, as long as at least one other thing works out for him that he's also been thinking about these last few years in prison.

He arrives at The Cloisters Hotel and knocks on the door of his favorite hotel suite, which overlooks the ocean. After a few moments, all is indeed right again in the world as his sweet Mabel opens the door, and seeing his smiling face, she can't help but welcome him into her arms.

CHAPTER 64

♦ ♦ ♦

The following day, after using the fanciest toilet he's had access to in years, Ed splashes water on his face and styles his hair in the large mirror in the hotel suite bathroom. Getting his look just right, he quietly tiptoes naked through the natural light pouring into the hotel room, which reflects off the ocean surface out in the distance, and slips back gently into bed with his wife.

He looks over to see Mabel, who is awake, smiling at him. She has the covers up on her, but her bare shoulders are exposed, and he can feel under the covers that they are both still in a state of desire left over from being apart for so long.

She welcomes him to nuzzle next to her. Simply feeling her bare skin touching up against his is a remembrance that moments like this are really all he needs in life. He'll find more money, but there is only one Mabel.

"Where should we start on your first day back?" Mabel asks him. "We can walk on the beach. We can stay here in the room. We can go back to our house."

"Your house."

"Right, my house. You can help me in the garden. All is right again now. Not a worry in the world."

All of that certainly sounds lovely to Ed, but it isn't exactly his plan.

"I'm going to rent the office space Oscar just vacated," Ed says. "I already have my mail being forwarded there. I might need to borrow just a little money from you to set up the office. I'm hoping you'll help me decorate it just like you have all my other ones. I have a notebook full of ideas. I'm hoping to pitch you a few of them. I'm curious to hear your favorites on the list. All require very little capital to get started, but all have big payoffs which we need to make the investors whole."

Ed would have continued on and on, but Mabel pushes away from him and gets violently out of bed. He assumes she is going to use the bathroom but instead starts to quickly put on her clothes.

"We don't have to get started just this moment," he says. "Come back to bed for a moment. I'm not that anxious to get going. I can make other priorities."

He puts his hand on her shoulder, but she pushes it off as she continues to get dressed. He's finally realizing now that he has upset her. From behind, he puts his arms around her and squeezes her until she can't move. She eventually stops struggling and seems to accept his embrace.

"What would you have me do?" he finally says.

"Live with me," she says. "Be with me… in the moment. Live out the rest of our lives together. Enjoy our family and our friends. I have enough saved up that we shouldn't have any real cares in the world. Claire and I even built a rental home in town that already has a paying tenant. We have income this time around, Eddie. We don't have to start a new business. We're all set."

Ed wonders how much equity Mabel might have in that rental home versus debt and how much they might be able to borrow against it, but instead of asking for the specifics, he's smart enough to let that question go.

"I have something to show you," Ed says.

He hops out of bed naked and rummages around his briefcase before pulling out a printed newspaper flier of some sort. He hands it to her to look over.

The first thing she notices at the very top is the banner that reads "Lewis Journal Volume I." After a quick scan of the content, her face turns from one of interest to one of pure terror.

"It's just a way for all my investors to keep tabs on me," Ed says. "It costs them just a dollar a month to subscribe, and, in return, I'll keep them abreast of what I'm working on to pay them back."

"But you don't need to pay them back," Mabel says. "Oscar settled all the debts. Everyone is fine. They have moved on with their lives. You apparently haven't moved on, but they have moved on. The mission was to build Atascadero and it is built."

"Nonsense," Ed says. "The investors and people of this town are counting on me. It's just that I can't afford any longer—now that the donations have run out—to mail them updates and respond to all their letters. This journal takes care of all of that and gives me just a bit of income to set up shop and get my enterprises going again."

What Mabel does next, Ed could have never expected, as she rips the journal into shreds. She tears it into as many small pieces as possible.

"You are banned from promotional mailers for life," she says. "For life. Suppose the judge or Fulton or anyone sees this, Eddie. You'll be…. Don't you realize what you'll be?"

"What do you mean?" Ed says. "It's already in the mail. It's already been sent."

"Sent where? To whom?"

"Hattie brought me the entire mailing list to Seattle," Ed says. "The whole prison helped me. We used the little press we have there to print copies of it and sent it to the entire mailing list on the prison's dime. The guys worked around the clock for me the past few days. We used the last cash I had left from donations to get it in the mail to everyone to thank the investors and to give them a way to stay in contact with me just by subscribing to the new journal. It's all set. It's done. It's fine."

But Ed can tell by Mabel's face that it is not fine with her. She's desperate to get dressed as fast as possible. No matter what he says, she isn't listening to him. Occupied with trying to get her to face him, he doesn't hear the knock at the door. Or the subsequent knocks. Or soon the pounding.

Mabel is crying hysterically, trying to get fully dressed and get out of the room, when suddenly, the door smashes open. That clearly startles both Ed and her as armed marshals storm into the room, guns out, and tackle Ed, still naked, to the ground.

In what seems like no time at all, they drag him out in front of the hotel, where all the other guests have gathered now to see him shackled and loaded naked into the back of a paddy wagon.

Ed notices the disappointed looks on the faces of the Atascadero residents, most of whom he knows personally, who are also staying at the hotel. In front of the crowd, he also sees Inspector Fulton's disappointed face, who Ed now realizes is both among the marshals and part of the raid.

Ed's last image he remembers of the scene at the hotel is the look of utter heartbreak on Mabel's face as she attempts to close what is left of the battered hotel door and retreat back into the room to establish some form of privacy and dignity.

Even more than his own embarrassment of being shackled naked in a police wagon, Ed already knows the last image of Mabel's face is what will haunt him for years to come.

CHAPTER 65

◆ ◆ ◆

For the next fifteen years of Ed's life in prison, he's not even allowed access to a mirror. No sunlight and no mirror.

Ed puts on his gray jumpsuit and doesn't even attempt to comb what is left of his hair at this point. He's not allowed to have a comb anyway. For a time, he would attempt some sense of order to his appearance by combing his hair with his fingers. But in recent years, he doesn't even bother any longer. In fact, he has no idea what he actually looks like. He can't remember the last time he's seen his own face or even his own reflection.

Each morning, on the walk to the cafeteria, just about everyone he passes goes out of their way to bump him into a wall, a door frame, and even into a trash can. Any food globbed onto his plate is back to being bland and terrible, not just for him but for the entire prison.

Gone is the prison farm. Gone is the office work program. Gone are the smiles, especially on the faces of the other inmates and the guards. Certainly, not on Walter, who can only be seen these days by anyone up high, overlooking the yard, and at a distance with no relationship with any of the inmates. Ed overheard a guard say one time that Betty had left Walter and McNeil Island for good shortly after Ed was returned to the prison.

Ed hasn't spoken to Walter or been in his office since he was first brought back. Walter wanted Ed at the time to witness him having to pack up his prized "Best Prison" trophy and mail it back, given he'd been forced to return it over the issue with Ed's printed newsletter.

Not only was the prize rescinded, but Walter also had the honor of telling Ed that the judge had updated Ed's sentence so that Ed is now banned for life from using the mails in any way, shape, or form. He's now been entirely cut off from society. Walter had the great privilege of informing Ed that he is one of the first Americans to be entirely and lawfully denied First Amendment rights.

Upon his arrival, Ed was assigned to cafeteria duty, but inmates refused to eat off of any plate he served. He would glob food on their plate, and they would toss the plate right back at him. After that, he was given latrine duties, but again, the inmates would just toss his mop and water bucket at him—or worse.

Eventually, Ed was assigned laundry duty alone in the basement. Every day after that, week after week, month after month, and then year after year, Ed spent washing jumpsuits and towels. Just for fun, on occasion, Walter would assign the least desirable prisoners in the penitentiary to accompany Ed in the bowels of the facility.

A good day was when no one spoke to him. A bad day was most days when the other prisoners working with him got bored and tried to shove him into the wash bins or worse.

He never really thinks about what day or year it is any longer. But he is reminded of his birthday each year because that is the day he is granted his only access to the outside world. That is the day Hattie continues to visit him for some reason he'll never understand.

It's always the same. He's shackled to a table even though all the other prisoners in the visitation room are free to move around and visit their wives and families.

When Hattie sits down, she gets out a comb and works to make him presentable. He puts up a fight each time, arguing it isn't necessary, but he must admit he does eventually enjoy her gentle touch on his scalp. Occasionally, she rests her hands on his face. Sometimes she brushes up against him, trying to get his hair just right. But mostly, instead of any form of arousal, he feels sorry for her instead of feeling what he should be feeling, which is gratitude.

"Why do you even bother coming?" Ed says.

"That's nonsense," Hattie says. "I look forward to it."

"Why do you still live in Atascadero?" he asks. "You said Rose is living in Sacramento now with her new husband. They are all building houses now or something with Larry and Lawrence. Why don't you join them? I'm sure Lawrence would love that."

"No, no," she says. "I love my house. I'm proud of my house. I love my town. I visit Sacramento often. I'm fine. Don't fuss about me."

"Or get married or something," he says. "Do something."

"Maybe one day. Like you always say, it's just a matter of timing. The timing just hasn't worked out yet."

That's an understatement for both of them to say the least, Ed thinks to himself.

Each visit is also exactly the same in that at the very end, Ed can't help but to ask about Mabel. Hattie will never tell him anything until he asks. She'll tell him that Claire is still in the same routine and that the new U.S. Route 101 multi-lane freeway is, unfortunately, planned to cut right through Ed's beautiful mall and sunken gardens in the center of town.

She's quick to tell him that a few more factories have opened in town and that Mare is still as ornery as ever. But never anything about Mabel until the very last moment, right before the guards announce the last call.

"Is she still going to San Diego?" Ed finally asks.

"She isn't, actually."

That's the first news that has made Ed happy in years.

"Does she ever ask about me after you visit?" he asks.

"She has no idea I visit. I've never mentioned it. Maybe someone has told her. I don't know. But it doesn't come up when we run into each other."

"Why doesn't she travel to San Diego any longer?" he can't help but ask. "Do you know why?"

"I do," Hattie says. "J.H. passed away this past spring."

She can tell by Ed's face this is fascinating news on a number of levels.

"Rumor is, and it's just rumored," she says, "that J.H. may have left all that money to Mabel. But you'd never know it if it were true. Her routine is still exactly the same. Gardening, renting out homes, volunteering. Everyone in town still loves her. She's exactly the same. Nobody really has any idea what is true and what isn't."

For the next year, while Ed is dealing with being bullied and just generally trying to get through his time in prison, he'll play back his conversation with Hattie over and over again in his mind. More importantly, he plays over what he plans to say to Mabel when he is eventually released.

He's going to walk up to her and say, "There are only two things in the world that matter to me. You and whatever it is you'd like me to do for you. I only do your bidding from here on out. Nothing else."

He says those three sentences over and over again in his mind. Over and over again. The only reason he is still alive now is for the chance to maybe get to say that to her.

"I only do your bidding from here on out. Nothing else."

CHAPTER 66

◆ ◆ ◆

Ed still has no sense of time. Other than his daily routine, he's only reminded of the season or time of year when Hattie comes to see him on his birthday.

Today, however, the guards find him in the laundry room to tell him he has a visitor. Oddly, it doesn't feel, for some reason, like it's been a full year. Regardless, Ed doesn't bother to mess with his hair or his appearance as he follows the guards to the visitation room, where they shackle him like always to an empty table.

Ed watches all the other visitors come in. It is primarily inmates' wives. On occasion, their mothers. Sometimes their kids and families. Ed watches everyone pair up, but he's still sitting alone and shackled when a man in a freshly pressed three-piece suit approaches him.

The man's face is familiar, but Ed can't quite place him. It's been over fifteen years, and he's had no visitors other than Hattie. This man is older, probably in his 60s, like Ed is now. The man kind of looks like an older Fulton, which then allows Ed's mind to drift a moment, wondering if Fulton has any siblings and, if so, what their personalities could possibly be like. Then Ed's mind shifts to wondering what Fulton wears if he's not working. Ed's only ever seen him in uniform. Does Fulton own any other clothes?

The man sits down in front of Ed, but it isn't until he speaks that Ed realizes it is Fulton.

"Eddie, you look a mess," Fulton says. "We're going to have to clean you up somehow. But we have a few days to do it."

"Where is your uniform?" Ed says, "Don't tell me you…."

"Retired," Fulton says, still instinctively reaching for the buttons on his sleeve that are no longer there. "I requested a leave of duty to come get you, but at my age, the request wasn't accepted. So, I was forced to retire."

"Come get me?" Ed says.

"Yes, to come get you."

"You mean visit me?"

"I'm here to take you home," Fulton says. "You're being released into my custody."

"I don't understand anything you are saying."

"I'm not doing this for you. I didn't retire for you. I retired for…I had to retire for Claire. It is at her request that I took a leave of absence to come get you."

"For Claire?"

"For Mabel, actually. She is very sick. You need to come home, and the judge and prosecutor have allowed it. I'm here to take you home to Mabel."

Ed is now lost in thought. Not about Claire asking Fulton for help. Not about Fulton giving up the Postal Service for Claire. Not about the fact that he's apparently about to get out of the hell he's been in for God only knows how long. But his mind is spinning, given he's just learned the love of his life is sick. He is so lost in that thought that he doesn't realize he is mumbling out loud.

"There are only two things in the world that matter to me," Ed says. "You and whatever it is you'd like me to do for you. I only do your bidding from here on out. Nothing else."

"You're speaking nonsense," Fulton says. "If anything, you should say that to Mabel, not me. Let's go back to your cell, collect your belongings, say your goodbyes, and head home."

"I don't want anything from here," Ed says, "or to say anything to anyone."

"Fine, we have just one stop to make, and then we'll get there as fast as the train allows."

"No stops."

"Claire insisted on one other thing. She gave me the money for it."

"What could that possibly be?"

"When was the last time you looked in a mirror? I'm to find a barber and a tailor and to clean you up before we arrive. Claire insisted."

Ed couldn't care less about any of that. He just wants to see Mabel. But he also knows that Fulton has been a civil servant his entire life and is used to taking orders. Ed's intent is to live the rest of his life in the service of Mabel. Clearly, Fulton now serves Claire, so he gets it.

"Let's leave immediately," Ed says. "But there is maybe one last thing I'd like to do before we go."

"And that is?"

"Get these off of me," Ed says, referencing his shackles.

Fulton brings over a guard to unhook Ed for the last time. As soon as the handcuffs are released, Ed comes around the table and gives Fulton a huge hug, which draws the attention of the entire room.

Many in the room have never seen two grown men hug before. They clearly don't like witnessing it. Ed couldn't care less. Fulton would like the hug to end as well because not only is Ed entirely disheveled, but he also smells terrible and has lice crawling around in what is left of his ratty hair.

Unfortunately, Fulton thinks to himself, it is now going to take them even longer to get home. Ed is going to need a delousing, full shower, shave, haircut, and an entirely new wardrobe.

And so is Fulton.

CHAPTER 67

A few days later, Ed and Fulton step off the train in Atascadero to zero fanfare. There are no banners. No crowds. No well-wishers. There is no interest in them whatsoever as they walk from the train station to Mabel's big white house, which still stands out compared to all the other homes and buildings that now exist.

Along their walk, Ed doesn't recognize any residents they pass. He thought he might have recognized one woman, but all these years later, he couldn't be sure. He notices that most of the lots are built now, but he estimates it is still only maybe fifty percent of what he had envisioned all those years ago. Los Angeles and San Francisco have dwarfed Atascadero at this point in 1935.

On the train ride, Fulton caught Ed up on world events. Fulton thinks Ed would have loved the Roaring Twenties. Fulton said it was amazing for the overall economy, not to mention for real estate and consumer goods. The Dooley Doll factory and all factories were booming. Fulton found the growth of the mails in that decade to be especially unprecedented.

Fulton also explains that as great as the Roaring Twenties were, in the last six years, the economy has suffered possibly the greatest depression America will ever know. Ed learns that the downturn immediately after the Great War was nothing compared to now. If that weren't bad enough, bolstered by rhetoric that the Treaty of Versailles was unfair and too stringent, a new Nazi political party in Germany is threatening a second world war that promises to be even larger than the first.

As disappointed as Ed is to learn all of this, the thing most disappointing to him, which causes him to pause a moment even though he's so close to finally seeing Mabel, is seeing for himself the construction of the new U.S. Route 101 multi-lane freeway that has cut Atascadero's mall and beautiful sunken garden into two sections. The powers in D.C. literally decided to slice the town in half, even separating the Community Center from the Administration Building.

Alphonse especially would have been disappointed to see this, Ed thinks, given the new highway is being constructed right over the site where Ed had always promised a community theater would be built. Now that motion pictures have sound, it would have been marvelous to watch movies in that spot. If things had been different, Alphonse might have been preparing to direct a new musical on the stage, maybe with Lt. Malone assisting. Who knows, there might have even been a behind-the-scenes role for Kramer.

When they finally get to Mabel's home, the first to greet him on the porch is a teary-eyed Hattie. At first, Ed thinks Hattie's tears have to do with Mabel, but they don't. She's just happy to see him. All these years later, her smile is still identical to when he first met her at the train station. From her perspective, even to this day, she can't help but be starstruck every time she sees him.

"You're all cleaned up," Hattie says. "The best I could ever do was comb your hair over a bit. Fulton has returned you to glory."

"Glory?" Ed says. "If glory were old and bald."

"That's the first thing I noticed," Claire says, now stepping out on the porch.

They all look fifteen years older, but Claire barely does. It seems she'll always be blessed with perfect skin and a perfect figure, and along with it, a jaw set in stone. Ed opens his arms to hug her, but she's not interested in that at all.

"She's waiting for you inside," Claire says to him in a matter-of-fact and all-business tone. "Choose your words carefully, as always."

"Absolutely," Ed says.

"Very carefully."

"I hear you. I will."

He leaves them all on the porch and heads into the house. The first thing he notices is what used to be his office is now a parlor room designed for sitting, reading, and entertaining. Ed will learn soon enough that what used to be the headquarters for the entire operation is now a place for tea parties, charity fundraisers, and general socializing. Mabel's entire home has been completely re-designed to serve her friends and community. He is surprised to see, though, that his old desk is still in the corner of the room. That's all that remains of his time here. At least, he thinks, she kept something of his.

He makes his way up the stairs to the master bedroom, where he finds the door shut. He's not sure if he should knock or open the door when he hears Mabel's voice inside call out to him.

"Dearest, is that you? Come in."

He opens the door to discover the curtains are all drawn back to allow as much light as possible to enter the room. Ed notices their bed is propped up a bit, allowing, he now realizes, for Mabel to lie in it and see the entire town out her windows. It's an even better view than Ed used to have downstairs in his office. In fact, he's not sure he ever took the time before to look out these windows. He was so busy back then that he often came to bed after it was dark and got up in the morning before the sunrise. He can't recall ever having entertained this vantage point before today.

He expected Mabel to be in bed, but she isn't. He turns instead to find her standing, having just gotten up from a chair. He never imagined she'd be so mobile. She's older. They are both older and grayer. But it is her frailness that captures his attention. She's still so much taller than him, but she's way thinner now. It appears to be an effort for her to spread her arms for a hug. He is scared, though, to fully embrace her. He's afraid he'll crush her in her current state.

"You can't hurt me," Mabel says. "Squeeze me. Love me. I can take it. You can't do any more damage than this cancer has already done."

Now having been given her permission, he obliges, but he still can't risk their full embrace of old. All the greetings from their past are going through his mind now. The charade they used to play on Fridays in Nashville when he returned home to their tiny apartment from being out selling door to door to farm wives all week. When he used to wash up in their little tent after a full day of Atascadero tours. When she came through for him in the courtroom and sat by his side for the world to see. The time they went skinny dipping in the lake they used to have. They've had a lifetime of memorable embraces.

He can't control the tears that are pouring out of him now. He has something to say to her. Words he has memorized for years, but he can't stop blubbering.

Mabel has to help him sit down on the edge of the bed. He should be helping her sit, but here she is again, putting others ahead of herself. He is able to take hold of her hand and get her to sit next to him while he finds the strength to say what he needs to say.

In all the years in prison, Ed has rehearsed his little speech, longing for the chance to deliver it. He's now realizing he forgot to imagine what her reaction might be to what he's about to say. In all the years of rehearsing his lines over and over, could those words really be about him and not her?

What does she want from him? He wants her to know he's so very sorry and he really will change this time. But what does she really want? All he had to do was ask Claire. Or even Fulton. Why hadn't he done that?

He looks at his wife's beautiful but frail face. She's waiting for him to say what he needs to say.

"There are only two things in the world that matter to me," Ed says. "You and whatever it is you'd like me to do for you. I only do your bidding from here on out. Nothing else."

Mabel just smiles at him.

"Well, it's about damn time," she says.

CHAPTER 68

One might think Atascadero is too big now for the entire community to attend a single event as they used to in the past. Only the residents who've been here since the beginning know Ed personally, but the entire town knows Mabel—the wife of the founder of Atascadero, who lives in the big white house whose doors are always open to the entire community. Two months after Ed has returned home, the entire town does indeed turn out for Mabel's funeral.

Ed was able to meet or reacquaint with nearly all of them over the last two months as they dropped by at some point or another to bid their farewells to Mabel. There was some trial and error, but Ed eventually learned how to entertain. He learned to make and serve lemonade. He even figured out how to wash all the glasses afterward. He learned those skills, along with a bunch of other simple domestic ones he had never done before, all while keeping his word and being of service to Mabel.

He learned to wash dishes. To clean the house. To make simple meals. To sweep the porch. To buy groceries. To tend the garden. One night, he even prepared an entire meal from scratch for Mabel, Claire, and Fulton. All the way from planning the menu to cooking the food, serving it, and even cleaning up afterward all by himself.

He'd never once before performed any of these tasks in his life. The only thing that Mabel didn't have to teach him to do was the laundry. He is an expert at laundry from his time in prison. She may have even learned a trick or two from him in that department. Everything else he learned as quickly as he could from her in the little time they had left.

Mabel also taught Ed how to make small talk. After he served lemonade to guests, she would often grab his hand and indicate he was to sit with her and join in on the conversation, despite there not being an agenda. By complying, he now knows everyone in town. He knows their names, their kids' names, what they do for fun, and their opinion on whether there will be another world war. He even knows their views on California, its promise, and what it is actually shaping up to be.

Often he listened to them talk about local newspaper articles, including a recent trend of automobile crashes being caused by deer dashing out in front of headlights given that cars are more routinely driving at night.

Sometimes, Mabel's visitors brought along letters with them from early residents who had moved away and asked that they read a story or memory to Mabel for them. Surprisingly, Ed didn't miss his old career since returning home. Serving Mabel and taking care of the house, he quickly learned, was an occupation in and of itself that, if done right, required the totality of his time and efforts. But he did miss one thing from his former life. As the guests read letters, he realized how much he missed receiving mail.

When the letters were opened in front of him, he imagined it must have felt to him like it felt to a recovering alcoholic who had to sit in a room where alcohol was present. He's in the room. He's listening. He's participating. But the entire time, he's wondering what it would feel like not just to hold a letter again but to find a letter addressed to him. Never again would he be able to feel the excitement of discovering his name on an envelope, wondering what could be in it, and enduring the surprise of opening it. It is the only daily reminder of his former transgressions.

Fulton took his new occupation very seriously by sitting on Mabel's front porch every single day until the mailman arrived. Fulton was the first to inspect the day's delivery, making sure there was nothing accidentally delivered for Ed, before bringing it to Mabel.

At first, Fulton just set the mail near her, but over time, as she grew frailer, Mabel asked Fulton to open the mail for her using a beautiful letter opener she had purchased in an antique shop years ago. Fulton found the letter opener to be one of the shiniest things he had ever had the privilege to handle. Nothing could match the buttons he used to get to wear on his postal uniform, but it quickly became the best part of his day—retrieving the letter opener from the drawer to see it glisten in the sunlight.

Ed fantasized that, just once, a letter to him might one day slip through from somewhere, anywhere. Maybe someday Fulton will let his guard down and miss one. But Ed knew that was crazy thinking. As long as Fulton is alive, Ed will never see a piece of mail addressed to him ever again.

A few days ago, Ed had Mabel all propped up in bed overlooking the city through her windows when she started to get up, saying she could use some water. He implored her to lay back on the bed as he ran down the stairs to fetch it. When he came back up, she had passed. He wasn't sure what to do, but then he realized what she would do. He simply took her hand in his and admired the view out the window of the city they had designed together. He built the buildings, but it was Mabel who made it a community.

It's not until Ed walks back to Mabel's house after all the funeral festivities are over for today that something dawns on him for the first time. The big house is now his. Her bank accounts—whatever is in them—are now his. He's no longer a ward of the state. Or a servant to his beloved wife. He may not have access to the mails, but he does now have assets.

He returns home to find his entire family waiting for him at the house. He's forgotten they had all made plans to visit privately together after the public events are over. Everyone is there; George and Lucile and their kids; Marcella and Larry and their kids; Rose and her new husband, Bill, and their new kids, along with Rose's daughter she had with Teddy. Hattie and Lawrence are there. Claire and Fulton. Even Ed's brother, John, has showed along with his estranged wife, Marguerite.

Ed doesn't pick up on the fact that they were all waiting for him to finish thanking well-wishers and return home. Instead of greeting them, he races upstairs and all the way up to the attic. He had heard Mabel mention one time she had stashed away some of his old belongings. He rummages through boxes, wondering if maybe, just maybe, she has kept something in particular he has in mind. It wouldn't surprise him at all if she had thrown it away or burned it, but he has to see.

In the boxes, he finds old copies of the *Woman's Magazine*, the *California Illustrated Review*, the wartime *Illustrated Review*, dozens of the other women's magazines he had published, brochures about Atascadero, brochures about Palos Verdes, a piggy-bank replica of the People's Bank Egyptian building, American Women's League pamphlets, and even an old box of Bug Chalk. She was generous enough to keep all of that for him, but what he was really looking for he finally finds in the bottom of the last box—his old idea notebook, containing all his business ideas since they were first married. He'd last seen it in the hotel room he shared with her at The Cloisters. Despite his being hauled back to jail that day, she kept it for him. She could have thrown it in the ocean or burned it or worse. But his sweet Mabel didn't.

He leaves all his former magazines and business paraphernalia strewn about in the attic, holding his prized idea notebook as if it were made of gold as he heads back downstairs to the parlor.

All he wants to do is grab some paper and pens and sit at his desk to go through the notebook, looking for the biggest ideas that do not involve in any way, shape, or form the use of the mails. Most ideas in the book he recalls do require the mails, but he remembers many in there do not.

As he barges into the parlor, it again takes him a moment to realize that everyone has been waiting for him. All eyes are on him. He finally stops and looks at them. He has no idea what this is about. Do they want him to say something? Or do something? Or serve them lemonade? He's entirely unsure what is going on until John finally stands up, holding legal documents.

"Mabel asked that I be the trustee of her will and estate," John says. "I've never been able to turn down that sweet woman in my entire life. So, of course, I accepted. I helped her put her wishes down on paper years ago, and we refreshed them again a few months ago. She asked that you all gather after her funeral, and, well, here we all are, finally."

The word "finally" is clearly a nod at Ed, which he finally picks up on, along with a few sly smiles from some of the adults in the room who have long known him.

"There's not much to Mabel's will, actually," John says. "It's pretty simple. First, how generous of her to have set aside college funds for every single child in this room to be administered by me. There's plenty for all of them and even ones that may yet come."

All the parents are certainly appreciative, but it is Claire especially who is visibly choked up by this gesture, thinking back to what brought her to Atascadero all those years ago. For the first time since Ed has known Claire, he watches in awe as emotion overcomes her. So much so that her own twins and even Fulton don't know how to console her. They've rarely had to before. They all rally to hug and support her.

It takes a while to get Claire settled as John continues.

"Mabel would also like her antique letter opener to go to Fulton as a symbol of both his storied career in the Postal Service and his continued duty to support an old friend."

John hands Fulton the letter opener, and now Fulton is all choked up with the twins and Claire trying to console him. Ed is still thinking about the phrase "continued duty to support an old friend." Is that old friend him or Claire or Mabel? He makes a mental note to ask John later what Mabel meant.

"Mabel also added something recently to the will," John says. "This is addressed to you, Eddie. I'll read her exact words."

Ed is still holding his notebook. Subconsciously, he tries to hide it as John continues.

"It reads, 'Dearest Eddie, I loved you from the moment I met you, and that love has never wavered. There have been times over the years where I didn't always like you, but I always loved you.'"

All eyes are on Ed now. He smiles. He can't deny he often gave her reasons not to like him, and he has always loved her. But she's never given him a reason not to like her. Ever.

"'I married a dreamer,'" John continues reading Mabel's words, "'and I never want you ever for the rest of your life ever to stop dreaming. To that end, I have a feeling you are going to get out your old notebook of ideas at some point.'"

His family realizes that must be what Ed is already sheepishly holding in his hands. His instinct still is to try to hide it, but it is too late. They all see it. The same sly smiles appear again from the adults in the room who really know him.

"'Please never stop filling that notebook with ideas until the day you die, and then come see me in the afterlife and tell me all about them. I can't wait to hear them. I don't know what they'll let us do in heaven, but if your ideas are about helping people, we'll do everything we can to help you make them happen, just like we did in our time together on Earth.'"

Now Ed is losing his composure. She sure did, Ed thinks to himself. It was her loan to him in a hospital all those years ago that led to his empire in St. Louis. It was her loan again in her pottery studio at their home in University City that led to Atascadero. She's always said if she had money, she'd be his first investor, and she always has kept her word throughout their entire marriage. By leaving him the rest of her estate, she's about to do it again.

"'But I was never good at keeping you in check, and I'm no longer on Earth to try. As such, all the rest of my accounts, rental homes, my home, and all of my assets I'm leaving to my sister Claire and not you, Eddie. I'm sorry, Dearest, but not to you.'"

There are audible gasps in the room as all eyes are on Claire to see if she knows about this. Though the college funds were a surprise to her, this news appears not to be a surprise as Claire is now looking rather sternly at Ed. All eyes go back to Ed as John finishes.

"'Eddie, there is just one stipulation in that Claire must always give you a room to sleep in as long as you tend to the house and garden, never open your own bank account, and never actually start a new business yourself. As long as you stay in the moment and cherish your friends, your family, and your community, you'll have a roof to live under at no cost for the rest of your life. Claire has agreed to see to all this for me. Yours truly, Mabel.'"

All eyes remain on Ed, still holding his notebook of business ideas. Since Ed first saw Mabel at the dance all those years ago, he has loved her. That will never change. He's also never once in his life had a reason not to like her. As she pointed out, he's given her reasons not to like him, but he's never once not liked her.

That is, until today.

CHAPTER 69

♦ ♦ ♦

Ed wakes up every day back to not caring much about his appearance, but he does at least make a half effort with a comb each morning. He can barely bring himself to look in the guest room mirror. As a result, his shaving routine is infrequent, to put it generously.

He never wants to have to put on a jumpsuit again in his life. He doesn't have any need for a three-piece suit now, either. His daily uniform these days is dungarees, an old shirt, and an apron since Claire runs a tight ship all day, every day, ordering him around the house. Every morning, he takes a deep breath before opening his door to find, like clockwork, a list of chores tacked to it, which dictates his entire day.

For the first few weeks after Mabel's funeral, Ed goes along with Claire's tasks, thinking it will wear off eventually and she'll give him access to Mabel's assets. Over time, surely, he thinks Claire will have felt she has done her service to Mabel, and he'll be out on parole with her, along with a little money. But as time goes on, it is becoming abundantly clear that not only does Claire, along with Fulton's help, seem intent to see Mabel's wishes through forever, but the two of them appear to be optimizing the process as they go along by creating even more complicated tasks for Ed to complete each day.

He can only imagine Claire and Fulton must have secret meetings where they discuss how each day has gone. He envisions them discussing what went well, what didn't go well, and how they can improve on his imprisonment. He's certain they are holding regular retrospectives and reveling in the optimized torture it generates.

His primary fantasy these days is to one day take the daily list of chores Claire has prepared for him, put it in an envelope, seal the envelope, address it to himself, show it to Fulton and Claire, and then put it in the mailbox. In his fantasy, he then pictures their faces as he's hauled back to the penitentiary, all because they are taking their new roles as his warden way too seriously.

Most evenings, Hattie, at least, shows him some kindness as she comes over along with Fulton after dinner. The four of them play card games, and it is always the same. Claire and Fulton team up against Ed and Hattie. Not only do Claire and Fulton almost always win, but they are relentless after each game, talking to each other about the different hands they played and what they could have done differently.

Ed can only beat them on occasion by taking crazy risks with his cards. His partner, Hattie, barely seems even to realize there is a competition going on. She's more interested in having a conversation with Ed across the table while ignoring the other two.

But it is later in the evening after Fulton walks back to his nearby home and Claire goes up to bed, that is the only fun part of his day when Hattie sits out with Ed on the front porch. Ed waits until he is sure Claire is asleep to get out his ideas notebook.

"Do you have the new packaging samples?" Ed asks.

"I do," Hattie says, reaching into her purse and pulling out a small box.

She loves seeing the excitement come over his face as he looks over the artwork and the "Deer Whistle" lettering imprinted on the box. It has taken them a few times to get the image of the deer just how he wants it, both in the headlights of a car at night and also just off to the side of the road and out of danger. A deer whistle is affixed to the car's hood, and a few lines coming out of it match perfectly the lines coming out of the deer's ears, showing the deer has stopped because it hears the whistle.

"Even with the lines, I still think people are going to assume they'll have to listen to the whistle while they are driving," she says.

"Good point. Good point," Ed says. "How about we add 'Only the deer can hear it' to the packaging?"

"I can have them add that, but there's just one issue."

"I know it will cost more," Ed says. "And I can't thank you enough for covering all the costs to date, but we're equal partners on this thing. We're going to sell truckloads of these. They are going to fly off the shelves at all the stores and even restaurant cash registers around here. You can trust me on this."

Hattie watches as Ed's imagination is racing, holding the prototype box in his hand. She's always loved how his mind works. Actually, she loves more than just his mind. She loves him. As a result, she still does his bidding without question and without reward. She even fronts the money. Today, however, she finds herself compelled to ask him a tougher question.

"Why do you do this?" Hattie asks.

"To save lives," Ed says. "I'm tired of reading about people getting hurt in car crashes around here when something can be done about it."

"No, I mean, why do you live here? Here in this prison Claire has built for you." Hattie says. "You can just walk away. I have a house right down over there. You do remember that, right? You've never called on me. I'm right over there. You even sold me the lot all those years ago. What's stopping you?"

She makes a fair point, Ed thinks to himself. Why does he stay in this house? For that matter, why does Claire? Why doesn't Claire move to Sacramento where both of her daughters and her grandchildren live? For that matter, why doesn't Hattie move to Sacramento for the same reason? His whole life, Ed has wondered just that about all old people. Why do they stubbornly stay rooted even when their kids move away?

He tries to articulate to Hattie his attachment to this home and to Mabel's memory and to, even after all these years, secretly finishing out his original mission. He thinks he's doing a good job at explaining his thoughts, but the more he talks, the more Hattie's face changes from one of disappointment to confusion to outright concern, which Ed feels is an overreaction.

The more he talks, the more consternation Hattie shows on her face. Suddenly, she's snapping her fingers in front of him as if she's trying to get his attention, which is odd since he's right there sitting in front of her, having a conversation.

She opens the front door and yells into the house to Claire to help her. Claire doesn't answer, so Hattie decides to run up the stairs to get her, but in doing so, Ed notices Hattie left the Deer Whistle box just lying out in the open on the porch.

He goes to reach for it, but everything is suddenly backward. He reaches to his right, but his hand is somehow going to the left. He takes a step with his right foot, but somehow it is his left foot that moves. Everything is backward.

After some maneuvering, he is able to stand. But for the life of him, he can't seem to get his body over to the packaging to pick it up. Instead, he falls in the wrong direction slamming into the front window of the house, but not hard enough to break it. He tries to turn away from the window, but instead, his body turns toward the window. He just can't get used to making himself go in the opposite direction.

Through the window, he sees Hattie coming back down the stairs with Claire in her nightgown fast behind. Ed still needs to get back to the packaging so Claire doesn't see it when he suddenly notices his own reflection in the window.

His first thought always is where did his hair go and how did he get so old. Everyone tells him he's going to have to get over that, but it still surprises him every time he has to face the reality of looking at his own reflection. But what is especially odd is how the right side of his face looks. Or is it the left side of his face? Regardless, it is drooping. As if all the muscles on that side no longer work. Then he realizes that the reason he's going in circles is because one of his legs and one of his arms are drooping, too. It's the oddest thing.

But he still has to get to the packaging, so all he can think to do is just to fall in the other direction, which he does. Claire and Hattie almost catch him, but they aren't quick enough as he falls right on the packaging, flattening the box.

The rest of that evening is a blur as he remembers bits and pieces of them sitting him up, of Fulton coming over, of someone fetching a doctor, of someone asking him questions, which he answers, and they all act like he isn't making sense even though he clearly is.

All he wants is to try to get Hattie to pick up the packaging before anyone sees it. Finally, the doctor arrives and gives him some kind of sedative.

His last thoughts are of wondering if Hattie is going to remember to grab the packaging or not and of people telling him to quit trying to get up and other people saying the same word over and over to him, which is harder to hear now that the sedative has kicked in.

But as he drifts off to sleep, he can finally make out the word everyone has been saying all night. Something about him maybe having a stroke.

CHAPTER 70

Over the next year, Ed learns the meaning of the phrase "good news, bad news" as he uses his left arm to pull himself up high enough to get a good look at his drooped face in the master bedroom mirror because today is the day, he's told, he needs to learn to shave on his own.

The good news is he's now back to living in the master bedroom of Mabel's house. He's got the best view of Atascadero, and he can see the comings and goings of the entire town. He also hasn't had to do many chores in over a year. His mind is perfect, and he can communicate well enough now with a pencil and a pad of paper.

The bad news is the entire right side of his body doesn't work. The left side is great. His manhood appears intact, not that anyone has ever asked. But for the life of him, he can't get the right side of his body to cooperate. Thus, he can't speak.

Claire, under the experimental guise of physical therapy, still makes him do some chores involving his left hand. She makes him fold napkins, pop peas out of pods, and sprinkle sugar on strawberries. He uses a special railing that George constructed so he can lower himself down the stairs on his own and then crawl back up.

Ed is certain Claire and Fulton are still doing that thing when they get together to discuss even more ways to continually push the limits, as they now have him washing, dressing, combing, and even going to the bathroom by himself, all with just the use of the left side of his body. Shaving, he's told, is next.

The worst is that every day Claire makes him write with his left hand and practice his penmanship. He's right-handed, which makes that especially difficult. Not to mention that if he ever did finish an actual full-length letter, he's still not allowed to send it. But being able to write is helpful for him to at least communicate on occasion.

They are also all back to their evening card games again, in which they cut him zero slack, even making him shuffle cards and deal when his turn comes around. Claire and Fulton are still as relentless as ever about winning. Hattie still couldn't care less about anything except for always making time for Ed and sitting out with him on the porch at night after Claire goes to bed

It seems they got lucky that Claire never found out about the deer whistle, but Ed can no longer risk discussing his business schemes at the house. So, in the afternoons, Hattie instead often wheels Ed down to what's left of the mall area next to the Administration Building where they can workshop ideas in private.

While she's pushing him Ed jots down note after note of things he'd like Hattie to research and do for him. When they get to the mall area he's ready to show his thoughts to her, except there is some kind of large gathering going on this particular day with tables and chairs set up in all directions on the mall. Ed doesn't pay much attention to the crowd as he's thinking about different ways they can market the whistles when Hattie finally stops pushing his wheelchair and kneels down in front of him to get his full attention.

"Do you even know what today is?" Hattie says.

That's a good question, Ed thinks to himself. Tuesday maybe? Thursday? What's it matter? They have work to do.

"It's your birthday," she says. "Your seventieth birthday."

He had absolutely no idea. More importantly, he has his notes to show her.

"You see all those people down there?"

Now that she mentions it, he does.

"They are going to yell surprise in just a minute, and you are going to act surprised and gracious," she says. "I'm telling you now because you've been through so much, and the last thing I need to witness is you having a heart attack. Do you understand me?"

It takes him a while to comprehend what she is saying, but he does. *What terrible timing.* He only has so much time left to get his new business off the ground. If he could talk, he'd tell her to turn him around, but instead she wheels him right toward the crowd.

As soon as they get a little closer, the entire mall of people yells "SURPRISE." Everyone Ed knows is there. Surprisingly, everyone in town is there, along with his entire family. He's slowly coming to terms with the fact they won't be getting any work done today.

Ed notices that even the twins are there with their families having come down from Sacramento. Rose's new husband, Bill, who treats Hattie like his own mother, gives her a huge hug and a kiss, and leads her over to greet her grandchildren. He's no substitute for Teddy, but Hattie certainly has grown to love him nonetheless.

Of course it is Lawrence who is the first to run over to Ed with his hand outstretched. Ed attempts to shake it with his good hand, but Lawrence slightly moves his hand further away.

"You almost got it, big guy," Lawrence says. "Keep going. Keep going."

Ed is about to stand up on his good leg and strangle him.

"We got to get you back to one hundred percent," Lawrence says, still slightly moving his hand out of Ed's reach. "Come on, big guy, you can do it."

What Ed would prefer to do is punch Lawrence in the balls, but he stretches a little further and does, indeed, eventually, shake Lawrence's hand. Lawrence is happy with himself.

"I knew you could do it. I knew it, " Lawrence says, now leaning down in front of Ed to say something privately.

"I've never properly thanked you. Larry is still upset about the merger and all that and having to move, but you taught us everything. Do you realize Larry is now the largest homebuilder in Sacramento? That's because of what we learned here and from you. You're just a gift to so many people, and I wanted you to know that."

Well, Ed thinks, that is very kind of Lawrence to say that. If he could talk, he would tell Lawrence it is the other way around. He learned from him that he doesn't always have to go big in business. He can start small and kind of bootstrap his way through it by selling a few and then rolling the profits into more sales. Not all businesses have to take on investors. It is Ed who should be thanking Lawrence for reminding him to start simple and work his way up, which he intends to do with the Deer Whistle.

Lawrence eventually gives way to others who have lined up to talk with Ed. Next up is his brother George.

"Listen," George says, leaning in close to Ed. "I know you know this, but you've always been and will always continue to be my idol. Remember, I was a laborer before you took me under your wing. Now I'm leading national sales again at my new company, and I'm next in line to be the general manager when the current one retires. I could have never had this opportunity without you. Do you realize what you've done for Lucile and me and the life we've been able to give our kids? I'll never be able to thank you enough. I'm still learning from you. I still wish I could be more like you in many ways."

If Ed could talk, he'd tell George it is the other way around. Watching George have success in his career, despite having to move twice because of him, while also making time for his family, is inspiring. Ed never did that. It was always work first and foremost for him. No, he should have been more like George.

Next in line is brother John, who takes Ed's good hand in his.

"There's one thing you'll always be able to do that I can't," John says. "And that is to draw a crowd. Look around. I could never do what you do. I can service a contract after it is signed or tell you all the risks, but I could never make the actual sale or even come up with the idea. I'll always be in awe of you for that. Always. And that's why Mabel always loved you more than me. I can get the job done, but you're the steak and the sizzle everyone loves."

If Ed could talk, he'd tell John just the opposite. Anyone can get up there and make promises. But John is the person every salesman needs. Someone to sort out the details and actually deliver on them. Ed has always considered himself lucky that he was the first to talk to Mabel. If John had gotten there first, there is no way Ed could have ever competed with him. No way.

Just about everyone at the party comes up and talks to Ed at some point, and it is all the same. They gush and gush about what Ed has meant to them through the years. Each time Ed longs to say it is actually the other way around, but he just can't make his mouth form the words.

Eventually, Mare quiets down the entire party as she has something to say to everyone.

"I'm excited about today," Mare says. "But maybe not for the reasons you might think. This is the first time since I've been in Atascadero that I get to do all the talking, and there is nothing Ed over there can do about it."

The entire party bursts into laughter as Ed can only shake a finger at her in jest.

"But I'm also excited to make a proclamation today in Atascadero," Mare says. "From here on out, March 4th will forever be celebrated right here on this mall. Starting today, March 4th, in Atascadero, is to be forever known as E.G. Lewis Day."

With that, the entire crowd erupts into applause. Ed has no choice but to soak it all in. His entire life, he has indeed attracted a crowd. He's also then had the opportunity, until today, to say a few words. This crowd is used to that, and they quiet down as if they are expecting him to say something. But, of course, they must be forgetting he can't.

It's at that moment that Claire and Fulton walk up to Ed, kneel down in front of him, and take his notebook out of his hand. He's afraid they are going to read it or take it permanently away from him, but instead they flip to a blank page and hand it right back.

"You think we were just making you write with your left hand to torture you? We were just preparing you for your next big speech," Claire says. "Write down what you want to say to all these people and I'll read it for you."

She puts the pencil in his hand and has the paper all ready for him.

"However, it is true that no one in the world infuriates either Fulton or me more than you do."

"And we'll never fully trust you," Fulton adds.

"But we'll always root for you," Claire says. "You make it very hard for us not to continue to love you."

"And we would have never met without you," Fulton says. "Neither would the majority of the people gathered here today."

Fulton actually takes Claire's hand in his, which surprises even her. Ed can barely keep himself together looking at them and all the other couples holding hands. Now that he thinks about it, most of the couples did meet because of him.

"Now, you've never passed up an opportunity to give a speech in your entire life," Claire says. "Don't miss your chance now. Go ahead. What do you want to tell all these dear family and friends who have gone out of their way to celebrate you and all you've accomplished?"

Ed looks out again at the crowd. They are indeed eagerly waiting for what he has to say to them. Ed begins to scribble as Claire has trained him, but he instead puts down the pencil, in what Claire initially thinks is out of frustration, until she realizes he'd much rather just attempt to say it.

"Go on then," she says. "Give it a try."

Ed musters a deep breath and goes for it.

"It," he says, wondering if he's making any sense.

But he can tell he is making sense as Claire and Fulton suddenly nod in encouragement. He is apparently making sense for the first time since his stroke.

"It," he starts over, "is…me…who…should…thank…you."

Tremendous cheers ring out from the crowd. They are all elated that he successfully made the effort to speak, and they couldn't be happier for him. After soaking in their applause for a moment, Ed then takes Claire's hand in his and pulls her closer.

"Almost…," he says, pulling her even closer. "Almost…pulled…it…off."

Claire just shakes her head. If only Ed could realize that all his idols like Hearst and other 'successful men' like that can't take their castles or artwork or statues or gold or even their young girlfriends with them when they leave this Earth.

"You have an entire day named after you," Claire says. "And a mall full of people who love you and will forever view you as a martyr who sacrificed his freedom and his wealth to build a community here that is even better than the one you promised in your brochure."

That sentiment is more than Ed can process. It's certainly not how he's ever viewed himself. He's fixated, always, on what he's yet to accomplish.

"Look around," Claire implores, "you've achieved your mission. If this isn't having 'pulled it off,' then what is?"

CHAPTER 71

◆ ◆ ◆

That evening, Claire, Fulton, and Hattie have another surprise for Ed. Claire called ahead to a restaurant in a neighboring town and made a reservation for Hattie and Ed for dinner. Hattie picks Ed up in her auto. Just the two of them.

The only downside is Ed has to use a wheelchair, but otherwise, it is an amazing feeling for him to be driven away from the house and out into the world, away from the prying and watchful eyes of Claire and Fulton.

At the restaurant, Hattie gets him all situated at the table as the waiter comes over to take their orders. The waiter takes Hattie's order and then asks her an additional question.

"And what would he like," the waiter says to Hattie.

"Ask him yourself," Hattie says.

"My apologies," the waiter says, turning to Ed. "What can I get you, sir?"

"Have…read…papers bout…car crashes…deer?" Ed asks, slurring his words but annunciating enough of them clearly here and there for the waiter to understand.

"Um, you are referring to news stories about deer jumping out into car headlights?" the waiter says. "Yes, yes, I have read that. It's a terrible new trend."

Ed smiles, though the waiter can't really tell as only half of Ed's lip is moving. The waiter now notices Ed is holding out something for him to grab. The waiter takes what turns out to be a rectangular packaged product from Ed's hand and starts to catch on now that he's not going to be taking his food order anytime soon as the waiter puts his notepad and pencil aside to take a better look at the box he is now holding.

The waiter looks over the imagery on the package and eventually forms a smile on his face.

"How smart," he says. "I almost hit a deer the other night driving home. So, you put this whistle on your hood, and it scares them away?"

Ed nods, but his nod kind of makes his head go to the side as if he's saying no instead of yes. Hattie picks up on the potential for confusion and can't stop herself from helping him out.

"That's right," Hattie says to the waiter. "The deer can hear the car coming from far away. Ed here invented it himself."

The waiter is smiling and nodding, not noticing Ed shoot Hattie a look as if to say, "I got this. Stay out of it." She gets the hint and tries her best to stay quiet going forward.

"But the only thing is," the waiter says, "I wouldn't want to listen to this thing whistle the whole time I'm driving. That would drive me crazy."

"Look…pack..ging. It…on…it." Ed says.

The waiter doesn't understand him. Ed says the same nonsense a few more times. Hattie is doing everything she can to not say anything, but eventually, the waiter has to look to her for help. She just kind of motions her eyes at the packaging. Eventually, the waiter gets the hint and looks a little closer.

"Oh," he says, now reading the smaller print on the package. "'Only the deer can hear the whistle.' So smart. Love it."

The waiter starts to hand the box back to Ed when he thinks for a moment.

"Wait. Would you be willing to sell this one to me?" he asks. "In fact, do you have more? What if we bought a few from you and we try to sell them up by the cash register? Just think of the lives we might save on our customers' drives home, even tonight."

Ed is doing that thing again where he is enthusiastically nodding yes, but it appears instead he is nodding no.

"He's saying 'yes,'" Hattie says, unable to help herself. "Yes, we have a display box of a dozen whistles in the trunk of my car."

"Great. I'll talk to the owner about it now. I'm sure I can talk him into it."

As the waiter leaves, Hattie can tell Ed is pleased with himself. Very pleased indeed. After they finish eating and after a conversation with the owner, Hattie fetches a whole display box of deer whistles out from the trunk, and Ed shakes the restaurant owner's hand as Hattie collects money from their first sale.

As Hattie helps Ed into the car, she can't ever remember him being so happy. He's almost a different person now, mumbling on and on about all the other area restaurants they need to visit over the next few weeks and insisting she keeps all the money they just made and use it to buy more inventory.

Hattie loves seeing him excited. As she situates him in the car, she can't help herself and takes real liberty, even while he is still trying to talk, to kiss him for the first time squarely on his lips.

This is something she's been wanting to do since they first met. The timing was never right. But when will it ever be better than today? Now's the time, she decides. After a few moments, she leans back from the kiss to gauge his reaction.

At first, by the expression on his face, she thinks she's made a terrible mistake and tries to hurry up and shut the door. Instead, he reaches his hand out, grabs hers, and gives her a squeeze in appreciation. However, he doesn't seem to realize he just grabbed her hand with his bad hand, and she doesn't let on to tell him. She just wants him to keep improving without overthinking it. It is all she can do now to shut the door and not let him see her jump for joy.

She carries the wheelchair to the back of the car and opens the trunk to put it away, thinking this may be shaping up to be the best night of her life. Today might be even better than the day she stepped off the train in Atascadero and met him for the first time.

The best decision she ever made in her life was escaping to California. She was so nervous that day seeing Ed for the first time in person after reading about him for so many years. She just had to meet the only man brave enough to stand up not just to Ted Sr., but years earlier to Ted's father and that dirty web his father had spun in all his years as a senator.

She was so nervous when she spied Ed sitting there that day at the train station drinking his coffee that she almost introduced herself to him by her married name—Platt. That could have changed everything and ruined what had become her new life.

She shakes her head, thinking back on all that as she gets the wheelchair situated in the trunk. As she does so, the waiter quietly meets her, holding the full display box of Deer Whistles. Making sure she is out of view of Ed, Hattie takes the box from the waiter and gives back the owner's money.

"I can't tell you how much we appreciate this," Hattie says.

"Our pleasure," the waiter says. "That was smart of Claire to call ahead."

"Smart is an understatement for that woman," Hattie says.

When the waiter has left and is out of view, Hattie shuts the trunk, gets back in the car, and Ed surprises her by again taking her hand in his. He's back to using his good hand, but she's still excited to take it. Ed talks and talks and talks all the way home, delivering more and more words successfully with every sentence he attempts.

Hattie has to give credit where credit is due. This entire plan to get Ed talking again was actually Fulton's. The more Ed tries to talk, Fulton surmised, the more successful he'll be at it. Fulton's entire hypothesis is that a salesman just needs a product he believes in and an audience to sell it to.

Hattie and Ed make plans to go out for dinner again next week and every week after that, which is just fine with Hattie. It's absolutely fine with her. She can think of no better way to spend her days and no better person to spend them with than Ed, who will always be her hero.

As they drive back home, Ed admires a Deer Whistle, which Hattie fastened earlier that day to the hood of her own car. He loves nothing more than looking out at his inventions. He loves the design. He loves the new packaging. He loves everything about this venture. He's confident Mabel would love it as well.

The success of his life's mission has always simply hinged on timing, Ed thinks to himself. That's all it has ever been for him. *Just a matter of time.*

AFTERWORD

◆ ◆ ◆

E.G. Lewis quietly lived out the rest of his life in Atascadero in Claire's home until his death on August 10, 1950, at the age of 81.

His obituary ran in newspapers across the country, celebrating his successes and his failures in Connecticut, Missouri, and California and highlighting his advocacy for a woman's right to vote in his numerous publications, which reached millions of subscribers across the country.

Claire died nine years after him and is buried next to Alphonse. Their grave markers are set next to Ed and Mabel in the Atascadero Cemetery on a beautiful hill overlooking the valley.

Today, Atascadero has a population of 28,000, with around 11,000 households, and is part of the San Luis Obispo-Paso Robles metropolitan area. The city welcomes visitors.

The Administration Building, registered in the U.S. Register of Historical Places, serves as Atascadero's City Hall and is available for tours. On an upper floor, Ed's old desk is roped off and permanently on display.

The stretch of Route 41 that connects Atascadero to the Pacific Ocean is a fun but narrow drive and is now named the E.G. Lewis Highway.

Other locations mentioned in this book that are still standing include the Printery Building; Stadium Park, where the amphitheater and tent city were located; the mall and Sunken Gardens, including "The Wrestling Bacchantes" statue from the 1904 World's Fair; the Community Center Building (now a church); the Dooley Doll Factory Building; and a house Mabel and Claire built and rented out

The U.S. Navy took over the Cloisters Hotel property during WWII, and today it is a housing development known as the Cloisters, along with a large public park.

J.H. Henry's big white home, which served as the Headquarters House, was demolished in 1965 to make room for a shopping center. Around that time, the Atascadero Historical Society was formed to prevent further such travesties from occurring. The society also maintains a museum inside a restored colony home, which today houses photos and artifacts of Atascadero's history, including copies of the *Illustrated Review* magazine and early real estate brochures of Atascadero.

William Randolph Hearst died in 1951 at the age of 88 while still legally married to Millicent but living with Marion Davies. Like Ed, Hearst also ran into financial issues with bank loans, and upon his death, his family donated his castle to the State of California for use as a tourist attraction. Today, the Hearst Castle attracts 750,000 visitors annually just 40 miles northwest of Atascadero.

Every year in Atascadero, on the Saturday closest to March 4th, E.G. Lewis Day is still celebrated. The historical society in University City, Missouri, refers to E.G. Lewis as Eddie. His family in Atascadero refers to him as Ed.

ABOUT THE AUTHOR

◆ ◆ ◆

Doug Villhard is a professor, entrepreneur, investor, and philanthropist. After decades of starting and selling companies, he is supposed to be retired, but instead is having too much fun heading the #1 ranked entrepreneurship department at the Olin Business School at Washington University in St. Louis.

Doug, Diane, and their four children live just outside of St. Louis in Glen Carbon, Illinois, where they co-founded Father McGivney Catholic High School.

When Doug isn't writing, teaching, investing in startups, or serving on boards, he's perpetually working toward achieving a respectable golf score.

Visit DougVillhard.com to download a book club discussion guide and to watch a video of the author discussing what was fact and what was fiction in the telling of this story and his first book, *Company of Women*, a prequel to *City of Women*.

www.ingramcontent.com/pod-product-compliance
Lightning Source LLC
Chambersburg PA
CBHW021212310726
48971CB00006B/1537

9 798986 537825